Lessons in Love

Emily Franklin

nal
jam
books

NAL Jam
Published by New American Library, a division of
Penguin Group (USA) Inc., 375 Hudson Street,
New York, New York 10014, USA
Penguin Group (Canada), 90 Eglinton Avenue East, Suite 700, Toronto,
Ontario M4P 2Y3, Canada (a division of Pearson Penguin Canada Inc.)
Penguin Books Ltd., 80 Strand, London WC2R 0RL, England
Penguin Ireland, 25 St. Stephen's Green, Dublin 2,
Ireland (a division of Penguin Books Ltd.)
Penguin Group (Australia), 250 Camberwell Road, Camberwell, Victoria 3124,
Australia (a division of Pearson Australia Group Pty. Ltd.)
Penguin Books India Pvt. Ltd., 11 Community Centre, Panchsheel Park,
New Delhi - 110 017, India
Penguin Group (NZ), 67 Apollo Drive, Rosedale, North Shore 0632,
New Zealand (a division of Pearson New Zealand Ltd.)
Penguin Books (South Africa) (Pty.) Ltd., 24 Sturdee Avenue,
Rosebank, Johannesburg 2196, South Africa

Penguin Books Ltd., Registered Offices:
80 Strand, London WC2R 0RL, England

First published by NAL Jam, an imprint of New American Library,
a division of Penguin Group (USA) Inc.

First Printing, March 2008
1 3 5 7 9 10 8 6 4 2

NAL JAM and logo are trademarks of Penguin Group (USA) Inc.

LIBRARY OF CONGRESS CATALOGING-IN-PUBLICATION DATA:
Franklin, Emily.
Lessons in love / Emily Franklin.
p. cm. —(Principles of love)
Summary: During fall term of her senior year at Hadley Hall, Love Bukowski faces myriad challenges
including boyfriend issues, choices about college, her long-lost mother and sister's return, and the loss
of her private journals.
ISBN: 978-0-451-22309-8
[1. Interpersonal relations—Fiction. 2. Mothers and daughters—Fiction. 3. Sisters—Fiction.
4. Boarding schools—Fiction. 5. Schools—Fiction. 6. Massachusetts—Fiction.] I. Title.
PZ7.F8583Les 2008
[Fic]—dc22   2007034876

Set in Bembo • Designed by Alissa Amell

Printed in the United States of America

For Asa

Chapter One

You know how many songs state the greatness of summer? Too many.

Or too many for me to count, because I have only an hour before I have to report to orientation.

Consider "Summer Breeze," "Summer Lovin'," "All Summer Long," and the perennial favorite, "School's Out for Summer"—what do they all have in common? A certain joy, a gleefulness (even though it's sometimes cloaked in cheesy lyrics) that filters into not only your ears but your entire system as soon as the first notes escape from the speakers. Your limbs go loose, your hair cascades (even if it's suddenly short, like mine), and your summer self takes a long, lung-expanding breath. These songs belt out what we already know: Summer is a time for freedom and romance, long days and less concern about the mundane qualities of the other seasons.

Looking around my room, I feel the chilled September air that wafts through my open windows. Along with the subtle temperature change, my body registers the dread of that first homeroom bell. Hard to believe that in less time than it takes to tour a college campus I'll be moved out of my bedroom and into the Hadley Hall dorms. Taking in the contents of my soon-to-be-former place of residence, and the changing light on the trees outside, it's pretty clear why no one writes kick-ass songs about heading back to school: The return to academia has nothing compared with summer.

Maybe I'm just mourning August's passing. I haven't quite let go of that feeling of waking up in the summer, stretching my legs out under just a sheet, the slight grit of sand by my feet, and knowing that the rigors and rules of school are far off. Those days when all the possibilities are waiting outside the screen door should you choose to roll out of bed and find them.

"You could make a mix of fall songs," Chris says from my doorway when I express my woes. Look of the moment for him is that of a golden boy at Harvard circa 1970—very *Love Story*. And yet he's single. Chris has been on campus on and off over the summer, so he's past the settling-in point. I, on the other hand, am disoriented about orientation. I'm not a new student but I'm new to the boarding life, and from the sounds of it, life away from home is an adjustment.

"Which songs, exactly, were you thinking would grace that playlist? Genesis? 'Evidence of Autumn'? All those songs are good, but such downers." I fold my sweaters and stack them into a long red duffel bag. It's not a long walk to the girls' dorms from my on-campus pad, but too long with all the stuff I'm bringing. As if I'm a regular boarding student, Dad has offered to drive me over to Fruckner, aka my new abode. Somehow he thinks he can bypass the weirdness of his title as headmaster of the school and be, for the drop-off, just a normal father seeing his daughter off for her final year of high school.

"Aren't you forgetting something?" Chris asks. He eyes my room the way I do, like it's a person and we're saying good-bye to it.

"Oh, right," I say and run back for my Hadley sweatshirt. I'm not big on the name brand—school, hot label, or otherwise—but my tattered zip-up is a must-have. Admittedly, I have visions of sitting on Fruckner's fire escape (not allowed) at midnight (past lights-out curfew) with Chris or Jacob (major violation of gender/visitation rules, as all boarders must be in their own rooms by nine p.m.). Not to mention that the boys' dorms are way far from the girls'—a long-standing item of contention among the Hadley masses. Then again, the school was built more than two hundred years ago, when walking the three-quarters of a mile to class was considered a luxury (girls grew their own crops then). Now it's just a lesson in how to be late for first period. "I wouldn't want to be without my only Hadley item of clothing," I say. "Don't want to look like a misinformed freshman."

Freshmen are of two camps: Either they have an entire Hadley wardrobe from ankle socks to ski hat or they have nothing, thinking this makes them above it all and cool. Personally, I couldn't give a crap about what items someone purchases from the price-inflated campus store, but I do love that fall feeling of sliding into this sweatshirt, tugging at the frayed cuffs, and sometimes chewing on one when I'm deep in thought.

"Not that," Chris says, pointing a toe to my sweatshirt. "Those." He gestures to the towering stack of journals near my bed. Each one contains a part of me. A part of my life until now. I like to see them amassed; they feel substantial. Like all those days and weeks that passed, all the ups and downs and jokes I had, really happened.

"No way am I risking taking them to the dorms," I say and pat them protectively. "I should probably move them."

Chris laughs. "Oh, like someone's going to break in here and read your innermost thoughts?"

"No . . . ," I say, bitchy on purpose. "But it could happen." I unstack them—the orange one from when I first got to Hadley, the black one, the composition notebook I schlepped through England, all of the books—and slide them under my bed. "They can take up residence with the dust mites and stray socks."

"And what about you?" Chris has his hands on his hips, ever the team leader.

"Oh, I think we both know where I'm taking up residence. In the land of hell . . ." I start to think about it: the small room, the new roommate who won't be assigned until later today, and the suspicious list of "new rules" that will be revealed at our welcome picnic tonight.

"I can always come back if I forget something, right?"

I survey the room, fighting the urge to cram everything—
each pencil, all my music, the books that line my shelves,
the photos I have fake-organized in boxes rather than al-
bums because I'm too lazy to deal.

"You know what they say." Chris raises his eyebrows.
"You can never go home again."

I nod. He means it to be funny—it's not like I'm off to
hike unexplored territory or discover new frontiers—but
it hits me that he's right. I won't come back to this room
the same girl I am now. And when I do return, it won't necessarily feel like home any longer. "I gotta go." I check my
watch. "Half an hour and it nonofficially starts."

"It?" Chris questions my pronoun.

"It. Senior year."

He grins and I mirror the expression. "Isn't this when
we're supposed to rule the school?"

"Okay, Pink Lady, we'll see." I shrug. Those last few
traces of summer cling to me like leeches, if leeches were
pleasant: the Vineyard and remeeting Charlie, my now-
boyfriend who is precisely eighteen long miles away
at Harvard; the earth-shattering reentry of my missing
mother, Gala, into my life, not to mention my sister, Sadie;
the fun times with Chris and our friends Chili Pomroy
and her brother, Haverford, Chris's longtime crush. Why
does summer flick by in an instant while school stretches
endlessly? It's not just the time in actual days; it's that feeling that summer exists on its own—not entirely conse-
quence free, but close. "Everything counts now," I say, and
Chris gets just what I mean. Kissing Charlie in the waves

at night, that was fun. Kissing him when he comes to visit next weekend, meaningful. Singing on the rooftop with Jacob Coleman, my "old friend" who defies categorization, sweet. Seeing him at the picnic tonight, loaded. "It all feels heavier."

"That's September for you." Chris swipes a hand through his hair, and then looks at mine. "Think people will be surprised about your new look?"

With my palms I smooth out my newly cropped locks. Chris rough-chopped my hair on the Vineyard and no one's seen it yet. At first I kept reaching for the hair that wasn't there (and other bad rhymes), but now, after a few days of shampooing and air-drying, I'm into it. Plus, I look different. I feel different. "I have no idea. I like it, though, and it's actually going to be nice not to blend in with all the other *long hair makes me feminine and sexy* girls on campus who use their hair to get attention."

"Oh, like you never used your flame-colored dead cells to get noticed."

I grin. "Maybe I did. Once . . ." I kick my overstuffed bag and yell down to my dad. I have to yell so he'll hear me over his Mozart concertos—he blasts music when he's practicing his opening remarks, which we'll hear tomorrow at the nondenominational chapel service. "We should head down." Chris nods.

"I got it!" Chris says as I pull the weight of everything—summer, fall clothing, books, and big expectations for senior year.

"What's that?"

"A song. About this time of year." He takes my back-pack for me.

"Okay . . ."

With a smug look and raised eyebrows, he says, " 'My Old School,' Steely Dan."

I stare at him and heft my duffel bag onto my back, stooping as though I've aged sixty years, which is entirely conceivable, considering the newest wave of back-to-school jitters that has found me.

"You know the lyrics to that?" I say from the middle of the spiral staircase. How many afternoons have I bolted out of class and back here? I won't be on this staircase again for a while. No signing out to home until Columbus Day, Dad has warned me—lest I get confused about my resident status. I sing the line. *"And I'm never going back to my old school. . . ."* At the bottom of the staircase, I turn to him. "So there."

"Fine—my mistake. I may be many things—but never let it be said that I'd like to challenge you in the realm of music."

It's funny he says that, since that's the realm I've been moving away from. Most recently, it's been writing that's taken up my creative thoughts. But I can't resist the urge to return every now and again to my previous passion. "And PS, there's a cruel girl in that song—but thanks for the reminder."

"I'm assuming you mean Lindsay Parrish?" Chris says her name slowly, enunciating every consonant.

"The one and only." My bag lands with a thud at the last

twist of the spiral staircase. "Can't say I'm looking forward to seeing her. Let alone having her as the dorm head"—I sigh—"and co–head monitor."

Chris coughs and my dad steps out from his office. "Is it that she's evil and manipulative and has it out for you and therefore doesn't deserve her positions or that she's . . ."

"What?" I pull my lips in, checking again to see if there's anything I'm leaving behind.

"Maybe it's not that she's high up in the school's echelons, but more that she'll be working—hands on"—Chris gives me a wink—"with Jacob."

"Ready to go?" Dad asks, his tall frame taking up space in the hallway.

I nod. We walk toward the door and I finally get it. What I'm leaving, what I can't bring with me, isn't my journals, my music, photos, or a comfy sweatshirt. It's the past few months. I step out the door with all the tangible items I can carry, casting off summer and heading full-on into fall.

Chapter Two

Dad drops me, gives the traditional hug (close to the chest) paired with a couple of deep breaths (to highlight how emotional it is to drop your child at school), and then waves from the driver's seat (the wave is upbeat, almost like a thumbs-up, perhaps to make me feel confident about my new venture and also to assure him he's done the right thing, ostracizing me from the house).

The first thing I see, other than the summer-tanned girls in shorts and tanks, all with boxes and piles of bags, is something even more surprising: boys.

The Hadley Hall campus is laid out the same as it has been for centuries: boys' dorms up on the main campus (they haul ass out of bed and go to the dining hall) and girls' dorms—three of them—down here. *Here* being the part of campus that used to be pastures and visions of agrarian life (girls then had courses in health, knitting, sewing, being a wife, and milking cows). Basically, you never see guys down on this side of Hadley unless there's a dance and they're doing the chivalrous thing, collecting their dates from the flower-trimmed porches of Fruckner, Deals, or Bishop. Or else they're having a snowball fight as flirtation, since foreplay's highly limited. Or they're part of a serious campus couple and engaged in one-on-one intense conversation in the common rooms or on the grassy oval of lawn that unites all three dorms.

But now there's tons of them. Boys, that is, all clumped on the oval either talking with friends or playing abbreviated Frisbee (the oval's not that long), or just sitting on their suitcases, waiting.

I shuffle with my stuff over toward Fruckner, wondering what the situation is that demands such a gathering of testosterone, but figure my curiosity will have to be kept in check. Right now, I have to check in.

"Bukowski, Love." Lindsay Parrish holds her clipboard and puts a mark by my name (a hex?) as soon as I'm through the door.

"Present and accounted for," I say, and then wish for a retraction. While I might want to be a writer, I'm badly in need of an editor. *Present and accounted for* is redundant, right? Or, no, it's fine. Or maybe I should stop thinking about that and start wondering why Lindsay sounds so . . . normal.

"You can place your personal items in the common room," Lindsay cruise-directs me. "Past the staircase on the left."

Like I haven't been here before? Like I'm really new as opposed to seminew? Like she and I don't already have a sordid history of mean pranks (her), rude remarks (me), and general mutual dislike (both).

"Okay." I put the first of my bags in the corner of the common room and wait for Lindsay to say anything else. We take a moment to eye each other—no doubt she's checking out my recently restyled hair, my attempt at summerizing (read: hints of color on my face, arms, and legs, and brighter reddish blond hair at the front). Like a well-preserved painting of royalty or something equally pricey but cold, Lindsay Parrish looks remarkably well. Her skin is tan enough to prove she's partaken in the outdoor pursuits of the wealthy (polo, pool parties at estates) but not enough so that she looks like she waited tables outside or hauled yacht lines. (Oh, note to self: tell Charlie about boating reference!) Her subtle bronze makes it perfectly clear she'll never be a camp counselor teaching water-skiing, never ask if someone wants cole slaw or fries with that. Only the discerning eye can tell that, true, she's dressed to look like anyone else at Hadley, in a tank top—but it's one of those hundred-dollar ones Arabella showed me in London. And sure, she's wearing a fairly standard-issue canvas skirt that sits on her hips, but it's not one you could find at a mall. It's the kind Lindsay has made for her by her mother's personal tailor.

"Good summer?" I ask, being polite in the face of weirdness.

"Lovely. Thanks." Lindsay looks up from her clipboard again, smiles without showing her teeth, and then leads us back to the front door so she can keep registering people.

"The picnic is in an hour. After that there should be a little bit of downtime before the room draw." She waits for me to come up with something equally banal. I'm semidazed, though. Where is the tried-and-true class-A bitch of yore? Where's the girl who publicly humiliated me, stole Jacob (even though, true, technically he wasn't mine to steal); and threatened me and Chris last spring after Chris made her dip into her personal trust fund to give to my Aunt Mable's breast cancer fund?

"Well, it's official," I say to Chili Pomroy when I've heaved my bags into the common room. "Lindsay Parrish is either medicated or else she's been invaded by alien beings who erased her former personality."

"Maybe she found inner peace this summer," Chili suggests. She's got black-and-white prints, framed rather than rolled, with her, along with an antique lamp. She's one of those boarders who see their dorm rooms as potential apartments, complete with new curtains, rugs, and home makeovers on any and all furniture. "Didn't Chris's old boyfriend Alistair head to some ashram in India?" I nod. Chili shrugs. "Maybe La Lindsay went to the same one."

"You could be right," I say, but my brow is furrowed. "I wish I could accept that. . . . Maybe she's on best behavior for check-in day, what with parents around and everything."

"Or maybe . . ." Chili looks at me and I know from her expression what she's thinking.

"Calm before the storm?" I ask, and she nods. Maybe

senior year is all about that misleading calm. You enter thinking that this year, finally, will be different. It's the last one, after all. And it starts with a placidity that's akin to an early morning sail. Only midway out do you find that the winds have picked up with colleges, misplaced family members, and people you can't trust. Maybe it's a sucky analogy, but that's my hunch. That all this moving-in chatter, the jumble of *hey, how are you*s and suitcases and potted plants and *you look great*s are just a cover for later when we all get slammed.

Outside, parents shuttle their kids into dorms, and I wonder what it would be like if my whole family—that is, my dad, my until-recently missing mother, Gala, and my incredible newly found sister, Sadie, were here. Probably, the world would cease to spin. It would be that bizarre. For the minutes I think about such a reunion, I feel off-kilter and actually stumble on the wide steps by Fruckner's back door.

"You know what I can't imagine?" I ask Chili.

"Going back to sophomore year?" she asks, pouting. She wishes she could fast-forward to seniority.

"No. Parents' Weekend." In the Hadley calendar, an entire fall weekend is blocked off for "special visits." Parents are not required but "very strongly encouraged" to attend classes on Friday, visit all day on Saturday, and come—along with their children—to a formal dinner that night, followed by a big brunch on Sunday. Of course, this sounds lovely in theory. It sounds lovely if you have a family from a television show. But if, say, your parents are divorced and loathe each other (Harriet Walters), or your parents are married but still loathe each other (Chris, whose dad cannot come to grips with his son's sexuality, while his mother totally overcompensates), or your father's head of school and your mother's been absent for almost eighteen years all the while hiding a sibling (me), it sounds hellacious.

"I think it sounds fun!" Chili says, sounding every inch her sophomore self.

"You would, what with your adoring parents and their matrimonial multicultural bliss." I tug on one of her curls. I am forever doing this because my hair is so straight and her coils are fascinating, and she lets me even though it's annoying.

Chili and I hunker down in the shade between Fruckner and Deals to partake of possibly the highlight of back-to-school: watching people arrive and talking about them. Not in a bad way. Not in the mean way. More in the random notable: "Hey—Marty McCallister grew seven inches." "Lissa's going out with Brad Winston—happened on the Cape." "I'm not sure about advanced calculus with Peterman—it sounds too hard."

Chili turns to me. "What happened with *your* class requests?"

I keep looking at the steady stream of arriving students and shrug. "Not sure. Only new students—such as yourself—get the honor of knowing in advance."

"Why do they do that?" Chili tucks her legs to her chest, looking small, her eyes bright against her dark skin.

"So we can't moan about it. See, new students don't

know which teachers to avoid and which to hope for. They don't know that having lunch fourth period means you're starving by eighth. Whereas we"—I point to my breastbone—"we know all too well the highs and lows of Hadley and could easily tie up the phone lines with complaints before opening day."

"So you don't know about Chaucer's Advanced Creative Writing," Chili gestures with her chin so I see Mr. Chaucer walking toward Bishop and herding some of the boys with him.

"Not yet. But the chances are slim. I have to present my case in person." I'd love to be accepted into his small circle of students who are truly talented writers, but I haven't even taken one creative writing class, let alone the three that are prerequisites for his group. Limited to five students, the class meets at night and feels more like a members-only talent club than a class. "Rumor has it Chaucer allows snacks," I say.

"So, you're trying to get in so you can have brownies and graham crackers?" Chili elbows me and I laugh. I keep laughing, for no good reason except it's funny to be sitting here, at my school but doing something—registering—that I've never done before, with my friend from the summer.

"I'm so glad you're in Fruckner," I say and laugh more.

"Wouldn't it be great if we were roommates?" Chili sighs, overdramatically. "We'd be studying and talking, hanging out and not having to deal with anyone else . . ."

"You know we have no control over it, right?" I mime

picking a name from a hat. "You do the roommate draw, and bam—that's it—your fate is sealed for the year."

Chili lowers her voice. "You nervous that you'll get Lindsay?"

I stick out my tongue then reel it in fast. "It seems too obvious, doesn't it? Like, oh, two enemies room together and learn to love each other's differences. . . ."

"This movie of the week brought to you by feminine products and diet aids," Chili says, doing voice-over.

Then we pause. "It could happen," I say. The thought of bunking in with Lindsay, of deciding what configuration to make our beds, hearing each other's conversations, knowing the comings and goings—it's all too much to bear.

"Whoa," Chili says. "Just—wait—hold everything." She has her tongue pressed to the inside of her mouth, making a lump on the outside as she sucks in air through her nose. I follow her gaze to the oval, where a certain boy duo is kicking a soccer ball.

"Hey," I say and smile at Chili. "Jacob . . ." I use my hand as a visor, checking him out as though he could have radically changed since I saw him on the Vineyard. Hard to believe it was only a few days ago, really, what with the change of scene, the stress level that's already entering the airwaves, and the fact that my stomach gave just the smallest of leaps when I saw him. I switch tacks right away. "Jacob's with Chloe Swain. Did you know that? Oh, yeah, you were at the fair with us when it happened." I pause and think about catching Chloe and Jacob in surprise lip-lock in the hall of mirrors at the fair on the Vineyard. "But,

anyway . . ." I look again. "Charlie's visiting this weekend."
Saying his name brings a smile to my face. "He's so . . ."

"Am I allowed to have a turn to gush?" Chili raises her
eyebrows and crosses her arms over her chest.

"Sorry. Just . . . I have a lot of words—and no place to
put them."

"It's called a journal, and according to Chris you have
tons." Chili turns back to the oval, and then her tongue
resumes its place on the inside of her mouth. "Who. Is.
That?"

I pay attention to Chili's verbal punctuation because
she's not usually interested in the male species. Or not in
an overt way. "He's—he's just . . ." I pause, giving her space
for words.

Chili tilts her head. "You're the lyricist-turned-writer.
You tell me—"

I look over to where Jacob heads the ball back to—
"Dalton?"

Chili looks satisfied. "That's his name?"

"Him," I clarify. "People call him Him. Or Himmel. Or
Man."

"But not Dalton?"

"No, that, too," I say. "He's one of those many-named
guys—Dalton Himmelman."

"And he's . . ." Chili looks at them again, but this time
they notice.

"He's Jacob's best friend and he's . . ."

Chili blushes and for some reason I do the same. "Coming over here."

Chapter Three

♡

I manage to get through most of the crush of "welcome events"—registration, dorm meeting, boarders' tea (not to be confused with the picnic, which is just starting)—without all the knowledge that's been dished out to us giving me much pause.

"So," Chris asks when we're near the statue of the ugly fish behind the science center. He sticks his arm out like he's interviewing me. "Quick—tell me your thoughts about senior year thus far."

"I don't know, you know?"

"With language like that you're hoping to get into Chaucer's class?"

This provokes a smirk from me. "It's just—I wanted a normal year."

"Look, you're talking to a guy who came out to the whole school, whose first boyfriend wound up at some ashram in India, and who is currently chasing the unattainable Haverford. I don't know much about normal."

I put my hand on the metal of the fish statue, thinking back to all the times I've jogged past before, or stood here talking, or walked by wishing for something—someone—I didn't have. "Normal. You know, like with a regular boy-friend and going to pep rallies."

"So you wanted to be a senior in a movie."

"Yeah." I look at the swell of people all milling about in picnic form. "At least—I want to feel like things were more tied up from the summer. A clean break. But with Charlie and the sort of leftover weirdness between me and Jacob . . ."

Chris leans on the statue's fin and nods. "Like how Harriet Walters came back as a hippy, all leggings and dreads and crunchy fabrics."

"Right. But she's still Harriet. I wanted to be me, but more. Or less. Or different. Because I feel it."

Chris points to my hair. "You look it, too." Then he watches some people walk by, nodding at us, everything very familiar. "It's a repeat—this year—even though it's new. So I think it's our job to make it what we want." He glances at the crowds, knowing Chili's brother, Haverford, is in there, along with his steady, Ben.

I breathe in the hot air, the smell of cut grass, the grounds crew's hard labors of the past week to get the campus ready. "What if you don't know what you want?"

Chris twists his mouth and runs his hands through his hair. "Then you're pretty much screwed until you do."

"Thanks," I say and mime kicking him. "Thanks a lot." I think about being in the ocean with Charlie, about fooling around with him and where it could have led, where he thinks it might still. And maybe it will—but there's just the smallest part of me that isn't sure about any of it. How we met up at this formal gala, the Silver and White, on the Vineyard and how we were dressed up and it felt so glamorous, but so not me. And while I like trying on new hats, so to speak, I just wonder if Arabella was right. She said at the beginning of the summer that summer flings never turn into more, and if they do, they're always tainted with the knowledge that the waves, the beach, the pier, Paris, wherever you first met and kissed and seamed yourselves together, will always be better than the year-round environment.

Chris flicks the metal statue so it pings and pongs and then flicks my shoulder so I stop thinking. "Change of subject. Which of the new rules is the worst?"

"I don't even know," I say, looking out at the sun-kissed masses. "I remember my first day here—at this picnic—and how everyone looked like golden retrievers." As if on cue, Malty, one of the campus hounds, presents in front of me, and I reach down to pat her. I love dogs.

"You love dogs." Chris nods, watching me fluff up Malty's hair, pat her soft ears.

"Being allergic to cats gives one a natural affinity toward other domesticated creatures."

"Is that what it does?"

"Yeah, that, plus making all feline lovers seem automatically off-limits." I say this and then think it sounds funny. "Do you get that?"

Chris crouches with me, so we're the same height as Malty. "Yeah, like one of those things where if someone likes dogs it's sort of a mental point in their favor. Like on your list of ideal qualities in a datable."

"Well put." I hug Malty, resting my face on her clean, fluffy back, not caring that her hair will show up on my clothing for days to come. "I like Malty probably the best of all the resident dogs."

"Oh, yeah?" Chris asks. "Can I just say how bizarre and seniorlike it is that we're talking about dogs when there's clearly so much campus gossip and general buzz to catch up on?"

I nod, take a brief look at the crowd of students waiting for toasted hamburger buns, the others in the vegetarian line waiting for grilled zucchini sandwiches, and think about how this scene looks just like the catalog pictures. Maybe there is truth in advertising. Then again, I notice that the staff photographers aren't around during the slushy hell of Farch (February–March), and they never snap up two girls bickering outside the dining hall, or the tongue probing that happens toward the end of a campus dance. But now they're having a field day, with the tank-topped masses all aglow from summer break, the guys with Frisbees, the girls with their arms around one another, happy to be reunited.

Malty pants, waiting for me to stop patting her so she can grub for food. "Malty's the best. She's friendly without being exuberant, gentle but not a pushover, athletic but not particularly graceful . . . and cozy."

"Can a being be cozy?" Chris shrugs. "Sounds like you just described yourself."

I think back. "*No*. . . . Well, maybe a little. Okay, yeah."

This gives Chris an idea. "Let's go randomly poll people about their favorite animal and ask them why and then laugh as we share the private joke that they're really describing themselves."

"Oh, good fun," I say and pat him on the back. We head off in search of our pathetic though amusing psychological game, passing by Harriet Walters—my constant classmate who waves but remains in her heated talk with my dad, who also nods—and Chili, who along with her brother sits listening to Jacob play the guitar. Chili is clearly smitten with Dalton Himmelman, who, rather than being Jacob's sidekick, is more his counterpart. Dalton's part of that breed of boys who is witty as well as book smart, slightly goofy, but good-looking enough to pull it off. Chili has positioned herself as any girl with a crush and a brain would—off to the side so it seems like she's checking out Jacob's mastery of the instrument when really she's just vying for the seat closest to Dalton.

"We can go over there if you want," Chris offers, looking to the widening circle around Jacob.

"I was going to say the same thing to you." I squint at Chris. "Isn't your boyfriend right there?" I make reference to Haverford Pomroy with my toe.

"Isn't that *your* boyfriend right there?" Chris points with his toe toward the strumming offender—Jacob.

"Hey—you're the one messing around with a taken guy," I say, my voice full of warning. Chris and I hashed all this out over the summer—I'm not fully approving of his fling with Haverford, since Haverford has been in a long-term relationship with Ben Weiss.

"And you're the one drooling over Jacob when your mythical boyfriend is—"

I clutch Chris's shoulder. "Hey—don't compare your fling thing with my steady one."

Chris sighs. "Right. Sorry. When are you seeing Charlie, anyway?"

"As fast as this week can fly by—he's coming here on Friday." My shoulders slump. "What the hell am I supposed to do with him on campus? This whole time, when I asked him to come, I kept thinking we'd be at my house." I look through the trees, past the soccer field, and can just make out the yellow of my house by the field hockey grass.

"Welcome to boarding life, babe." Chris slips his arm around my shoulders. "There's always Friday Night Flicks."

"I'm supposed to take a college sophomore to see a rerun of an edited PG movie?" It sounds so lame I have to laugh. "I think dining hall food and homework sounds better."

We walk around, interviewing people—teachers, boarders, and day students—feeling like we've gained secret knowledge into their psyches. Then somehow we wind up with Cordelia—a fellow faculty brat whom I used to know—and Lindsay Parrish. Inside my body, a roiling as I wait for Lindsay to break—to show her true colors. But again, she is placid, listening to Cordelia talk about her favorite lizard.

"Izzy, we called him," Cordelia says. Her corkscrew curls are long now, mellower, and she looks older.

"Izzy the lizard?" Chris asks, and I have to fight cracking up because his tone is so serious. He looks at me and has to look away. "And what qualities did Izzy possess that made him your favorite?"

"Well, first of all, we couldn't tell if Iz was male or female . . . ," Cordelia starts. Cue laughter from Chris that he disguises with a cough. "But he—or she—was always getting into other people's business, whatever you call that. Nosy, I guess. And she'd let you stroke her but then she'd suddenly bite—she was feisty. I liked that. . . ."

It's amazing, really, how accurate people have been in their descriptions. I make a mental note to remind Chris that he hooked up with Cordelia not once but twice back in his hetero days.

We're about to move on when Cordelia stops me with a hand on my forearm. "One more thing—Izzy was slimy." I can tell from her wistful expression that Cordelia's back in the age when she had Izzy as a pet, but the rest of us are right here in the now.

"What about me?" Lindsay asks. "Do you want to know which animal I prefer and why?"

Chris bites his upper lip, his signal to me that we can bolt if I so choose. But I'm feeling lazy, and tired from the unfamiliar back-to-boarding routine, so I tuck a strand of my short hair behind my ear and wait. "Sure."

With a serenity bordering on psychotic, Lindsay stares me straight in the eyes. "I like Gloria."

"The cat in Deals?" Cordelia asks. She's probably taking notes on all this—to use for later and so she can be more like her Hadley idol, La Linds. Gloria is butterscotch colored and I do my best to avoid her, like I do all cats.

"Yes. She's superbly beautiful, choosy about whom she likes . . ." Lindsay pauses and swings her eyes over toward Jacob's circle of friends. The group has widened so it's all-inclusive—with faculty members nodding in time to the Dylan lyrics like they have some hope in hell of retaining their youths, campus couples clutching hands, the stoners psyched that the buffet is endless and the tunes are good, and gaggles of girls swooning over Jacob and his posse.

It takes me a second to realize that Lindsay looked over there on purpose. As though she wants to make a reference to Jacob, to someone she knows links us, someone she knows still means something to me. But someone she's tied to with her position as Jacob's co–head monitor. "So, to recap and add on . . . ," Lindsay says, staring at me again. "Gloria is stunning, socially discerning, and"—she looks at Chris to make sure he's getting this—"she can hide whenever and wherever she likes, she never gets caught for any of her infractions . . ." That is true—cats somehow sleek through a room, knocking cups over with their tails or scratching your thighs with their claws, but they're hard to catch in the act. "And when you least expect it, Gloria's there." Lindsay's voice hasn't changed; her pitch is still calm and collected. But her eyes are hard now. "So that's why I like her. She has the power to evade, disrupt, and surprise."

Chris clues in and stops Lindsay in her tracks. "And all while looking like the sexiest feline ever to grace the campus. Got it. Fascinating. See you."

He pulls me by my shirt hem and we go to shake off her craziness, the impending roommate draw tonight, and the fact that classes start tomorrow, with some good old-fashioned lemonade.

By the time we (and by *we* I mean my fellow Fruckners and I) get back to the dorm filled with too much punch and too many hot dogs, it's nearly eight p.m. and time for our dorm meeting. Each one of the dorms meets individually on this first night before classes. Day students are dining with their parents or out having one last hurrah before capitulating to class, but we—the boarding population—are huddled in the common room like a vision of slumber-party comfort from a catalog.

There are females on every available surface—sitting on couches and the floor, perched on the arms of the sofas, leaning against the white-trimmed windows. Some are involved in back-to-school chit-chat, others are already complaining to one another about the bathrooms (they haven't been updated since the school ruled to allow girls to wear pants), and a couple are doing all that typical girl stuff, braiding hair and giggling.

Chili watches them with a mix of envy and ridicule.

"You know," I say softly, "if you want to go be with them, you can. You're new—*new* new, as opposed to fake new, like I am, and you should meet people."

Chili shrugs. "It's like I can't decide yet which camp I'm in—or even what the choices are."

I lean back onto the sofa from my position on the floor and breathe in, wondering why my dad insisted I join this life, why I couldn't be with him, doing our back-to-school ritual of going out to dinner and eating by the harbor. "Well, that's understandable," I say to Chili. "But you will, just give it time. I know that's one of those annoying things people say when you're hoping they can spell out an answer for you, but it's just the way it is."

"What about you?" Chili stretches her legs out so they're under the narrow cherrywood coffee table. In a few weeks, there'll be outdated magazines, some with pages torn out, on this table, along with random textbooks and someone's overly lined *Scarlet Letter*. Certain things about dorm life I already know—those details I sucked up from visiting Arabella or Lila Lawrence my first year. There's a particular grace and sleepy sameness to prep school life—like if you page through the yearbooks from any given decade, the only things that are markedly different are the haircuts and cut of the jeans, though even those two things cycle through, too.

I furrow my brow, thinking about the day last spring when Jacob and I cracked each other up while looking at college catalogs and thinking basically the same thing. "You know, I just sometimes wonder . . . ," I start to say to

Chili as Lindsay and Mrs. Ray, the dorm mother, come in the room and silence is ushered in with them. "Am I making a difference anywhere? Are we all just repeating the same classes and conversations as the people who graduated before us?"

Photos line the school and dorm walls: black-and-white grainy pictures and later the colored ones, of head monitors and award-winning students, times gone by. Part of me feels like it's great to be part of tradition (Go, Hadley!) and another suspects that this, like anyplace where masses of people grow up, is a treadmill that drops you off at one place and swings back to collect someone else.

"Today is a day that changes history," Lindsay says, gathering everyone's attention—even mine, since I figured she'd start with the standard room draw and then move on to dorm rules and how important bonding is and so on (perhaps while giving me an evil look).

All the hair braiding, massages, and whispers about summer and the picnic fade as Lindsay, looking poised and still dressed in her outfit while the rest of us have downgraded to sweats and aging T-shirts, tells us the news.

"As many of you know, it's long been considered unfair that the boys of Hadley have no commute while we, the fairer species, have to trudge nearly two miles every day, even in the middle of winter."

No one points out that it's good exercise, or that many a Hadley girl has used this distance to the dorm to their advantage—no teacher can ask you to go quickly and get the homework or book you left in your room, since by the time you'd return, class would be halfway finished. Only Chloe Swain, who up until right now I hadn't even seen since she's blocked by a few other girls on the far side of the room, speaks up.

"Sometimes," Chloe says, "it's kind of an advantage to have the space from campus."

She doesn't say why, exactly, but if memory serves (and mine usually does), I seem to recall a rumor about Chloe and her old boyfriend Matt Stone (a guy who should have added a *d* to his last name). Chili leans in. "What did Chloe mean by that?"

I shake my head and whisper, "I don't know—sometimes people sneak back during the day and, you know . . ." I turn my attention away from Chili's ear and toward the front, where Lindsay is outright glaring at me. There. Finally. She broke, and over nothing—just a little whispering. I look her right in the eye, determined to meet her intensity, but as soon as our eyes meet, her face changes back to bland. Her smile is even, her face turned slightly upward to me, giving her the appearance of someone open, concerned, and patient.

"Regardless of any potential benefits the girls have from our distance to campus, the primary concern for me as co–head monitor is to make sure certain issues are addressed. Over the summer I worked with faculty and administration, and the first big item on my list . . ." Lindsay looks at Mrs. Ray, ever the dorm mother in her long corduroy skirt and maroon cardigan, and takes a breath. "Bishop House is no longer a girls' dorm. As of tonight, for the first time since its construction in 1801, Bishop will have boys in the beds."

Cue laughter from girls who hear *beds* and *boys* in the same sentence and may as well be playing spin the bottle.

Mary Lancaster raises her long arm. She's center for the Hadley girls varsity basketball and will probably be recruited by more colleges than she can handle. "Where are the Bishop girls?"

Lindsay nods. "Good question, Mary. Bishop has most in common with Fayerweather—both in size and . . ." She pauses. Over and over again at Hadley you hear that dorms don't have personalities, or that assignment to them is random, but we all know it's not. Lindsay covers her faux pas by giving stats. "Both Bishop and Fayerweather have the same square footage, the same demographics in terms of upper and lower classes, and—most importantly—the same number of beds."

Mary slumps in her seat. "Well, it doesn't seem fair . . ."

"Just because you want all of Whitcomb here instead . . . ," starts one of the girls.

"Not all of Whitcomb," Becca Feldman says. "Just one person."

This inspires general mayhem as everyone has an opinion about which boys would be best to have close by. Naturally, those in relationships want their boyfriends' dorms nearby.

"Enough," Mrs. Ray says and actually stomps her foot. She's American but sounds imported from a country that defies naming. She was the one who caught Harriet Walters last spring when her boy toy of the moment, Channing, tried to shimmy up the drainpipe à la metallic Rapunzel. Mrs. Ray has a few nicknames among the students—Sting Ray (it hurts when you get caught), Manta Ray (she flies low under the radar but is an ominous presence), and Charles (as in Ray Charles—she turns a blind eye to those she favors). "What Ms. Parrish is informing you is a done deal—Bishop and Fayerweather have successfully traded. Lindsay—you may continue."

Harriet Walters, my English-class buddy and fashionable feminist, speaks out first. "The most important thing is that some kind of statement has been made—equality won't come easy, but it's worth it."

People either ignore her or raise a fist in recognition of Harriet's ongoing efforts to debunk myths about campus feminists. She's cool, and well-heeled, but one of those floaters who move easily between the studious and the stoned, the fashionable flirts and the fleecies (the group of kids who always look as though they're about to hike up a mountain).

"Before we get to rules and regulations, I'm thinking you guys must be anxious to draw names. . . ." Lindsay's tone is that of a camp counselor. I have to remind myself that we're not going boating and making God's eyes out of string, but rather, about to find out our rooming situations for the entire year. My whole senior year.

Fear and anxiety undulate through me. As a day student, I had none of this. My room was my sanctuary, my own space to which I could retreat whenever I wanted.

Now I'll have someone else—who?—around all the time. Someone who will see me and all my moods, be witness to every visitation. With a clutch I realize that whomever it is will get to know Charlie, or at least know about him. And that freaks me out—sharing info with my friends took me a long time. I'm naturally kind of a listener, not a sharer of my feelings, so the knowledge that one person—or two people (there are triples)—will be in my face like that, sucking up knowledge about me that I haven't even chosen to share, is discomfiting.

Like everything else at Hadley, roommate draw is a tradition—but one, up until now, that I've never seen.

"You sit here," Lindsay says, patting people's heads like we're playing duck, duck, goose. "And you over here . . ."

We line up in order of height (again, Hadley is centuries old; clearly we've moved on to more innovative ways of grouping), which is sweet and kind of quaint.

"I'm so glad you're short," Chili says to me.

"Right back at you, Tony," I say.

The two of us are toward one end of the footage spectrum (I have the pleasure of being one of the bookends), while Lindsay and the other height-endowed Fruckners are on the other side. Mrs. Ray bends our lineup so we're arch shaped.

"With this ribbon," Mrs. Ray says, displaying a silky light blue tether in her palms, "we will sing the Fruckner House song."

She unfurls the length of the ribbon so that we're all holding on to it. Once everyone has her spot, the shortest person—that'd be me—moves next to the tallest. In this case, all five feet plus of me are standing next to Mary Lancaster, aka the Giantess. She's one of those women who looks as though she should be hauling logs by a chain or else doused with fake tan and rubbed down with baby oil before playing pro volleyball. She's not large, just elongated and permanently joined at the hip with Carlton Ackers— better known as ACK! He's her counterpart in height, middle-range grades, and jocky pleasantry.

"Hi," I say to her, because it seems like I should at least ack(ACK!)knowledge that we're now nearly holding hands on the blue ribbon.

"Hey," she says, looking down at me with her cow brown eyes. It's always so strange to be in close proximity to someone who has been on your periphery for ages. As though I should know she has freckles on her nose, but I didn't. Or how she has a claddagh ring with the heart turned in, to show she's unavailable (which she has been since before I even got to Hadley); I wonder if Carlton has the same one.

All of Fruckner stands united: the girls from different cliques and grades, with various personality meshings and conflicts, from all over the globe (technically I am the closest, what with my dad being up the street, and Gretchen Von Hausp-Akala, who is half German, half Aboriginal, holds the record for farthest—her parents live in Tasmania). As my fingers feel the silk and the writer in me glances over my shoulder at the framed photos of all the girls who have been in this circle before me, I'm torn again with the meaning of it all.

Last year and the fall prior to that I was at home now, flicking through reruns and organizing my pens either with my dad or my aunt Mable. Now I have neither of them. Dad's retreated to his house, and Mable's gone for good. And now I'm supposedly part of something else, but I don't feel it. I watch the other girls—even the new ones—who start to sway as Mrs. Ray leads the house song.

"At first these words are unfamiliar, their grandeur quite . . ."

I half listen to the old song and half study the faces of the Fruckners. Everyone seems caught up in all this, happy, like we can go from sitting in the common room as a jumble of feelings and social spheres to now—suddenly, and with the aid of only a $2.99 ribbon, united as one, like the song claims.

"United as one, we stand together, girls eternally grateful for our time together in Fruckner House." Mrs. Ray smiles as the senior girls, who've been singing this for four years, get teary. This is the last time they'll have this ceremony. Then I notice Mrs. Ray glaring at me. She goes so far as to raise her eyebrows, questioning my lack of emotion.

Hello? I just got here. A blue string and herd of hormones isn't going to make me well up. But she continues to glare, so I bow my head and stare at the loose threads on the Oriental rug, hoping if I focus on the blues and reds of what's under my feet, my dorm mother will think I'm trying not to cry. When I look up again, she seems satisfied, and I hope—strongly—that I've covered my ass with regard to her wrath. Dorms each have a place on the strictness scale, and it's known campus wide that Mrs. Ray is far off to the side that sucks. My plan is to fly under the radar—not too this, not too that. Sounds boring, but in this venue I'm hoping it'll keep me from getting double duties and hawklike viewings.

"I can't believe this is the last one!" senior Mandy Bohner says, the tears already dripping down her cheeks. "Not that I want to be in high school forever, but . . ."

"I know—I *so* get that," Lindsay says. She sounds sincere; enough so that I wonder how much Hadley really does mean to her. Maybe her life in New York and the Hamptons and wherever else she jets off to isn't so great. Or maybe it is, and this is another one of Lindsay's ways of blending in, being like the rest of us.

The rest of us except me, that is. Rather than feeling swept up in the moment, encompassed by newfound companionship and camaraderie, I feel only—what is it? Not disdain, not like I'm better than all this, and not as though the ceremony is lame. All the girls hold hands, the ribbon slipping to the floor as true embracing takes the place of the symbolic string. That's it: I feel left out.

"Now we adjourn to the living room for biscuits," Lindsay says, with Mrs. Ray hot on her heels. Clearly, Mrs. Ray is psyched to have such an elegant counterpart.

"Biscuits?" Chili asks me as we're walking from the common room to the small living room.

"Don't look at me—I'm totally out of the loop," I say.

Mary Lancaster elbows me. Normally, such a gesture would register in someone's side. Our height difference is so great, her elbow winds up on my shoulder. "You're not that out of it," she says. She looks at me again with her soft brown eyes, and I know instantly why she's a good captain, a good team leader. Her voice is its own pep talk without being peppy. "You only feel that way now. Give it two weeks and you'll feel differently. Okay?"

I have no reason to nod except that she sounds so confident that I think maybe she's right.

Set up on small silver platters, heaps of biscuits are arranged one atop the next, a steady pile.

"For those of you who aren't familiar with the rules," Mrs. Ray says, clasping her hands in front of her cardigan like she's in choir, "everyone must pick a cookie—help yourself to chilled tea, of course, or milk—and eat it."

The resident too-thin girls pull their cuffs down over their hands and get fidgety while others dig right in. They'll have the same problem during the year when Mrs. Ray bakes her famous cakes. One of the Fruckner traditions is called the unbirthday—when on a random day, each girl is showered with cards, small gifts, and her own cake for an unbirthday party. Since Lindsay's in charge of this, I'm sure my cake will have a stone in the middle, but maybe she'll prove me wrong.

The cookie extravaganza is in full swing. What this has to do with drawing a roommate name I still don't get, but I reach for a cookie—only exactly at this moment Lindsay Parrish is reaching for the same one.

"I think this is mine," Lindsay says, her voice honey coated. She doesn't let go of the biscuit, though, so I don't either.

My fingertips are pressing into the sides of it. "Does it

matter?" I ask. Lindsay purses her lips. Clearly, it does matter. But why? Then the shouts begin. All around me, girls say names and jump up.

"I have Francesca!"

"Oh, my God, Jen, I'm with you!" Melissa Lindstrop and Jennifer (who up until now has spelled her name Jenn with two *n*s) hug each other.

Then it makes sense. With my hand still on my chosen cookie, I watch Delphina Chang pick a biscuit up, bite just the tip, and extract a slip of paper from the middle. "I have Yolanda Gomez."

Yolanda makes her way over and they stand as a duo until a girl I don't know says, "I have Yolanda Gomez."

"That's one triple out of the way," Harriet Walters says. She's notably removed from the flurry of papers and crumbs.

Lindsay, her voice as low as it can be while still being audible, hisses at me, "Let go. I mean it, Love."

"Ah, the truth comes out, Parrish. You haven't changed at all." I look at her, my hand now firmly gripping the biscuit. She and I have to stay very still, near the tray, so neither of us lets go. Quickly, I flip through reasons why she wants this cookie, and only one makes sense. So I speak to her, hoping to prove the problem. "You fixed this, didn't you."

Mrs. Ray comes over to us. "Is there a problem here?" She smiles at Lindsay and raises her eyebrows at me.

"I had this cookie first," I say.

"Biscuit," she corrects.

"Of course," I say, kissing baked-good butt just so I'm not chastised. "And Lindsay won't let go of it."

Mrs. Ray doesn't know whether to be amused or concerned. "Lindsay, as dorm leader, and school co-head monitor, it would behoove you to defer to your underling."

She said *underling*? Nearby, Chili puts her hand to her mouth to stifle a laugh. I'm Lindsay's underling? "But, Mrs. Ray, I believe I had my hand on this biscuit . . ." Lindsay emphasizes that she, of course, uses the correct word for the crumbly pale shortbreads. "And it's really Love who needs to back—who needs to choose another one."

"So we're in a biscuit duel?" I can't help but feel like the whole thing is ridiculous. Here I am trying to find meaning in the ceremonial aspects of moving in, only to experience warfare over something the size of my thumb.

Lindsay's fingers tighten on the biscuit.

Mrs. Ray turns to me, perhaps realizing I don't know how the system works. "The chef baked these today—only half of the girls' names are printed once; others, twice; one, three times for the quad room on the top floor. Some biscuits are blank. It makes more sense once all the names are out. You'll find that the actual rooms are noted with a colored dot on the bottom of the name fortune."

Delphina Chang holds hers up for me to see—a purple dot. Mrs. Ray scurries out of the room, and then returns with an envelope, which she tears open. "Purple . . . you three are in the back-hall triple."

Delphina sighs. "Great—the farthest from the bath-room . . ."

I glance at the tray—only a few biscuits remain, and my hand is sweating now from holding on to the shortbread. I notice Lindsay's pointer finger, bare of polish but with a sculpted nail, scooting toward mine. *She's actually going to pinch me,* I think, and open my mouth to say something, and she stops.

"In the olden days," Harriet Walters says, "this was a formal tea—with name biscuits and gloves. See, if you pick someone, they're automatically your roommate."

Mrs. Ray continues, "All the biscuits are identical from the outside; this way we can really be assured of a random—and delicious—draw."

Maybe I would find this amusing on another night. Perhaps this tradition would be one that could spur on a journal entry about how Aunt Mable would like this, or how my newfound mother, Gala, would appreciate being told about the evening, further evidence to our bonding. But right now, all I have inside is nerves and suspicion.

Harriet Walters has her hand subtly perched near the side of the other tray. She makes a pointed look at the biscuit near her and motions for me to do the same. Looking closely as Lindsay makes nice-nice with Mrs. Ray, I see that the biscuit in question has a small mark on it, a barely discernible *L* scraped into the side.

"You planted this," I say before I think whether this will mean certain doom.

Lindsay's caught off guard. "What?"

Mrs. Ray's mouth flips into a frown. "How could this be?"

"If Lindsay will let go, I can show you."

Mrs. Ray looks at Lindsay. Lindsay shakes her head. "Really, this is uncalled for. She's ruining the tradition."

Mrs. Ray sighs. "Lindsay's correct—this really is a most unsuitable accusation for this special night."

All the girls are gathering around now, those with roommates, those without, waiting to see who will back down.

"I'm not accusing Lindsay," I say. "I just want a fair placement. It's my belief that she has orchestrated this entire thing to her advantage."

Lindsay gives a scoff, then a laugh that's full of disbelief. "You're so out of line, Love. You think you can show up here—your first night at Fruckner—and take over?"

This doesn't sit well. A couple of sneers from girls and a dubious look from Mrs. Ray let me know I'm on the verge of getting lambasted. I look at Harriet Walters. She's one of the smartest girls I know and also has that rare quality of being impartial. She would make an excellent judge.

"Here," Harriet Walters says and holds the biscuit she's been biding time with up for inspection. "I took a course in forensics over the summer. . . ." She turns to the side and comments ("Good for college apps") before continuing. "This biscuit has an *L* on the side. See?" Mrs. Ray goes over to inspect.

A look of panic crosses Lindsay's face, and before I know what's happening, she grabs the biscuit. "She took it!" I yell. The whole scene is so surreal, I don't know whether to laugh or cry or run home, pound on the door, and demand that my dad let me back in.

As it turns out, none of that happens. Lindsay squishes the cookie so no one can tell if she'd drawn an L on it or not. "Harriet—the one you have means nothing. It looks like an *L*? It could be a unicorn. Or a star. Or"—her voice is thick with sarcasm—"or . . . the slip of a baker's knife." She crosses her arms over her chest, revealing a chunky gold bracelet on her wrist, the kind that on me would look as though I were masquerading as a superhero but on Lindsay looks elegant and refined. I am screwed.

"It doesn't matter if you crush the evidence, Lindsay," Harriet says. "It's math—an equation. You might have bashed the evidence, but show us the paper inside."

Lindsay is foiled. Mrs. Ray holds her palm out and reluctantly Lindsay puts the paper there. "It's blank." Mrs. Ray looks confused. "That's impossible. The biscuits are . . . they're meant to either contain no paper, or if they do . . ."

"Of course it has no name," Harriet says. "She planned this. Lindsay wanted the only single in Fruckner." Harriet points upstairs like we can see it from here.

"But that room is specifically for the person who is last to be paired up," Mrs. Ray says. Her eyebrows meet as she clenches her jaw and furrows her forehead. "Lindsay?"

Lindsay does what any deceitful person caught out might do. "I have no idea what you mean. I didn't make the cook—biscuits. I'm just playing along like everyone else."

Playing along, I think and make a mental note to tell that to Chris later. It's exactly what she's doing.

"Look," I say, my voice finally filling up with real emotion after feeling disconnected all night. "I didn't ask to be here. I'm supposed to be in my own bed, with my own family, waiting for classes to start tomorrow. Will someone just please tell me where I can go to unpack my stuff and go to bed?" It's the truth. It might not be exciting. It might not make me seem supercool, but right now I just don't care. I only want to find my footing and move on.

Mrs. Ray snaps to attention. Without uttering a word, she pairs people up by their draws, consults her list of rooms, and sends off the various duos, trios, and one quad.

"So this is what we have left," she says, circling us like we've been hauled down to the station for questioning.

"Mrs. Ray, I really think that I—"

Mrs. Ray cuts Lindsay off. "It would be in your best interest to be quiet now, Ms. Parrish."

The final five: me; Chili—who looks terrified in her baggy sweats, her fingers raking through her ringlets, a nervous habit; Harriet—ever calm and convinced that good will triumph over evil; Lindsay—glib rather than shamed; and Mary Lancaster—who, from the looks of things, couldn't give a crap.

Mrs. Ray looks at her list, then turns to us. "Harriet Walters, you may go to room twenty-two."

"But that's—" Lindsay clamps her mouth shut but is clearly distressed at being overruled.

"That's the single," Mrs. Ray says. "Please go get settled."

Harriet gives me a wink, and then starts to do what everyone else in Fruckner is doing—hauling their gear from the storeroom and common room up to their new digs.

Suddenly, a new realization hits me. Odds are very good that I will be Lindsay's roommate. All those jokes about it over the summer could come back and smack me in the butt. *Please, no.* I imagine being a prisoner in my own room, with Lindsay peering over me while I work, plotting against me as I sleep.

Mrs. Ray opens her mouth and points to me, and my whole body clenches. Just as she's about to speak, Mary Lancaster—long and lanky and leaning against the wall while eating leftover biscuits—saunters over. "You know what, Mrs. Ray?" Mary puts her big palm on my shoulder. "I've been here the longest out of this group. I think as long as we're reshuffling"—she sounds like she's calling the team in for a huddle—"Love's in a bind—she's new but not new, you know? So she'd benefit from being with someone who knows the ropes—"

Lindsay sees her opening and rips it. "Like me. I'm well versed in the Fruckner code and . . ."

Mrs. Ray rubs her nose, looking tired. "I've had it—this night is such a special occasion . . . and it's been sullied by . . ." She stops herself and clears her throat. "Mary, please take Love to your double . . . room fourteen. Second floor." Mary grins, having scored numerous points apparently, and pulls me out of the room with her.

I'm psyched and relieved, all of my limbs slightly shaking with the myriad emotions of the past few minutes.

"You," Mary says, hefting a monogrammed duffel over her shoulder and a laptop bag around her neck, "are in for the most awesome surprise. We scored big-time on the room front."

She doesn't ask for thanks, though I'm grateful that she potentially pulled me from Lindsay's wrath. She just nods for me to follow her up the stairs to the room we'll share for a year. Only when I'm halfway up that flight, my wrists straining with the weight of my bags, do I realize what's on the other side of the coin. Downstairs, looking small, left all alone with Lindsay the Pariah, is Chili, who looks at me but doesn't wave.

Chapter Four

My alarm buzzes, hauling me from my brief sleep into the present:

As of today, I am officially a Hadley Hall senior.

Poppy Massa-Tonclair, my writing professor in England—who is also a world-renowned novelist—told me once to treat my eyes like a film camera. I do this now, waking up in the position I fell asleep in, on my side, with the blankets pulled up, my feet exposed to the morning air.

Just as Mary Lancaster told me, the room is a pleasant surprise. More than that. Catalogs always depict boarding school rooms as bookshelf lined and paneled with dark wood, but the truth is, most of the Hadley dorms were redone in the seventies, when the students were politically active and rallied against the "old regime." Along with scrapping the no-pants-for-girls rule, they also succeeded in "modernizing" many of the dorm rooms to reflect the current styles. Flash-forward to now, and either the rooms are total kickbacks to that hazy dazed time—with fading paint on the walls and shag rugs in the closets—or they are minimally overhauled at the request of the many parents who visit and find their kids' digs grim. Your basic Hadley room is a square, plus or minus a window, with two twin beds (or three if it's a triple), white walls, and standard-issue dressers that with three narrow drawers were, when the school had uniforms, useful, but now hold virtually nothing.

So that's what I'd prepared myself for: plain white room or moldy oldy.

But with my camera eye, I take it all in: the odd shape—like a V with a flattened point, four windows, hardwood floors, freshly painted white walls, and wonderful light. The quality of light is important to me—this much I learned from my squalid room in London. My natural happiness is much closer to the surface when I'm closer to light—and if it sounds high maintenance, I can live with that.

At this moment, the campus bells have yet to ring, mottled morning sunlight ripples on the hardwood floor, and on the other side of our room, Mary Lancaster is asleep with her back turned to me, all five feet eleven inches of her spread out on the too-short bed.

"Hey," she says, sensing that I'm awake. She rolls over so we're facing each other, but still in sleep position. "What's up?"

I don't know Mary, not really. She's the kind of acquaintance that if we passed in the hallway we might say hello—or not—and if we were seated next to each other in class, we'd probably smile but not exchange much in the way of conversation. So to suddenly be plopped in a room with her, in my pajamas, with all of senior year rolling out before me, feels slightly odd. But also kind of good. Fresh.

"I was just thinking of how blank this room is now," I say and sit up. I brought a duvet (white with a white swirled pattern on it) and white sheets. I'm in a phase of all white—purity of mind while I sleep. Or maybe it's because my mind hasn't been filled with such pure thoughts now that my relationship with Charlie has turned from summer fun into full-on romance.

"You mean, like no posters or anything?" Mary scratches her head, pulling her collarbone-length hair into a ponytail and stretching. Her hair is the color of fancy chocolate, the kind with cinnamon in it, or something equally sweet and appealing. "Because we can get some, if you want. . . ."

I shake my head and stand up. My feet register the cool floor, instantly bringing me back to summer and waking up in the apartment above Mable's café, where the sunlight was so intense I once burned my soles. "More like—nothing's happened yet." I look around the room. We haven't figured out where our standard-issue desks should go, nor the future of our wardrobes and beds. I haven't even looked out the windows properly since it was dark when we came in last night and my bed—right now—is far from the windows.

Mary gets out of bed and walks over to me, her baggy Princeton T-shirt hanging off her shoulders, the orange of it clashing with her red plaid boxers. She points. "Shirt is from my older brother, Dan, Princeton class of way before

us, and these"—she plucks at the flannel of the boxers—
"are Carlton's." Just saying his name makes her smile.

"You guys are really serious, huh?" I ask.

"Yeah," Mary says. Then she sighs.

"What?" I begin the search for first-day apparel, wishing I didn't care what I wore, but knowing I do. Kind of.
A little. Some. Anyway.

"It's just hard, you know? Carlton—he and I have been
together since the first day of freshman year. And now it's
like we're looking at places—"

"Colleges?" I ask, and Mary shoots me a look like what
else could she possibly mean.

"And who knows? I could wind up at Stanford and he
could be at UConn . . ." She tightens her ponytail.

Hearing her say *Stanford* makes me think of my own
noninterview out there, how I could have applied—or at
least looked—and how the rest of my life seemed to take
over. My heart skips one normal beat when I think of how
crammed fall will be—with college visits and Charlie visits
and all of the usual Hadley events, how I could be facing
the same situation if things with Charlie continue on track.
With a Harvard boyfriend, I could limit my choices to the
Boston area, but what if I do that and then we break up?
How do you know when something's serious enough to
plan around?

I know I'm getting way ahead of myself and that right
now I have to get dressed for senior meeting, where we'll
get our class schedules and a calendar of senior events, and
basically hang out while the underclassmen listen to my

dad's speech. It's a bizarre feeling to know I'll miss it. I mean, he's been my definition of home for so long, but it makes sense somehow—like if I'm here, in Fruckner, and he's at home, then we're really apart. And if I'm a senior, it's just one more step to fully breaking away. Pangs of sadness come through me while I watch Mary rifle through her bureau drawers to find clothing for today. Maybe I can't plan around anyone or anything just yet.

"You could always look at colleges together—you and Carlton," I say. Jeans are too thick for this time of September—it feels chilly now but by noon it'll be T-shirt weather, with kids basking in the sun on the quad. I need something in between. I settle on a simple chocolate-colored linen dress with red flip-flops Chili and I bought at a tiny seaside hut near Menemsha. Chili. I know I'll have to deal with her sooner or later—and I just hope she's not angry about the room situation.

"Hey, Love?" Mary asks when she's back from the shower and I'm all set to go. My backpack is first-day light: one notebook, several pens, and a further plea I typed out to Mr. Chaucer about his Advanced Creative Writing class.

"Yeah?" I figure Mary wants to do the roommate thing—hug or bond—but instead, she pulls me into the center of the room.

"I thought about it—and you're right. About this room, I mean. For four years I've gotten here and just settled into my random room and dealt with everything. But now—it's senior year." She has one of those wide smiles that highlights her pretty features. "Two things. No, wait, three."

"First?" I say, putting my backpack on my bed so it doesn't seem like I'm rushing out the door, despite being totally obsessive about not being late.

"First—we meet back here after school, before my practice, to rearrange the furniture."

"Is that, like, Fruckner code for something, or do you really mean . . ."

"I really mean—bed there? Table here? We'll set it up just right."

"And the other two things?"

"Oh," Mary says, a slight blush creeping into her tawny cheeks. "I guess I just wanted to say that I'm glad—you know—that out of all the other girls in Fruck, that you're the one I'm Frucked with." She laughs.

"Nice," I say and laugh, too. Then, because I never said it last night, I add, "And thanks—by the way. I'm not sure if you're fully aware of the extent that you saved my ass— and the rest of me—from a year of hell, but you did. So, thanks."

Mary nods. "I get it."

I pull my bag from the bed, wondering where all the items in the room will find homes later. "So, I'll see you later?"

"Wait." Mary tugs on my hair, and then walks with me over to the front windows, which are blocked by our desks. Over the summer, the handymen and -women, the campus cleanup crews, come into the dorms and repair anything that's damaged. They also apparently rearrange everything so that it's in the least convenient position. As is, my bed is blocking the nonworking fireplace (my head was in a chimney last night), Mary's bed takes up an entire wall, the bureaus are shoved together, and these desks—which I've yet to even touch—are in front of three large windows.

"What?" I ask. "I know—I'm messy with my desk. It's a fault." I flash to Charlie and his immaculately arranged workspace on the Vineyard, how I bet his dorm room at Harvard is the same. The thought of that difference somehow makes me more weirded out than it should—but it's as though his perfectly organized desk is a reflection of his too-compartmentalized brain. And which part am I in?

"No, not that." Mary uses her body weight to slide one desk to the right and jam herself between both. "Let me move them."

I help her, not knowing why, and we succeed in creating even more displaced furniture, with both desks at an angle. "What exactly are we doing?" I check my watch. It will have to be breakfast on the go. Normal people would probably sit and eat and not worry about the first bell, but I'm not like that. I want to take my toast and be the first to arrive.

When you get to class first, you can just sit there and wait, watching people stream in while you're already comfortable in your chosen chair. None of those awkward *where will I sit* moments. Maybe it's that, or maybe—it occurs to me now—maybe I just like to see each class, each encounter at the student center, as a plot unto itself. So I'm there from chapter one, from the first page. I check my watch again.

"Who knew you were such a clock watcher?" Mary smirks.

"Who knew you were of the laid-back variety?" I respond. The only time I've been with Mary for more than a few minutes in line at the dining hall was watching her play for Hadley—where she's most definitely not mellow.

"Guess we'll learn," Mary says. "But before you go? What I didn't show you last night and the primary reason for my psychage?"

"Psychage?"

"I like to make up words," she says, unapologetic and grinning.

"Me, too."

"Anyway . . . you should know that room fourteen comes with its privileges. Other than just the gift of rooming with me, I mean." She laughs at herself and I join her, then follow her as she presses her nose to the windows. "See?"

Rather than simply providing a lovely view of the grassy oval enclosed by Deals, Bishop, and Fruckner, our room's windows are not what they seem. "What the . . . ?" I back up while Mary fiddles with a latch on the window side. With a few clicks, and a bump from her hip, the window reveals its true nature.

"It's a door!" I can't help but yelp. Two out of the three windows are attached, and swing open, just a crack now since the desks are in the way, but enough so that I can see the small step down to a deck.

Mary shushes me. "No kidding. This room is kick-ass

and built for boarding breakouts. . . ." She waits for me to react. "Don't get all headmaster's daughter on me, okay? Carlton and I didn't make it through three years of parietals without the occasional nighttime rendezvous."

"And everyone knows about this?"

Mary has a matter-of-fact tone. "Well, Love, the deck is made of actual wood—it's not invisible."

"And we're allowed out there?"

"No. But legions of Fruckners have gone out there to smoke or make out or just gaze at the stars."

"And that's your plan?" I look at Mary. She seems so varsity—so rules oriented and regulated, with her regular classes and steady boyfriend and group of sweet if generic friends.

"No. I mean, smoking is disgusting." She smiles. "But being social . . ." Mary closes the door-window and locks it, shoving the desks back in front of it. "Anyone can get to the deck—it takes a truly stellar planner to get down from there."

I laugh, ignoring the seconds ticking away, and lick my lips. "No way—I had my one run-in with the disciplinary committee sophomore year. . . ."

"Oh, yeah—with that guy—Robinson Hall?" she scoffs. "I bet that was time misspent."

"Tell me about it—but let it be noted that it quelled my taste for breaking and entering."

Mary crosses her arms over the plain red T-shirt she's chosen for today. "I'm not talking only about leaving here—who'd want to leave this palace?" She looks around our awesome room, and I have to agree. If I do get into the creative-writing class—or even if I don't—I can imagine many days spent writing here, tucked away from noise and chatter and yet still a part of campus. "Listen," Mary says, sounding every bit like she's thought this through. "I wouldn't ever ask you to risk getting in trouble. But just"— she slides cherry Chap Stick across her lips and shoves a notebook into her bag—"if you're ever in a position to . . . um . . . be in a position. . . ." She raises her eyebrows. "Just know, I'd be happy to vacate should you want a little night-time privacy."

She heads out before me, even though I've been waiting to leave. I take my backpack from my bed and I'm suddenly aware that I seriously have no idea what will happen in the space of these four walls and four windows (or, um, one window and a door). I could have fights in here, write the next American novel, find out if and where I'm going to college, pine for Charlie, play guitar with Jacob, even bond with my fellow boarders. And maybe, just maybe, I think, smoothing out my duvet even though my bed isn't in its final position, share this bed with someone other than just myself.

Chapter Five

♡

Ten minutes into History of Hadley, the required elective (a misnomer itself) for all seniors, and most of us are bored enough that we're engaged in other pursuits. It should be noted that the class is unmonitored, so there's no teacher keeping us here, but our section is shoved into a former lower-school classroom in plain view of all faculty offices. On our transcripts, the class looks rather quaint and official, pulling Hadley's name even further up the boarding school rankings—all this and no need to pay a teacher to slog through the course work. Basically, it's a waste of time that you can't really complain about because if graduation is actually something you want to partake in, you have to have been here.

Rather than try to escape, we're all content to while away the forty-five-minute block, crammed into chairs that were the appropriate size back in grade school.

I scan the room and watch the plot unfold. Channing is nearly asleep, his head a victim of that head-jerking dance that snaps him to attention every time his chin rests on his chest. Two girls write notes on a spiral-bound pad between them—one of the notes is probably about me, as I saw them gesture to my new haircut and immediately write something; then again, I could be paranoid. Other students check their class schedules or doodle.

My own class schedule is so messed up, I can't begin to know who to blame—except perhaps the computer that shuffles all the classes, requirements, and requests and spits out the index cards.

First of all, I'm listed as a freshman—which puts me in intro classes and their two-hour grammar lecture. Second of all, as I'm listed as a class IV (the technical term for a freshman), I have study halls, which you outgrow by sophomore year. And last—but perhaps of most crucial importance—denying my class I (the official senior term) status means that I can't take senior classes. Meaning: I have not secured places in Literature of the World (notoriously difficult to get into and taught by J.P. Kramer, who should have taught Ivy League long ago but chose to grace us with his cowboy-hatted presence instead) or French for the French (the class, after all your language requirements are filled, in which you get to cook, talk, read short stories, and debate—all in French). And of course, there is no record whatsoever of my trying to gain access to Mr. Chaucer's small Advanced Creative Writing class.

My next task: skip my next class—which is Ancient Civilizations, the basic history class for all IVs—and head directly to the dean of students to see what I should do.

I try not to let the schedule screwup ruin my morning, and instead appreciate the fact that as of right now, I don't have any homework. This bliss I'm sure will last all of one period, but it's like those last few days of break, when I just pretend the rest of life—real life—won't bombard me.

"We're supposed to have these," Harriet Walters says. She places her hand on the stack of leather-bound books on the nonexistent teacher's desk and begins to hand them out. "I've actually already read it."

"Of course you have, Walters," a guy named Jimmy Kapp says. He and Harriet have long dueled it out for top ranking in our class, even though—as per Hadley's handbook—we don't have class ranks. Jimmy Kapp—aka Jimmy Phi Beta Kappa—is the guy who'd lend you his class notes if you were sick in the health center, the guy teachers would choose to monitor study halls if they had to dash out, the guy who helped stage the fund-raising dance-a-thon and then ran the Boston Marathon last April. The guy you could find incredibly annoying if he weren't just plain nice, smart, semifunny, and quite cute.

Harriet shoves a *Hadley History* book in Jimmy's face. "A little light reading for you, Kapp. Just so you won't fail the test."

At the end of the semester, we have to take a test based on all the exciting knowledge we've gained from the ancient text. Basically, if you go to Hadley, or just hear about the school from a friend, you can pass—supposedly.

"You know no one's ever failed that test?" Jimmy Kapp says.

"Not true," Dalton Himmelman says. He's shrugged down in a plain white T-shirt, gazing out the window toward the quad, where lucky folks who have their free periods now are lazing about, flaunting their ease. Dalton is without his best friend, Jacob, which is unusual. Normally, I only ever see Dalton in the context of Jacob. Watching Dalton alone gives me new appreciation for him, his wry tone, his smirk, his from-the-corner comments. I guess whenever Jacob is around, I turn a blind eye to everyone else—or if not quite that, a certain muteness overcomes the rest.

"So, who failed, then?" I ask Dalton. He swivels in his tiny seat, giving me a look that for some reason makes me pay more attention to him.

"Funny *you* should ask," he says, but he doesn't elaborate. He's like that, filled with humor and proverbial peanut-gallery fodder, but then just as likely to withhold.

Jimmy Kapp shrugs. "Everyone passes."

"Not Parker Addison," Dalton says. He doesn't look right at me as he says this name, but there's an energy floating between us. Maybe he knows Chili likes him (read: she is among the legions of girls—and a few guys—who track Dalton's every move with their crushes). Or maybe he and I are just on some bizarre wavelength.

"There are lots of rumors about that guy," Harriet says. "Who knows what's true about him?"

I could speak up and say that I know about him. At least a bit. He's Charlie's brother, and though I met him under rather unfortunate circumstances this summer (read: I thought he was Charlie and tried to grope him), I do know that most of those rumors—the stuff of campus lore—are true. But I don't say that—because to say that means to admit how I know him, and to do that is to be one of *those* people. And while I want my relationship with Charlie (and, by virtue of his being related, Parker), I do not want to be one of the Hadley heartbroken, who abuse the verbal privilege by bringing up their long-distance amour every chance they get. Those people—the ones who wait for the phone calls, the letters, the texts, the e-mails, all the while constantly longing for that long-distance love who begins to sound made-up. Is that what Charlie will be? Some summer myth?

I look down at my notebook, at my current list, hoping people will go back to being quiet—reading or ignoring the text.

The page in front of me is a list that belongs in my journal, but since I refused to bring along any of them—even the latest one—to the dorms for fear of them being read, I have only pages in my notebooks to fill at random.

NEW RULES THAT SUCK (not in any order):

- No cell phones (as of this morning all phones are to be turned in to the headmaster's office—hi, Dad!— only to be redistributed at closing of the day [day students] or Friday at four p.m. [boarders]).

- Required participation in Hadley Hugs—the hippy-earthy-crunchy procedure that was started in 1968 for valid reasons (country torn apart, people divided, racial tensions, and so on) but that culminates in the hugging of every single one of Hadley's students by every single other student. This is not optional as in prior years. Hadley did away with calling it "a nonrequired community-minded day" and got around the litigious parents and antitouching laws by making it an academic necessity. Basically, it's a morning of gropage that ends in either laughs, or tears, or gross-outs, or hook-ups.

- Maximum weekends away for boarders are capped at two per semester. This includes holiday weekends.

- In light of last year's (when I wasn't even a boarder!) infractions, all boarders are to remain on campus after school unless otherwise approved (permission-granted examples include doctor's appointments, college interviews, and parental visits—provided you've asked permission *in writing* beforehand). If my mother visits, which she has promised to do, she'll have to plan in advance. For a woman who came into my life after a near-eighteen-year absence, forethought might not be her strong suit.

Then there's:

THE NEW RULES THAT ARE GOOD:

- Extended parietal hours (this is highlighted in the reissued handbook as though it's a major coup on the students' part—however, the giant "exten-sion" is exactly one-half hour. Instead of vacating opposite-gender dorm rooms at nine p.m., you can stay until—gasp—nine thirty! But then again, a lot can happen in thirty minutes.

- Increased community service. Hadley makes sure each student does a certain amount of hours, but this year the boarding population has to work to-gether on a project that varies by dorm. We have a meeting tonight to make suggestions as to Fruck-ner's focus. I'm all for it.

- Bishop House swap. It's not just equality; it's an influx of boys down to our sector. Not that I care from a potential-suitor perspective (read: Charlie Addison is plenty for me), but Mary Lancaster's psyched because her boyfriend, Carlton, is now our neighbor.

- Bishop House swap reverse—the girls of Bishop are now on main campus.

- Exams are no longer prior to winter break, so they don't hang over your head at Thanksgiving. I pre-dict this will lead to a nonproductive, social, fun few weeks post-turkey and pre-menorah (or what-ever your choice of seasonal bush). Then again, it could lead to complete disaster in terms of reentry in January.

I draw a long arrow from the last point on my Good list to the end of the Bad list, then begin a doodle that's short-lived: little cursive lowercase *e*s all linked together. I miss Charlie. I don't want to pout about being apart, but I wish we weren't, that we could do the Cross-Campus Couple Shuffle. The CCCS takes its form in hand-holding on the way to lunch, leaf fights in the fall, snowball tosses in the winter, hallway canoodling (Note to self: Add *canoodling* to the list of words I dislike), and general gooey displays of affection. Just as I love cotton candy but don't partake in public, I'm realizing that though I'm a pragmatic person, and have no desire to get it on with my classmates watching, I do relish the thought of having my boyfriend close by.

I look up from my line of fake cursive and check on Dalton Himmelman just to see what he's been doing to fill the time. He's not looking outside or asleep; rather, he's got a number two pencil (Are there any other kinds? Of course, but they never get mentioned) in his mouth and a composition book open in front of him. He doesn't catch me watching him, which I'm glad about—if for no other reason than I can't explain my slight fascination with him other than his connection with Jacob. Dalton takes the pencil from his lips, twirls it like a Lilliputian baton, and then writes furiously for about twenty seconds. He's still writing, his sandy hair suspended from his forehead, when his eyes shift up and lock on mine. I figure he'll glare at me or look away, but he just smiles at me while his left hand keeps moving across the page. I wish I knew what words link on his paper to form whatever thoughts are in his head—no wonder Chili has a sudden and deep crush on him. He's that kind of guy—the guy in a movie who'd be the hot best friend, the character they don't explore but whom you can't shake off when the lights come on in the theater.

Thinking of Chili makes me doodle her name now on my pad. I stop short of making hearts or stars above the two *i*s in her name because it seems so typical of high school doodles. She and I walked to campus together this morning, silent at first, and then all of a sudden talking through bites of a breakfast bar (her) and seven-grain toast (me). Overlapping, we both said we were sorry and then wondered why we were apologizing.

"Maybe because I could have intervened and gotten it so you and I were roommates. Now you're stuck with La Pirate."

Chili turned to me, her first-day-of-school new orange V-neck bright against her dark skin. "Let's face it: Probably you wouldn't have been able to change anything, and quite possibly you could've made it worse."

I chewed the crusts of the bread—my favorite part—and stopped to shake a pebble out of my flip-flop. On the way to main campus there's a gravel driveway leading to a huge cemetery, the kind with old, tilting gravestones. The place looks either poetic and nearly picturesque in that Ye Olde New England way, or else totally creepy. "How could it be worse?"

Chili looked at me, polishing off the last of her bar. "You and LP could be together. Hey, she might take pity on me—"

"Or try to convert you to her wicked ways."

"But with you she'd have been out for blood right away."

We stared at each other before she went off to the main assembly and I went toward the senior gathering. I don't really think she'll be turned into one of Lindsay's drones, but I guess you never know. And I like that she and I are both protective of each other. "You're sweet, anyway," I said.

"Just get me Dalton Himmelman's attention and we're even." Chili grinned, and with a flick on my arm—she's big into flicking as a form of greeting and departure—she was off.

So I'd made amends about the rooming fiasco, but what about Dalton? You can't exactly demand that someone take notice of another human being. But I guess I could try. Jacob and I are supposed to be resuming our multilayered friendship: I like him, he likes me, he hooks up with Lindsay Parrish while I'm in London, now I'm taken, we never get together, that sort of thing. So maybe that's my in with Dalton. Maybe this week, after any sense of newness has worn off and we're back to business at Hadley.

The bell rings and I realize that my first period of senior year is over. Never again will I have another first period of the year here. Finally, the solid understanding of how fleeting each day is gets to me. That feeling other girls had with the ribbon ceremony last night fills me up until I want to scream, *This is it!* Everything now is a countdown.

My thoughts must show on my face, or else Dalton Himmelman can read minds. Beside me in the doorway, he doesn't touch me but bites his lower lip and studies my eyes. "You okay, Bukowski?"

Everyone calls me Love. I'm not one of those girls—whatever breed they are—who get called by their surnames. And I don't play sports, so I never really hear my last name as a point of reference other than on an attendance sheet, which prep schools don't have (they don't need to with a student-teacher ratio of twelve to one, max). I look at Dalton, about to feed him a line—*Yeah, I'm fine*—but he says more instead. "Kind of intense, right?" He looks at me as the rush of students swell the hallway. "The starting and ending of things at the same time?"

I nod at him, amazed at the perfection of how he summed it up, and before I know it, we're sucked into the wave of bodies, both going our separate ways.

Chapter Six

♡

By the end of the week I've been promoted from false freshman.

"I'm finally a senior!" I say to Chris and Chili on the way to lunch. The entryway to the dining hall is packed—it always is on fresh-fish Fridays. Students are queued up for the catch of the day prepared any way they like—pan seared, fried, baked, or breaded.

"Oh, I'm already baked," Trevor Mason says to the lunch lady. Chili, Chris, and I chuckle, taking in his standard Visine-clear eyes and wastoid physique. He and his stoner crew move as one loose-limbed unit, paving the way for us.

"Pan seared," Chris orders when it's his turn. Chili and I nod.

"So, what's it like to be a freshman all over again?" Chris asks.

"I'm done with that—so smart I breezed through to seniordom in less than a week." I smile, thinking back to that first day and how I'd been stuck sticking to my class IV schedule. When I complained, the registrar informed me that if I didn't attend the classes on my printout, I would be issued cuts. "It was insane, though. It makes me curious how all those colleges can keep track of all those applications—how the world doesn't just screw things up all the time."

"Oh," Chili says, snagging napkins for us as we head toward the seating area. "I think they do—only this time it affected you, so you noticed."

We sit at the end of one of the communal tables, leaning in close to talk, like we did over the summer. In my bag are notes and too many assignments, as well as postcards from Gala—my mother. She'd promised to send one every day, and so far, she has. Sometimes they're funny, filled with observations about what's around her, and other times they don't say all that much, more like the stamp and scalloped edges are meant to remind me she's out there, this roaming presence in my life.

My brown tray touches Chris's orange one, while Chili removes her plates from her tray and begins to eat like she's in a restaurant. The table is rectangular, light wood that's recently been shellacked. At the far end is a group of sophomores who take notice of us but keep to themselves. "That's true," I say, forking up a bite of salmon. "Maybe you only pay attention to errors when they're directed at you."

Chris eats and gives me a look as a couple of the sophomores glance our way. Chili looks at me and then at Chris. "What? What'd I do?"

"Nothing," Chris says. "It's just . . ." He waits for me to fill in, but I don't want to poke at Chili during her first week. She visited last year enough to know the ropes, but she's still fresh faced and easily bruised. "It's only . . . Love and I were talking . . ."

"You were talking about me?" Chili asks.

"No," I say right away. "No—not like that." I bite a roll, pleading a full mouth so Chris has to do this.

"We adore you, right?" Chris gives Chili his puppy look, all sweet faced and wide-eyed. "But you . . . we're graduating this year."

"With any luck," I add.

"And then I'll be left with no one, blah blah blah," Chili says, intervening for us. "Don't you guys think I know all this? It's not my fault if I gel best with older people."

"You make us sound geriatric," I say. Across the dining hall I see Jacob, and then wonder how it is at this distance, with his generic dark blue T-shirt, even from the back, that I can know it's him. Girls are more easily spotted—the hair, the clothing. Guys blend more, yet I can detect his still-tanned neck, the lank curls that have grown just a little longer since summer.

"Thanks for trying to protect me"—Chili looks at me—"again. But seriously, I can handle it. I'm sure I'll meet people in my classes. I just haven't yet."

"It's been a week," Chris says as though by that time she should have been well ensconced in the sophomore ways.

"When I was a sophomore, I was really good friends

with Lila Lawrence," I say, not to defend Chili but just as a reminder to myself and to Chris.

"And when she graduated you were all sad—it sucks when your friends leave you stranded." He's finished eating and stands up. "Look, Chils, all I'm saying is—get out there and see what happens. It's cool to live like a senior, but when it comes down to it, you're not." He smiles at us, semiunaware of how harsh he sounded. "I have a GSA meeting."

"Looking for a few good men?" Chili asks, putting a brave face forward.

"Always," Chris says; then he pauses. "Or just one."

I watch him walk to the clearing center, where you unload your tray of trash, utensils, and plates. "Notice how he just happened to clear when Haverford's there," I say, deflecting potential tension by turning the conversation back to a reliable topic like Chris's love life.

"If he wants my brother," Chili says, "he's being a dumbass about getting him."

My habit of packing up my tray before clearing has come back in full force. My garbage is crumpled together, my utensils already upended in my water glass for easy unloading. Maybe this method is abnormal, or maybe it's just part of my fiddling instincts (not the instrument—that I can't play—but I can twist, shred, or play with any objects left in front of me). I wonder if Mary was able to partake of fresh-fish Friday, what with the seven—count them, seven—Slim Jims she scarfed down instead of breakfast, courtesy of Charlie, who sent them as a care package with a note saying he'd loved eating them when he was a boarder. Sweet, though slightly misguided due to the fact that I don't eat things that claim to be meat but aren't—a fact I told him this summer.

I check my watch. Right now, Charlie is probably strolling by the Charles River, pondering whatever it is you ponder in college. (The meaning of life? Beer? Your awesome high school girlfriend?)

"You think Chris is really up for a relationship or just the chase?" Chili asks.

"Chris needs to get his priorities straight," I say. "It's one thing to want someone, but another thing altogether to sacrifice yourself to get them."

Chili throws up her hands. "Look, Haverford's no saint. He dealt with years of crap being varsity and closeted, and it's my belief that sometimes he turns all that pent-up denial and frustration on people he cares about."

"Like Chris?" I ask. Even though I don't necessarily abide by Chris's cheating behavior, I still get the emotion behind it. When you want someone, it's hard to turn that intensity off—even if you're hurting yourself and someone else (in this case Ben Weiss) in the process. I begin to tear my napkin into halves and then quarters.

"Have and Ben could break up tomorrow or they could last through college. Who can tell?" Chili tugs at her hair and looks down the table at the group of her classmates dispersing toward the frozen-yogurt center. By junior year, the daily urge to eat fro-yo subsides and the need to perfect the ideal wrap sandwich comes out. What senior year will bring foodwise is still open for discussion. "I'm gonna head out." She doesn't say *with them*, but I can tell from her body language that she's ready to infiltrate the class III masses. "I'll see you at home?" she asks.

"Right." I nod at her, and only in my mind do I add, *Not that Fruckner's home by any means.* Home is where my dad is—Fruckner's where my homework is. All twelve hours of it. Hadley's esteemed faculty have taken no time in assigning an overload that for me translates into chapters of reading, two papers to write this weekend when I was hoping to be carefree with Charlie, and science data to collect, not to mention finalizing my college applications. A huge load will be lifted from my brain and chest when I hand all of those envelopes over to the post office. It's so easy to forget that a week ago today I was on the Vineyard, still surrounded by the best that summer has to offer, and now I'm heavy headed with work and woes.

Due to my freshman-senior mix-up, I haven't yet pleaded my case to Mr. Chaucer. I check my watch and take a breath. Fifteen minutes and I can go to his classroom and hope to be heard. With my few free minutes postlunch and pretrial, I decide I can't wait until tonight to talk to Charlie and head to Foster's Hall to call him.

In the age before cell phones—an age to which we've suddenly returned now that the "new regime" has kicked in—Hadley installed pay phones around campus. My favorite one is an old-school phone box near the computer center, but since that's fairly central (and thus open for eavesdropping), I choose Foster's. Up two flights of stairs, through a set of double doors, I see the gleaming silver and black rectangle that will magically provide me with Charlie's voice.

I drop in my money, holding the receiver to my ear. The heaviness of the handle makes me nervous for some reason, as if cell phone calls are chatty and lightweight, so easy you can slip them into your pocket without a second thought, and these calls—the ones that take actual change, that carry heft in their bulky designs—they mean more.

"Hey!" I love that we're at the place now where we don't need to identify ourselves—even without the benefit of caller ID, we just know.

"Hey," Charlie says, breathy.

"You just run in?" I imagine him in tweed, all movie collegiate even though it's warm today, in the upper seventies, and I'm wearing a tank top and shorts to prove it.

"No." He breathes into the phone, sending shivers up my neck thinking of how his breath feels on my skin. Amazing that the phone lines can offer this kind of visceral reaction. Maybe doing away with cell phones is a good idea. Maybe we all talk so much and so often that we're becoming immune to the beauty of the planned phone call. Not that I scheduled this one, but with my cell I'm much more apt to be multitasking than solely focused on my call, certainly distracted enough that I might miss the chills Charlie's bringing to my arms as he speaks now. "I didn't just run in—I'm actually heading out. . . ."

I swallow and push the phone hard into my ear like that will shrink the miles between us. "Oh, yeah? Where?"

Charlie doesn't wait for me to finish asking before inquiring, "Did you meet with Chaucer yet?"

I check my watch. "Ten minutes."

"Nervous?"

"Very." I take note of how abbreviated out conversation is, how normally long-winded he is—at least, in person. "I'm really glad you're coming this weekend." Just because I'm the one to bring it up, I get stomach flip-flops. What if he cancels? What if he's one week back into Harvard life and already he's decided a relationship with a high school girl is out of the question?

"Me, too," he says. "I can't wait."

I breathe in through my nose, slowing my heart rate. My fingers entwine with the silver phone cord, and I smile into the receiver. "I can't promise much in the way of entertainment...."

In the background, I hear a swoosh of noise—the sound of water running and then keys jingling. "I don't need anything but you." He pauses. "And maybe some lame movie?"

I think about Friday Night Flicks—the A/V crew's answer to empty, campus-chained weekend nights. They show double features, which are watched by only film fanatics, the truly lonely, exchange students who don't know better, and couples who need the dark for purposes other than plot and dialogue. It never occurred to me that one day I might venture to Flicks, but with Charlie, I'm game.

"That I can manage," I say, my voice echoing in the vacant hallway. Following the noise of my words are footsteps. Instinctually, I turn around. Jacob.

He's at the top of the steps, the light from the arched half window behind him casting rays on him so his hair looks angelic, all of him illuminated. I wave using only the fingers of my empty hand, a small wave, like my body doesn't want to give in to the hello. Jacob nods at me. We've yet to formally greet since returning. Sure, there was the picnic, the nods in the hallways while we were otherwise engaged, and a few near misses on the grassy oval encased by Fruckner, Bishop, and Deals, but nothing concrete. No alone time.

"I'm kind of running late," Charlie says.

"Oh, sorry," I say, then wish I hadn't apologized for no good reason. I'm trying not to do that—if only so that when I am really sorry, it means something. "I mean, where are you going?"

I can hear Charlie lick his lips—he does it unknowingly, when he's thinking, or buying time. "Out—well, that's obvious. Um . . ."

Jacob takes a step closer. It's clear from his body language—hands in his pockets, his torso slightly back—that he doesn't want to intrude. "Hey." He says it almost as a whisper.

"Hey." I return the word to him.

"Who was that?" Charlie's voice is at a regular level, which jars me just slightly.

"Oh . . ." I stumble, wondering if I should say *no one*,

which would be insulting to Jacob and a lie, or just—"Jacob. Jacob Coleman?"

Charlie sighs. "Right. Your friend." He says *friend* like it's in italics, but then drops the potentially touchy subject. He was calm on the Vineyard when I explained my past with Jacob—and there's not much past there, when you actually do the math of it. "Anyway, I'll see you Friday—okay?"

"Sure—around five-ish? I want to make sure we get dinner before the dining hall closes." I then feel stupid for saying this, even if it's the truth—my life is, in fact, still regulated by school, while his is not.

"That's kind of early for me—with traffic and all. How about eight?"

My heart sinks. Eight means two hours of time together—maybe two and a half with weekend check-in times. "Seven?" I risk it. It's not a big risk, but still.

"Seven," Charlie says. Then, in the background, I hear the keys jingling again.

"Are those yours?" I picture his keychain, a metal ring encased with a red lacquer that's worn off around the edges.

"Nope—those are Miranda's. She's infamous for her massive set of keys." I laugh, thinking that Charlie's aware of his innuendo—I've got a pretty decent-sized set of keys, too—but he's serious. "She's got, what, twenty keys on here. . . ." He starts to rattle off the different locations the keys work, and it suddenly dawns on me that he's not alone. That this Miranda is probably right there, swinging her massive keys in front of his face.

"And who's Miranda?" I ask. He said her name like I'm supposed to know what it means. My heart flits and faults as I wait for an explanation.

"Miranda," Charlie says again. "Did I tell you about Miranda Macomber—M and M, some people call her. . . ."

I hear her laugh in the background. "M and M . . . ," I say, trying it out, wondering if I'll ever eat the candies again without thinking of this phone call. "But no. No, you never said anything about her." Jacob looks at me, waiting for me to finish the call but not wanting to overtly listen in. I try to keep my tone even—for Charlie's sake and mine. And maybe for Jacob, too, though I don't know why.

"You'll totally love her," Charlie says. "She's—you saw that picture on the bookshelf, right?"

I zing myself back to his cabin on the Vineyard, moving like a ghost in my memory of the décor. Photos of Charlie sailing with Parker. Charlie with his sister, Mikayla. "No—I don't remember any pictures of anyone there. Just on that red bookcase?"

Charlie clears his throat. I check my watch—five minutes and I have to be three buildings and four flights away pleading my case to Mr. Chaucer. "Not at the cabin," Charlie says. "At the big house—my parents' bookcase in the library . . . ," he says. "The Macombers and the Addisons go way back."

I thoroughly dislike when people group themselves into their family names—maybe because my family's small (and now kind of different—with an unknown sister springing up and my mother coming back). It gives this notoriety to *the Addisons* or *the Macombers* that reeks of monogramming everything.

"So she's a family friend," I say, using my wrap-it-up voice. I have to go, and now I'm pressured from all sides.

Charlie pauses. "She's a . . . Yeah, she's my friend." He takes a breath. "My old friend." It's those last three words that tell me all I need to know.

Miranda is his Jacob.

Great.

His Jacob who's already won a prize slot in the big house, with Charlie's uptight family and tight-knit social crew.

Charlie blows a kiss into the receiver, which has to count for something, but I don't do it back. The black receiver is even heavier now, after this conversation, and I place it back with a quiet click.

I stare at the pay phone like it just let me down.

"So," Jacob says as he takes a few steps closer to me. "We haven't really said hi yet."

I turn to him, taking in his presence, the easy way he walks, his side grin that whenever I see it wrenches a part of me. "No," I say back. "But now's as good a time as any." I check my watch. "We have precisely sixty seconds before I have to sprint somewhere else."

Jacob nods. "I accept those limitations."

Leaving the pay phone a few feet away, and the stairs that lead to the rest of campus to our left, Jacob and I hug. The postsummer embrace. He could be thinking about Chloe, his new girlfriend, or the fact that I have Charlie visiting or that he witnessed an awkward phone call. Or, like me, maybe as our bodies touch, Jacob is remembering sitting on the rooftop, the slight pink light fading as we sang together.

I pull back before the hug is too long. "Good to see you," I say and start down the stairs.

"Welcome to senior year," he says.

And maybe I'm imagining it, but I feel his eyes on me as I walk away.

Chapter Seven

Mr. Chaucer's room is probably bird's-eye center to the Hadley campus. The English rooms are light, airy, and on the third and fourth floors of Tennant. Unlike the standard science classroom, each of the human rooms (short for humanities—as though science is not only another building but another species) reflects its teacher. Mrs. Randolph's room is the smallest, crammed with artwork she's collected from her world travels; Mr. Hayward's is Afrocentric, colorful and then stark with black-and-white prints near the windows. There are others—Ms. Lucretia Melon, the resident Shakespeare expert, has a room so filled with old books that there's hardly enough space for students to sit. Often, they kneel on the floor or sit on the table, unable to push the leather-bound volumes off the chairs.

Mr. Chaucer's room isn't like any of those. Sophomore year when I had him for English, I was new—I thought his plain oak desk and the oval table on which years of graffiti had been etched were just his way of saying he hadn't yet settled in. I sat in that classroom for a year and never paid enough attention to the walls to notice that they had their own artwork. Probably I was too distracted by Jacob—class III English was where I'd first met him—and probably I was too caught up in Chaucer's electrifying teaching to notice that patchworking the walls were poems, first pages of short stories, laminated articles about Hadley kids who'd gone on to publish pieces in magazines, or win awards, or wrote in their best script back to Chaucer when they graduated and realized they'd never have another mentor like him.

All of this I'm noticing now, as I sway in my sneakers while I wait for him to enter. I drop my bag on one of the wooden chairs that's pulled out from the circular table and read some of the writing on the wall.

My Father's House, Summer

Deck chairs surrender to the sounds of
the Atlantic—the ocean and periodical—
both of which are steadies alongside the coaster
topped with iced lemonade and its perspiration
horn-rimmed glasses, a blue pen, and two loafers
All of these items, bundled,
like children, within arm's reach.

My heart aches reading this, my mind overwhelmed by the language. How incredible that a seven-line poem can distill this scene and present it so clearly that I'm right there, as it's happening. I love it.

"Good one, hm?" Mr. Chaucer comes in, collapses at his desk, and lets his weathered briefcase topple over on its side.

"I can't write poetry," I say. Actually, I can't write anything—but I figure that might not be the best intro when what I'm trying to do is talk my way into his five-person class that's (a) full and (b) filled with people who've done the required prior courses and who can write.

"What can you write?" Mr. Chaucer, like everyone, looks the same but different. His hair is thinning just the slightest amount—not on top but at the peaks—making him look like one of those Victorian poets but outfitted by Brooks Brothers or J.Crew.

"Well, that's the thing," I say and sit in the chair next to his desk—the one that you might sit in for a conference or if he busted you for plagiarism, the worst offense, according to Hadley's handbook. He faces his desk, his feet on top of it, and I face the wall, calming my nerves by looking at the titles of other poems: "Grand Idea," "General's Army," "Honeymoon on the Moors, 1963." Some of the authors are people I know, or knew of—seniors when I was a sophomore—but many are names that mean nothing, people who, long since writing these pieces, have graduated and moved on. "I want to have a great speech right now." I take a breath. "But I don't. In the movie version I'd be able to quote some famous author or politician and you'd be all . . ." Mr. Chaucer smirks, attentive with his arms crossed.

"I'd start the speech but then cleverly it would cut to the end of the scene, or maybe the perfect song would play over it—Tom Waits or the Jayhawks or Dvořák or Kate and Anna McGarrigle—and then you'd say I could . . ."

Mr. Chaucer sits up, puts his feet on the floor, and checks the clock. Last period is about to start. I have it free—my one blank spot all day—but his group of freshman English students is already clomping up the stairs, waiting to come in the room. They hesitate more than a sophomore would, and a senior would probably come in, sit at the other side of the circle (even though I know circles have no sides), and not worry about interrupting. But the class IVs—they don't know if I'm in trouble or just hanging out.

"Then you could what, Love?"

"Then I could just magically get into your ACW class." I use the abbreviated name, feeling that maybe that will make me more likely to get into the class. Then I realize this is how starstruck people feel when they see a famous person, like calling them by their nickname will really make them close.

Mr. Chaucer stands up and starts writing on the board. I watch the chalk spell out *naturalism*, *setting*, *foreshadowing*, and wonder what they're reading. "I wish I could tell you there is a magic way." He keeps his back to me, writing more. The heat of the day shows up on his back, leaving sweat marks on the cotton of his blue shirt. My own fore-head is rimmed with beads of perspiration—at least my hair's not long anymore. Then he turns around, waving in the students who linger outside the doorway. "Writing, unlike movies, can't do that magic. Of course literature is magical, but the fade-out, quick cut, music over, isn't going to work—at least not the standard forms."

I plead my case, knowing the red second hand on the large black-and-white clock is about to signal I have to leave. "I really, really want to take the class. I know I didn't take the other ones—"

"Why don't you?" Mr. Chaucer takes his seat at the table and looks up at me. "You could enroll in the intro to creative—"

"With all due respect, Mr. Chaucer, I don't think I'm at that level. . . ."

He makes a face like he's tried a dessert that's only decent, not great. "Okay . . . so, why, exactly?"

I spit it out while the freshmen watch, fascinated. "I'm way beyond the intro class, okay? I've been writing since I was five, only I never really thought about it as writing because singing—that other pastime—always overshadowed it. Then, last year, in London—I realized maybe it was *it*."

"It?"

"My . . . focus."

"So take level two."

"But . . ." I try not to whine. "I studied with Poppy Massa-Tonclair. I learned from her. She's amazing."

"I'm sure she is—she writes exquisite novels." Mr. Chaucer points to his bookshelf behind the desk and I recognize the spine of *72 Brook Avenue*, her first book, which won so many literary awards I can't keep track.

"And she thinks I should go for the Beverly William Award. . . ."

Mr. Chaucer bites his lip, nodding. I can tell he thinks this is a stretch. "It's highly competitive."

"I know—wait. Forget that. What I'm trying to ask is, what do I have to do to get into the ACW section?"

"Remind me why you can't take the standard level?" He turns to the students. "Copy what's on the board—I'll be with you in a second."

"Your sections only meet on Tuesdays and Thursdays, which conflicts with required History of Hadley and my science lab." I watch him open his mouth but cut him off—I have nothing to lose now. "And yes, I could fit Mrs. Randolph's section in, but she's not . . ."

"She's a great teacher."

Just for a second, I wonder if Mr. Chaucer and the former Ms. Gregory, now Mrs. Randolph, had a fling. You never know with these teachers—if they're neutered or getting it on back at their faculty housing. Even my dad dated within the faculty pool.

"She is—but she isn't you. . . ."

"I'll accept that flattery and advance you ten places," Mr. Chaucer says, miming moving a piece around an invisible game board. "But it won't get you into ACW. It would be a disservice to you. And to the students—they've been toiling at this for years, and this class is—"

"I know what it is," I say. I've passed by it once before—with my dad. On Wednesday nights, for three hours, three seniors and sometimes a very talented junior sit with Mr.

Chaucer—at his house—reading their work aloud, offering constructive criticism that goes well beyond the usual *It was good* or *I didn't like the ending*.

"Mr. Chaucer?" One of the freshman guys points to the board. "Does that say *definition* or *defepition*?"

"What's *defepition*?" Mr. Chaucer asks, humored.

"I don't know."

"Then go with *definition*." He turns back to me. "Okay. I liked your movie speech. I get it. Poppy Massa-Tonclair and so on. But I'm not going to be swayed by your actions, no matter how proactive they are." He motions for me to start to make my way out so his class can finally get started. The last bell rings. "You hand in to me—on Sunday night—a completed short story." He says that like I understand fully what that means.

"Sunday night . . ."

"At chapel dinner. You said you don't write poetry, so I'm assigning a short story. And I will read it. And consider it. And after that, and on the merit of that alone—not your project with Ms. Massa-Tonclair, not your ardency—I will say yes or no." He looks at me. I open my mouth to say something, but there isn't anything to say. "That's really the best I can offer."

I feel the room swell and recede, the eyes of all the students on me, my legs holding firm to their spot on the floor as though if I stepped one way or the other I would fall, failing already. I can't beg homework, or my two papers, or my boyfriend's impending visit, or the fact that short stories aren't my forte, or cry and say I'm a senior and this is my last shot at this class. All I can do is nod. "Sunday. Okay."

"Good. I look forward to reading it," he says.

"Me, too," I say, wondering what on earth I have to say.

After a dorm dinner from which Lindsay Parrish was notably absent, I retreat from the Fruckner common areas to slave away at my desk. I have yet to get used to my room. It's still, as Mary and I are calling it, a work in progress. There are various formations for double rooms—beds far apart (I hate you), beds pushed all the way together (we're best friends or the room is too small for anything else), beds in an L shape.

We've opted for beds semifar apart, not because we dislike each other but because we have the space. Plus, the theory is that when Carlton Ackers, Mary's joined-at-the-hip boyfriend, appears, they'll have more privacy. Her bed is to the right when you walk in, with her desk at the foot of the bed and her dresser to the right. She's covered the twin bed with a spread that has, for me at least, nautical connotations—light blue edged in green, something you might find at a beach house. So far, her walls are empty, but on her desk is a series of sports trophies—miniature bronze hands holding basketballs with MVP engraved or the word CHAMPION. Next to the trophies is a photo of Mary with Carlton, in front of the Hadley circle, where cars drive up and let students out. The photo isn't recent—they're maybe freshmen—and they are thrilled to be together, caught on film with his arms around her from the back. Her wide smile is turned toward him but her eyes are to the camera.

I do not have such a picture on my desk. Mable is there—the two of us dressed in tacky retro garb and caught midcackle—and my dad is, too. It's a black-and-white picture of him when he was at college, and I've always liked its simplicity and that it was taken long before I was born. I like the reminder of that—the world that existed before I got into it.

Mary's side of the room already hails her sporty, open personality. Her life seems easy to me in the way that any life that isn't your own can seem. She has decent grades, doesn't worry too much about getting a B on a paper, is well liked by all, plays sports, will no doubt get into a good school, and—from what I know—her family life isn't a shambles. All in all, easy. And I'm sure that's how mine could seem, too.

My side of the room is more cluttered—not messy, but fractured. Mary presents one complete vision: *I'm sporty and nautical, and I have a boyfriend.*

My duvet is white, and I'm trying for this airy country-house vibe that really works only if you (a) have a country house and (b) furnish it with Danish pieces that never function in real life.

Behind my bed I put up a little shelf. On that is another picture of Mable, one of Arabella, and one of Chris in which he looks moody and dapper—his thin white duke phase, he calls it. Seeing Arabella's photo tugs at my chest— her father's been ill. I try to imagine what she's doing right now, if she's with her brother—my ex—Asher. Or if they're with Angus at the hospital, or at home with Monti, aka Mum. I haven't wanted to plague her with calls, and with no cell phone, no calling card, and the time change, it's tricky to do even nonplaguing, i.e., regular attempts. We've e-mailed, but nothing big. Just the usual *we'll see, talk soon, loads of love.*

Loads of love and *loads* of work.

I put my book bag on the floor so it doesn't take over my desk and think about what to tackle first: papers, science lab, reading, short story.

I hate that my first full weekend back at school is going to be so pressured. Should I call Charlie and cancel? Maybe I should. Or maybe I would have if I hadn't heard about that charming old friend of his, Miranda. Even her name is old and wealthy—Shakespearean. I imagine she's dark haired with bright red lips, straight out of a sonnet. And in college. With him.

"I'm not canceling," I say to Chris when he comes to my room after getting parietals from Mrs. Ray.

"She's a tough one," he says of the dorm mother. "Not like Chet—he's cool."

"Well," I say, still at my desk, "we can't all be so lucky to get the fresh-out-of-Berkeley guy who wants to be everyone's buddy."

"Okay, Jealousy, what's the problem?" He sits on my bed, then looks out the window. "Shit—you have the palace? That deck—it's like Hadley legend. I heard—"

"I know, I know. People have bedded down out there,

stargazed, and smoked themselves sick. But from the assignment load I have so far, I doubt I'll even get out there. . . ."

Chris puts on a mock sad face. "Oh, woe is me. . . ."

"Woe is I. I am woeful. I feel like I have to choose between academic excellence or, um, not that but something
like trying my hardest—and getting into Chaucer's class
and seeing Charlie."

"Obviously, you don't have to choose." Chris leans back
on his elbows. "You just have to juggle, which you're good
at."

"But what if I'm not?"

He twists his mouth. "Sometimes I play these little
games—"

"Like where you make out with someone else's boyfriend?" I ask, raising an eyebrow.

"No, bitch, not that." He explains. "Like, if I had to do
this or this—which would I do? If I had to pick . . ."

"Give me concrete examples, please." ·

"Fine." Chris pushes his hair off his forehead. "If I had
to choose either leaving the Gay-Straight Alliance—or, um,
GAS, as I've been calling it now and then, which I only just
founded—but in return could have Haverford . . ."

"But those things aren't at all related."

"I know that," Chris says, exasperated. "But sometimes if
you compare the incomparable, you can see what's inside."

"So . . ." I reach for a hair elastic from the pile I have in
a mug on my desk. The mug is from Menemsha Potters,
where the brother of my college counselor, Mrs. Dandy-
Patinko, works, and the elastics are from when I still had

enough hair to warrant them. I pull my hair back into a half ponytail.

"Now you look like you're twelve."

"Thanks, Chris—feeling really ready for Charlie now. Great."

"That's what I mean," he says. "Like, if you could only have one of the following—(a) great grades all year, (b) a serious relationship with Charlie, or (c) kick creative writing ass in Chaucer's class—which would it be?"

"Could I just—" I always do that: try to quantify, qualify, or add extra info to totally unrealistic and hypothetical situations.

"No—no further questions. No justifications. You can't say, *do Charlie and I stay together* or *do good grades equal getting into the college of your choice*. Just pick."

Here's what I see:

Charlie kissing me, the two of us happy the way Mary and Carlton are in her picture. Me as part of a couple. A serious couple.

Then I wipe that away and see:

My report card, the grades in the upper ranges, glowing comments, that pride of work well done.

Then, right as I'm mushing Charlie into my grades, and my father's voice is swelling with my accomplishment, I see something else.

Or rather, I hear something else. A quiet voice, a soft tap on the shoulder. A voice I don't know yet, and then a bunch of empty pages. I see me: the Love that has been and will be, at a desk or in a library or outside—with a journal.

That happy me, documenting everything and churning out words that mean something.

Chris looks at me. "I knew it."

I blush, wondering if he really does know or just assumes I'd pick a love life. "What?"

Chris stands up. "You better get to it."

"I know," I say. "I don't even have a title yet."

Chris nods. All the years and places of our friendship sway between us—I'm so lucky to have him. Of course he could help me figure out what's most important. "You will . . . and when you do, if you want? I'm all ears."

Chapter Eight

Maybe I've been typing for two hours, or maybe one-plus, or maybe more. I don't keep track or look up from my laptop until I have that creepy feeling of being watched. Mary's not back from practice and whatever she did afterward, and I've enjoyed the space and quiet. My story isn't great. It might not even be good—yet. But it is pouring out of me; the fiction Mr. Chaucer demanded. The writing bliss has filtered from the page to my mouth, so when I look up and find Lindsay Parrish staring at me from the doorway, the first thing I do is wipe the smile from my face. Showing emotion of any kind around her makes me too vulnerable.

"Upping the dosage on your meds?" she asks, her fingers tracing a smile on her made-up mouth. She's dressed up, in a close-fitting skirt and tailored top, classic pumps in cream and navy.

"I thought you were the one in need of that," I say. Then, so as not to bend to her level, I add, "I'm working here, so . . ."

"I've been working, too. Had to wine and dine the Harvard dean. . . ." She fakes a sweat, running the back of her hand against her forehead. "Those college applications are so for the masses."

"Sounds nice," I say, keeping my voice flat. She wants me to chew on her power, to froth the way most people do, and I won't.

"Did I miss much?" she asks, faux worried. "I heard it was meatloaf night. Shame. I had roasted wild cod instead, and fresh greens, served with a—"

"I appreciate the menu, but I have to get back to work." I turn to the screen, hoping she'll leave.

"Right . . . people like you, you have to actually try, don't you?"

For some reason, this stings. Maybe more than it should. But I am trying. I do try. I turn to the screen and type *Amelia Lessing was the sort of girl who could stick you with a pushpin and be the first in line to offer you rubbing alcohol as a salve.* I turn back to Lindsay. "All you missed was the social action committee," I say, and Lindsay shrugs. "We voted. Fruckner's doing the guide-dog program."

"Dogs?" Lindsay humphs.

"Sorry it's not so glamorous—but your fashion fund-raiser didn't fly."

"Figures," Lindsay says. It's like she has nowhere to go. Then I realize that maybe she doesn't. She doesn't need to worry about getting into college, her mother's donated a new building or something here so she can't get kicked out (despite her best efforts last year when she passed out on the quad), and she's not big into extracurricular activities. She must be bored out of her mind.

Note to self: Do not feel pity for LP.

"Anyway," I say, "our puppy gets delivered next week." My dad said he'd pick it up—so maybe I can get special permission to go with him. The fact that I need to be signed out of the dorm even to go with my father is ridiculous, but I can't waste time on that now.

Lindsay stares at me, my attempts at decorating my room, the music I have playing (OMD—*Crush*, thanks to Mable's immense import collection), my work, my whole being, as though I'm from another solar system. One where things matter. She's going to break, I think, to cry or say something real.

And then, with her eyes narrowed, she gives a snort. "Good luck with your 'work.'" She makes air quotes. "I'm going to hang out with my cool new roommate."

And right then, in back of her in the corridor, I see Chili—dressed up, too, and waving to me as she heads into her room. Their room. So she accompanied the Piranha on her woo-the-dean dinner. This makes me nervous, but I don't have time for nerves.

I turn back to the screen, where the cursor is waiting for me to write a story worthy of that Wednesday night ACW group. My tendency, which I'm realizing as I attempt to write fiction, is that I suck at coming up with names. Either they sound unbelievable or else all the good names belong to people I already know. I let this distract me for a full fifteen minutes and then decide to steal/honor the real

Nick Cooper by creating a character who isn't like him but who shares his name.

Just past the edge of the field where the muddied footprints were was where Nick Cooper found the first signs of something wrong.

The real Nick Cooper is in India, or Morocco, or Dubai, or Lima, but he sends letters to me that transcend how we met. That is, he never brings up Asher Piece, Arabella's brother, or my time in London, and when I write back I seem to have so much to say about my inner workings and present life that I never bother with those lame *remember whens*. Mainly because we don't have much to remember together. So I use his name in fictional form because he's named after a Hemingway character (his real name is Nick Adams Cooper), and I know what it's like growing up with a heavy-hitting literary name (Charles Bukowski—no relation—was a famous poet).

I figure I'll be stuck once I've made up Amelia Lessing and fake Nick Cooper, but I'm not. I don't want to fall into the hellhole of high school writing that takes place in a classroom or dorm or coffee shop, so I fling my characters elsewhere: to a weird beach in Mexico I went to when I was little, with Mable. I remember a blue hammock, muddy paths after a torrential rain, and always the threat of panthers in the Yucatán. And that's what I want to have in the story, this threat lurking in the background, so the reader never fully relaxes.

I know that Charlie's coming and my work is piling up and I need to stop by and see my dad, and that at some point I might even want to attempt a social life, but for the minutes and hours I spend writing, my mind and body seem to exist only in the story.

When I next check the clock, it's almost eleven. I stretch my back, feeling the ache of having been hunched over. My wrists are sore (Note to self: Must buy gel pad so as not to lose feeling in arms), my eyes sting, but the rest of me is quite pleased. Not perfectionist pleased, but filled with something solid.

"What's been captivating you?" Mary Lancaster asks.

I jump upon hearing her voice. "I didn't even know you were there."

She's stretched out on her bed, propped up by a back-rest some of the girls call husbands, made of yellow corduroy, which completes her beachy side of the room. "I've been reading here for almost a half hour. You didn't even move when I came in, and I didn't want to bother you. . . ."

I stand up and do postrunning stretches. That's how I feel, exhausted and exhilarated the way I do after a great run. I tell her this. "Does that make sense?"

Mary nods. "That's why I didn't interrupt. You looked so . . . intense. Like, when I'm covering someone, or if I have a plan with the ball, there's nothing anyone in the stands can do to distract me—I'm all-the-way present there." She looks at me and lets her book fall onto her chest. "Is that what you mean?"

"Exactly," I tell her. "What're you reading?"

She shrugs. "*The Tempest*. Shakespeare."

I smile at her. "I like that play—but not as much as the other ones."

"Well," Mary says, arching her tanned bare feet, "I'd rather be . . . oh, there's lots of things I'd rather be doing than reading this. But"—she looks back to her book and picks up a blue highlighter—"work's work, right?" She starts reading, and then pauses. "Hey, you're all into books; tell me about this one."

I massage my head, save my work on the computer, and then go sit on Mary's bed. It feels both unusual and nice to be with a friend at this time of night. Normally, at home, I'd be by myself, flicking through late-night TV or else lying in bed watching the shadows change every time a car zooms by, either way trying to switch off my overactive brain.

"So"—I pick up the play—"*The Tempest*. There's a storm . . . and all these characters"—I point to their names— "they get carried ashore, where they meet Miranda and her dad, Prospero. He's the one who made the storm."

Mary takes the book back. "Thanks. I've been reading the first three pages over and over again, but it's not really my thing." She mimes a drop shot. "That's more my thing. Not that I don't like books—just . . . it's not that easy to relate to, you know?"

"Yeah?" I lick my lips and slick my greasy hair behind my ears. I need to shower to rid myself of my slime. "Maybe if you, you know, think about how it's a love story, and there's this conflict between the father and daughter—she falls in love with this guy Ferdinand, and Prospero doesn't like that . . ."

Mary watches me. "I think you should read it, tell me all about it, and then I'll write the paper." She waits for my reaction.

"Mary . . . I . . ."

"Relax, Love. I'm totally kidding. You think I'd risk any form of plagiarism or rule breaking?"

I'm relieved to hear her say that. I still don't know her well enough to get when she's joking, and the thought of cheating or doing someone's work for them really makes me queasy. "Speaking of rule breaking, what's up with you and your man?"

Mary's smile fades a little, but she tries to cover it up with lots of head tilting back and forth as she says, "Oh, Carlton's fine. He's always . . . fine. We're—we—we just have a rhythm. . . ."

I raise my eyebrows. "Meaning?"

Mary blows air out her lips and makes the sound of a horse whinnying. "All along, everyone talks about relationships and how great they are. How that's what you're supposed to want, and get, and stay in. . . ." She traces the pattern of her coverlet with her finger. "But it's . . . it's like a job, after a while."

I grimace. "That doesn't sound fine, Mary. . . ."

She shakes her head. "Don't listen to me. I'm just all PMS-y, which means you will be, too. By midyear the entire dorm will be on the same schedule. Believe me—it's not fun."

I sigh, tired, and smile at her, wondering if she had a bad night with Carlton or if she's just in a cranky mood. "Well, let me know if I can lift your spirits. I'm gonna jump in the shower now. . . ."

"Avoiding the rush in the morning?"

"That and it'll relax me before bed. I'm still not used to it here. . . ." I look around the room. Sometimes when I lie in bed, my body feels like it's pointed the wrong way, or I feel as though I've forgotten something—to take my vitamin, or brush my teeth—and then I realize it's just being in a new place, and how disorienting that is, until one day—or night—it just isn't anymore.

"I'll be here," Mary says and chews on her highlighter pen cap. "Me, Prospero, and Miranda."

Miranda, I think as I take my small bottle of shampoo and conditioner, my minisoap and extra-large towel. My dad ironed name tags on everything—one of his guilt-ridden efforts, no doubt—and I hold my own name as I walk to the shower. Miranda. Beautiful Miranda who steals the heart of Ferdinand. I wonder what Charlie is doing. If he's with her. If they're working side by side in the library, or out for a late burger at Bartley's. If he's talked about me.

I hang my towel up on a small metal hook and take off my clothes, and as I lather, rinse, but don't repeat (takes too much time and it's just a ploy on the manufacturers' part to make you go through the product faster and rebuy it), it hits me that maybe Charlie's thinking about me, too.

Of course, I can't call him now. No cell phones. Just a

pay phone in a room the size of a closet next to the common room. There's even a phone log so when the dorm phone rings, whoever gets it writes down who called and when and if there's a specific message. We all get to read about moms calling with news from home, or friends at other prep schools leaving coded messages like "Get the cookies—I've got the milk." It's yet another display of the lack of privacy afforded by the dorms. My plan is to be proactive and make the calls before they come in so as to avoid Lindsay—God forbid—talking to my mother or Sadie—the sister I hardly know—or Charlie.

It doesn't occur to me before I overhear Ms. Parrish in the shower that perhaps she already has.

I pull my name-tagged towel in with me to dry off. It's a ritual from home—I always stay in the stall, keeping the steamy air trapped in as much as possible, before I step out. Sealed off by the curtain, it's actually peaceful in here. And late. I'm working my way from head down to feet, noting how much less water I have dribbling down my back now that my hair's short, when I hear her voice.

"Anyway, you should've seen it—he was so checking me out." I swallow and stop rubbing my damp self as I listen to Lindsay. "You saw him, right? Talk about dating outside of one's echelon . . ."

I stay still, frozen and now getting a little cold, hoping she won't see that I'm right behind her in the shower area. The bathroom is large—with a wall of sinks topped by mirrors, and then at the back, changing benches and eight shower stalls separated by coral-colored curtains.

"Did you have fun?" Lindsay asks.

I can't see out the slit in the curtain to know whom she's with, but then I hear Chili. "I did. It meant a lot. Today was . . . kind of hard."

I wonder why and then realize she means the lunch with me and Chris and how we told her she needs friends her own age. We didn't mean to be harsh, and it wasn't meant to degrade our friendship with her, but now I'm guessing we—or I—wasn't clear enough. She goes on. "It's like Love wants the best of both worlds—me around whenever she's lonely and has no one else, but if it's a senior thing or with her boyfriend, then forget it."

Instant guilt combines with a certain aggravation. I mean, fine—feel that way and talk to me, but spew it to Lindsay? To the girl we dissed all summer? Chili was the one who came up with the various LP incarnations—Lame Priss, and so on.

"Don't worry about it," Lindsay says. "You've got me now. And you were great at dinner. You really showed how diverse I am—" Lindsay stops herself. "I mean, I like having friends with diverse backgrounds. Plus . . . he was into me, right?" Chili starts to hem and haw.

Ah, so Lindsay used Chili's mixed race to demonstrate she's not only old-guard money and stuck-up. And it probably worked. But how can Chili stand being used like that?

"At least you're honest," Chili says. "First Love screwed me over on the room thing—no offense, Linds—and then today . . . Well, never mind. At least we know where her priorities are."

They know where my priorities are? I'm not even sure *I* know. How can they be so sure?

I decide that lurking in the shower stall makes me an accomplice to my own demise, so I wrap myself in my towel, grab my shampoo stuff, and fling aside the curtain. Clearly, they're surprised. Lindsay's mouth—filled with her expensive European toothpaste (How necessary is it to import it from Portugal? Ever heard of Tom's or Crest?)—drops open, and Chili looks very embarrassed.

"Love, hi," Chili says, tugging at her springy hair, which I know for a fact means she's feeling caught and conflicted.

"Don't you mean good-bye?" I ask. "Isn't that what all that was, Chili? A see-ya to whatever friendship we had?"

Chili clenches her fists and looks at me via the mirror. "That's what *you* did! You and Chris—a traditional gang-up on the new girl right at lunch."

"We weren't ganging up on you!" I yell; then I realize yelling isn't going to help. So I talk calmly, keeping my towel tucked by my shoulder. "All we were saying is that we'll feel really guilty if—nine months from now, at graduation—you have no one to sit with while we're marching across the platform." I look at her. "My closest friend was a senior when I was a sophomore and it was great, but then it sucked—and I wished . . . Looking back I think I missed out because I didn't get to know other people."

"Like?" Chili asks.

"Like me." Mary Lancaster stands in the doorway, her

height filling up most of it, a green toothbrush poised in her hand like a microphone.

I smile at her. "Right."

"Oh, please." Lindsay rinses her mouth out and licks her front teeth. "You're just jealous, Love. Of the time I have with Chilton"—Lindsay uses Chili's full name and I flinch—"and that I took her out instead of you."

Instead of me? Um, that's an invite that would never come. "I don't need to wine and dine the chancellor—"

"The dean," Chili corrects. I shoot her a look.

"To make it into college . . ." I take a breath. "You know what? You guys should do what you want. I can't control you, can't make decisions for you, so I'm just going to deal with my own life." I turn to Chili. "Which I hope you'll be part of."

Chili smiles. "So you weren't giving me the brush-off?"

"Not at all," I say. Chili's relief makes me happy, and I'm glad that I didn't hide in the shower stall. I raise one eyebrow to Lindsay—my look of triumph—and start to walk out when I step on the hem of the extra-large towel and it comes right off.

Lindsay acts poised, her face icy as she regards me with a look one might give a toddler with sticky hands—cute, but no thanks. "Brush-offs aren't ever cut-and-dried, are they?"

Chili looks at Lindsay and then at me. Lindsay puts her hands on her hips, annoyed by my damage control with Chili.

I step in again, saying, "Really, Chil, I wouldn't just leave you high and dry."

"I'm sorry, Love." Chili frowns, suggesting to me that maybe there's more she's sorry for than just believing LP. Then she waves at the air, trying to move us out of the awkward space and into new conversational territory. "Oh, by the way, tomorrow's Harriet Walters's unbirthday," Chili says. Lindsay stands with her hand gripping her Euro toothpaste as though she wishes it contained ammunition.

"Yum, cake!" I smile. The best part of the unbirthdays is the sugar high—we've only had one so far, but the rest will be scattered throughout the year. Lindsay is technically in charge; she picks the dates, but Mrs. Ray bakes the cake. Behind Lindsay's eyes, the wheels of evil are turning. In a movie, this would be the part where sparks fly out from her pupils.

"What?" I ask her, annoyed by her presence and at myself for being flustered by her.

Lindsay remains focused, giving a shrug. "Nothing."

Mary picks up my dropped soap and shampoo while I—completely naked—try to stop slipping on the wet floor and get my towel back where it belongs. I don't have much public shame, in fact I start to crack up about this—it's so me. So klutzy. And I keep laughing until Lindsay oozes by me. Probably she feels defeated.

"Oh, Love?" She gives me the one eyebrow back. "I have a message for you. . . ."

Great, I think; now she knows my family business. "Who called?"

"No one," she says. Then she flashes her trademark evil face—a combination toothless smile and pinched forehead. "But Charles Addison and his—*ahem*—friend, Miranda, send their best."

Now it's my turn to be shocked. Naked and shocked. And definitely not laughing.

"Don't worry," Mary says as we lie in the dark. "Things have a way of working out, you know?"

I lie flat on my back, the window near me open for fresh air, my palms flat on the bed while my damp hair sticks to my neck. Did Lindsay make that up? She couldn't have, right? Probably her grandparents had tea with the Macombers, Miranda's clan, back when my relatives were being persecuted or working in factories in faraway lands. What bugs me, too, is that Chili did nothing. Was she in on Lindsay's name-dropping meanness? I shudder when I picture Chili falling into Lindsay's seemingly sweet guise of dinners, dancing, pedicures, and predatory nature. "Things have a way of working out," I quote back to Mary. "You're the kind of person who believes stuff like that."

"What's that supposed to mean? That I'm, like, dumb and simple?" She laughs. She points to her desk. "Sign Harriet's unbirthday card, by the way."

I nod. "No. It's just . . . how do they work out? When? Why? And what do I do to make it work out faster?"

"Man . . . You've got motor-brain." She whistles a song I don't know, and then stops. "Here." She hands me the card, which is nearly filled with messages and signatures that will no doubt brighten Harriet's day without the pressure of turning a year older. My own real birthday is creeping up. "Sign it and come with me."

In one second Mary's by the side of my bed in her T-shirt and boxers, her hair freed of its usual ponytail. She bangs the window.

"What the—" I sit up, leaning back on my pillows.

Mary knees open the window farther, then reaches for the side lock. It opens with a click, and the next thing I know I'm with my roommate, outside on the porch, staring across the people-empty oval, the barren porches of Bishop and Deals.

"Now, this is what I call chilling out." Mary lies all the way flat on the wooden slats, her body slim as she faces the night sky.

"Do you wish you were here with Carlton?" I ask. "It's mighty romantic . . . and now he's only a dorm away. . . ."

"Ugh," Mary says. "I guess part of me does . . . but part of me—I mean, space is good. You have a long-distance thing going on—definitely appreciate that while you have it. It seems like the best of both worlds."

"How so?" Sitting here on campus as a boarder makes Charlie seem even farther away. Without those summer freedoms of time and hopping in my car to visit him or hanging out all day at the docks, there's a gap where I should feel his hand on mine.

"You get to live your life, do your work, practice, whatever . . . and then see your person on the weekends. You know you have someone, but you aren't dealing with the hassle of constant contact."

I don't want to pressure her with questions about the state of her relationship with Carlton. They're a campus institution, practically, so to think that she might not be all happy in the coupling is surprising. Rather than demand to know what she means, I follow suit, lying back on the porch.

My shoulder blades adjust to the dips in the old planks and I settle in as though we're at the beach, or somewhere without homework and mean girls and stress. "Hey—stars!"

"You catch on fast, Bukowski."

I laugh, just a small laugh, the kind when you recognize something in yourself.

"What?" Mary asks.

"Nothing. . . . Only—you're maybe the second person to call me by my last name. Ever."

"Who's the first?" Mary asks.

Above us the stars blink and fade, seeming bright and then suddenly leaving. "No one," I say. "Just someone I met."

We lie there until we don't know what time it is, until the sky's shifted and the air is still unthinkably hot, and then—without saying we're ready to go back in, because we're not—we climb through the window and head for bed.

Chapter Nine

The bell rings at three fifteen on Friday and I can officially do the countdown to being kissed. Four hours. Four
hours plus or minus, depending on traffic, and that gap I've
been lugging around with me will be filled by Charlie's
presence. I've managed to put aside bad feelings and worries from the Lindsay incident—so she met him, so she met
Miranda, so . . . so what. Kind of.

And I've managed to do a rough draft of my short story.
Title: "What Wasn't There." Of course, this was at the sacrifice of all other homework, so I'm giving myself a few
blissful hours with my boyfriend before I trek back to the
reality that is my work. Not to mention the skulking pressure of the college process.

On Fridays, the day students linger and boarders either
rush for sports activities or hang out outside. Recently, the
temperature's been creeping up again, though, so the student center is the place to be with its cold drinks and colder
air. The old dorms (Fruckner, Bishop, Deals) are woefully

antiquated with their lack of AC. If you're lucky, you get a fan. Or—if you're really lucky—you get a balcony like me and Mary, even if it's technically off-limits.

I wait for my dad to wave me into his office so I can say hello before the weekend starts. He slams the phone down, takes a breath, and tries to look calm.

"What was that?" I ask him.

"Frustrating," Dad says, describing the emotion but not the reason for the phone call.

We're separated by his giant desk. On the top of it are folders and memos, papers to sign, the handbook, and a stack of messages on pink slips of paper. I touch them with my finger. "Lots of phone calls, huh?"

"Tons." He looks wiped out, his forehead sweaty and wrinkled, his shoulders downturned.

"You're always so pumped up at this time of year, Dad."

"Well, it's not normally ninety-plus degrees this time of year." He stands up, comes around the desk, and hugs me. It's the first hug we've had since he dropped me off at the dorms. First, I thought it was because he was busy, but now I think it's because we're both trying to make it work. If he treats me like his daughter the day student, it will only add to my dislike of the dorms, or serve as a reminder of what I don't have. And if I make him my dad instead of my head-master, it's like I never left home. And part of me wants him to miss me, to know that he can't have it both ways.

"So what's wrong with hot weather?" I ask. Then I think back to my restless night, kicking the duvet off, my T-shirt slicked to my stomach.

"What's wrong is—the overprivileged—"Dad stops himself, remembering we're in his office, not at our house. "Many of the parents feel their children are uncomfortable—God forbid—and are insisting on the installation of air-conditioning."

"Couldn't you put a window unit in each room?" I suggest, thinking it sounds so good—Charlie and I could sit there, in the cold air, doing . . . doing whatever we can do with the door open at least five inches and with three feet on the floor at all times as per parietal rules.

"It's nice of you to suggest, Love, but the cost of hundreds of those units wouldn't make sense—plus, until we upgrade the oldest dorms, the electricity supply can't take the mass."

Dad sighs and I see concern register all over his mouth. He goes back to his desk, clicks on the screen, and pulls up the weather site. "They say it could break tomorrow. Or Sunday. We'll see."

"And if not?"

Dad shakes his head. The phone rings again and he puts his hand on it to pick it up. "If not, I'll have to come up with something. Just hope for my sake we don't get a real heat wave." The phone blares again and my dad's secretary sticks his head in and points to the phone, meaning Dad has to pick up. "That—that would mean serious intervention."

I leave my dad to fend off irate parents whose kids have been calling home and complaining about the heat and how they can't study, can't think, can't sleep, and can't possibly achieve all that they're meant to without the aid of air-conditioning. Never mind that people survived centuries in these very buildings without it. As I take the stone steps two at a time and head toward Maus Hall—or as it's known, EEK!—I realize I never told my father what I was doing this weekend. That he never mentioned his plans to me. That while we hugged, we had that true boarding school experience. He knows nothing about what I'm doing and I know little of him.

The quiet of Maus Hall is a welcome change from the Frisbee shouts outside and the continual complaints of heat. Maus is cooler than many places, since it's built of stone, its walls thick. I take a seat on one of the brown leather chairs, enjoying the cool of it against my bare thighs, until after thirty seconds, I begin to stick to it. I check my watch. Four o'clock. Closer to Charlie every second. With the stacks of books around me and nothing but the smell of stale coffee and fresh college catalogs, I think about him. The real him—how we talk about books and joke, how good a listener he is about my family, the way he looked in his dinner jacket at the Silver and White event at the Vineyard. They called it an *event* to make it seem less glitzy and downplay the glamour so as not to disrupt the image of the Vineyard's kick-back style of wealth, but it's basically a ball. I wore a borrowed white silk dress that Charlie compared to moonlight, and we danced in our bare feet, outside on a custom-made floor while torches lit the night and fireflies competed for brightness. We kissed a lot then, and more, down by the dunes of Squibnocket Point. The thought of that night now gives me chills, and those delicious haunting stomach flips when you remember with your whole body, not just your mind.

Chris and Chili kept asking about what might happen with him—wink-wink, nudge-nudge—but I'm not sure. Not sure yet. There aren't that many things in life that you can't undo, but sex is one of them; you can't unkiss someone. You can't unsleep with them. And knowing my propensity for dwelling on everything over and over again, I just want to make sure—as much as doubtful Love can be—that Charlie is *it*. Not kind of it.

In a cotton ensemble worthy of its own category of clothing, Mrs. Dandy-Patinko, my college advisor, appears at the front of the room and waves me into her office. I peel my thighs—which have adhered to the leather chair—from the seat cushion and follow the swish of her skirt. It's billowy, with stripes in multiple widths and colors; a Technicolor umbrella turned upside down.

"It's SIBOF time again!" she says when I sit down. Statistical Information Based on Facts. The Hadley computer program that chews up all your personal facts—scores, grades, and nicks and chinks in your armor—and churns them around with the most recent admissions info from colleges in this country and abroad and—*boom*—presents you with percentages you may or may not want to see.

"How was your summer?" I ask, deflecting the college chat as long as I can. It's not that I dread SIBOF anymore—it's more that my own confusion about schools gets to me.

"Lovely," she says. "And you? Are you any closer to coming up with your list?"

Everyone else has one. The list. Maybe it has only one school on it or maybe it's your top twelve, but almost everyone does. "I don't," I say. "Have it yet, I mean."

Mrs. Dandy-Patinko squints at me, her brown eyes resting on my hairline. "My, it's hot . . . not exactly college-cruising weather . . ."

"That's true—it's always fall, really autumnal in those pictures. . . ." I point to the catalogs on her desk.

"Love . . . ," she starts. Her nails are painted a deep brown, chipped on the thumbs. I imagine her at night, with a bottle of polish unopened as she watches some game show.

"I know; I know what you're going to say—it's time. And I need to come up with a list. But the thing is—I wrote the applications!" I smile at her, proud. "I did them, just like you suggested. Over the summer. Recently, in fact. And I have a range, too, just like you said. Yale and Brown and Amherst and Florida State because of their writing program, although to be honest, this heat bugs me now and it's like this all the time there—"

"They have air-conditioning." She watches me like I'm my own tennis match.

"And where else—oh, I bagged UCLA for numerous reasons . . . My dad didn't really want me that far away, and my mother . . ." I stop. "I have family and I want to see where they'll be. And UVM and Bowdoin—it's so pretty in Maine and up there—and also New York, with NYU and Columbia. And also UCL, in London, and Oxford, too—because how *great* would it be to go there? Hello, punting and . . ." My mouth is open, but Mrs. Dandy-Patinko is quiet, so I clam up, too.

"And you've done all these applications?"

I nod. "And the supplements. I get too worried about how much work I'll have, and time management, so I tend to just plow through. Of course the finishing touches are pending. That's on my to-do list for the weekend." I pause. "And I need teacher recs . . ."

"Yes." Her voice is low, hesitant. "You'll need those."

I search her face to figure out what I've done wrong. She fiddles with the collar of her shirt, pressing the points down. I reach to do the same. I've found that in stressful situations I sometimes mimic the person I'm speaking with. Arabella first noticed this, and we had a sign—she'd sort of wiggle her pointer finger—to alert me. Now I notice it myself, but miss her wiggling at me. A recent e-mail from Arabella let me know her father, Angus, is doing much better after his ill health this summer. She sounded good, normal even, and I make a mental note to e-mail back. To tell Charlie when he gets to Hadley. "Did I forget something?"

"You've done absolutely everything," she says. "You'll need to tour, of course. . . ."

I pull my red book out of my bag and flip it open. "All set—a day tour at Harvard . . . and BC, then a weekend in Maine and Vermont, and the others I'll—"

"You've done it all." She sighs, still fiddling with her

collar. Then she clasps her hands in front of her and I fight the temptation to do the same. "But, Love, you can't apply to that many."

I stop, cross my hands over my chest, even though I had a sneaking suspicion that was coming. "Why not?"

"Because it's a fortune, first of all . . . and—before you say you earned money working this summer and can afford it—I'd like to suggest something to you." She smooths her clownish skirt and takes a plain piece of paper from a stack on the side of her desk. "Here . . ." She draws a couple of triangles in the upper right-hand corner. "That's UVM and Bowdoin. Then here—on the other side—is UCLA, which I know you've negged for now." She takes a deep breath and I wonder if it's inevitable that teachers pick up the teenage vernacular. Some sound sad, the slang betraying their years, but people like Mr. Chaucer and Mrs. Dandy-Patinko get away with it. Chaucer because he gets it and Mrs. DP because she's just so not currently in high school and so bedecked with quilted vests and loafers and kindness that it fits in an ironic way. Maybe I pick up details like this for future stories, or maybe, like the humor as defensive tactic, I sit here sucking up all this useless crap to avoid the true content of the conversation. "Love?" Mrs. Dandy-Patinko taps her Hadley multicolored pen on the desk. "You listening?"

"Yeah," I rejoin the college appointment as she's saying—

"And down here is FSU—excellent writing program—hot, though, you said. And over here are the New York schools, and . . ." She keeps going, filling up the page with arbitrary designs until I get her point. "What does this look like to you?"

"A bad map?"

"Exactly." Mrs. Dandy-Patinko nods. She hands the paper to me. "A *very* poor map. And your college search— it's not meant to result in that. You see, people find a school—a kind of school, a type, large and rowdy, academic or sporty, geographically desirable or one with an outstanding Latin American program. But they don't apply to everyplace."

I imagine playing pin the tail on the college, basically me in a blindfold deciding my future. "The only thing I know . . . or that I think I know"—I loathe my indecisive-sounding voice—"I want to do is apply for the Beverly William Award."

Mrs. Dandy-Patinko nods and breathes through her nose. I can't tell if she's happy about what I said or dubious. "Great. That's a concrete plan."

"Solid."

She taps her cheek, thinking. "You'll need to be nominated for that, just to apply. But you know that." She checks something on her computer screen. "And there are three runner-up awards, too."

I try not to take that personally, but I wonder if it's her job to remind me how unlikely it is to win the Beverly William. "Oh."

"You'll have to file the paperwork by . . . looks like this year's deadline is right after Columbus Day."

Sighs pour out, one after the other, as I picture Columbus Day weekend—usually fun filled and festive, instead plagued by applications, paperwork, and proofreading. The biggest part of the BW Award is the creative-writing sample. You can submit only one, and the travel grant stipend is pretty much based on that—whether the committee thinks your writing stands a chance in the real world.

"But the Beverly William Award is just one thing, right?" I pause. "I bet a lot of other Hadley people apply, too. Not to mention writers from all over the country. The world, probably." She nods. "So what does the other stuff say, that bad map? That I want to . . . ?"

"What it says to me is that . . ." She begins to tidy her desk, signaling to me that our appointment is over. "Is one of three things: Either you haven't found the right school, you haven't admitted to yourself what your real focus is and selected schools with the same leanings, or . . . or you need a break."

"A year off?" I ask. I blush. "I feel like you're telling me I'm not good enough."

"I think we both know that's not true," she tells me. "But, I guess we'll see how you react to your actual campus visits. Maybe you'll get snowed in at UVM and think, *Forget it*. Or maybe you'll check out Columbia's writing program and feel it's perfect. Or not. Harvard's the first interview on your list, correct? Then you can do a handful at the Campus Collegiate Conference." The CCC (unlike chocolate chip cookies—the other CCC) comes to town like the hellish version of the circus—you run from one building to the next interviewing with on-the-road admissions people, tailoring yourself to what you think they want to hear.

Mrs. Dandy-Patinko hands me a list of dates and times for interviews and visits and I nod, taking in the Harvard name—that esteemed centuries-old place that, right now, I equate with both the epitome of academia and booty. I smirk and remind myself that while she's cool, Mrs. Dandy-Patinko isn't *that* cool. Harvard. That Harvard. Only a couple of weekends away.

"So, what do I do now?" I stand up. By her clock I have only a couple of hours until my weekend—my *real* weekend, meaning Charlie—finally kicks off.

"You do what you're doing—think about it—about where you could really not just enroll but *live* for the next four, three, or six years, and . . . Love?"

"Yeah?"

"No matter how many places appeal to you? There's still one out there that's going to feel like home."

Chapter Ten

Charlie's mouth is on mine and his hands are doing the guy puppet show, snaking across my back as a team, then separating, with one on my neck, the other plunging down my already stretched-out V-neck. Then, just like that, he stops.

"What's the name of it?" He's slightly out of breath, as though we've been jogging for a while as opposed to pawing each other in the dark at the oh-so-very Hadley Friday Night Flicks. The audience is made up of freshmen, flings, and a few film buffs all folded into uncomfortable chairs built for test taking, not movie watching.

In the dark I look at Charlie's eyes, watch the screen's images flicker on his face. Then I turn for a second to the movie. "*A Room with a View.*" I point and do a quick recap. "See, she's the main character—and they're in Italy now, which is supposed to represent the feeling side of things for her, you know, the lusty countryside with passionate people. Lucy—that's her name—has to sort of choose between

Cecil, who's very uptight English, i.e., the intellectual side, and George, who's all lust and feeling. You can tell because George has floppy hair—that means he's basically out of control in movie terms. You know, visually."

I get all this out in just one breath, maybe two. Charlie raises his eyebrows, letting his hands drop from the ten- and two-o'clock position on me to his lap. "I did this comparison paper when I was at LADAM," I explain. "Of the movie and the book and all this E.M. Forster stuff."

I look at the screen, where, finally, in a moment of pure emotion, George grabs Lucy in a field of flowers and kisses her. I lean in toward Charlie and whisper, despite a glare from one of the film-heads behind me. She's already kicked my chair once "by accident," meaning it wasn't. I continue with my analysis. "It's also a study in agrarian life versus—"

"I didn't mean what's the name of this movie." Charlie plays with my fingers absentmindedly, as though they're not attached to the rest of me, tapping my knuckles, thumbing the side of my thumb. I wonder if he notices the peeling skin where I nibbled too far in science this week.

"Oh." I wait for him to explain, feeling stupid for my many ramblings about *A Room with a View*.

Charlie stands up, further annoying the girl behind us. Charlie deals with her with his newfound diplomacy. "One moment and you, too, will have a room with a view." He steps into the aisle and gestures with his head for me to follow. When I first met him, I doubted he'd have said anything to that girl. Or maybe he'd have made some sarcastic comment about how she could rent the damn thing any day of the week. But not the version of Charlie that's made to appease his parents, the Charlie who dropped his fishing rod and pickup truck and donned a tie and sports jacket on more occasions than necessary at the end of the summer.

Still, he isn't so reserved that he missed the opportunity to grope me in the dark, and in this I find relief. Not just that he still wants me after being dropped back into High School Land, but that he's not so playing by the rules that he's lost his ability to relate to the masses. And that in those masses, I'm still the one dating him.

"So, what *is* the title?" Charlie's voice echoes in the high-ceilinged corridor. The A/V room is in the basement of the science center, cloistered away from the thick heat outside.

"Of what?" I pause by a sculpture that's boxed in by Plexiglas. Hadley's forever trying to merge the artistic realm with the scientific, as though shoving a sculpture near the Bunsen burners and soapstone counters will solve everything.

"Man, are you out of it or what?" Charlie flicks his eyebrows up, then pushes past me. He opens a swinging double door that leads to my science lab and goes through. My heart speeds up, wondering if he's truly annoyed or just perturbed.

"I love that you just parade around here like it's your school," I say. And I do. That confidence to burst through doorways without knowing what's on the other side.

"Oh, it's definitely not that," he says. He doesn't need to

elaborate with more than a sigh. "This is Parker territory, for sure."

I'm about to object when Charlie flicks on the lights. Basking in the thoroughly unflattering green hue provided by the fluorescent tubes overhead, I watch his hand as he touches the wall. Set into the concrete (again, science is "hard" and "earthy" and so the building is made out of slabs of stone and concrete) are years' worth of names, each one given a plaque. "See? Here you go. Proof." He touches the thin rectangle that reads PARKER ANDERSON, then spins around so he's facing me. "So, what does a guy have to do around here to get an answer?"

"To what?" With my head tilted to the side, my hair barely touches my shoulder. Right now, I feel naked without it. I never knew how much I hid behind my red shagginess until now. "You've been enigmatic all night."

Charlie points to his chest. His pale yellow Oxford shirt is thin, rumpled, a plain white T-shirt underneath, his jeans faded. My lungs feel depleted of air when he's in front of me like this, like part of me wonders how I have him, or why. If suddenly he'll come to his senses and wonder what the hell he's doing with a high school senior with a lame haircut. Note to self: Graph confidence level and see how faltering of it relates to insecurities with new do.

"I'm not the enigma here." Charlie leans against the wall, his head turned toward me.

I shift my hands from my front pockets to the back, thinking about all the times I wore these pants this summer. They're not really cropped, not really full length, just really soft cotton in a color some catalog would call bleached sand. I feel like I've misdressed. We aren't on the beach anymore, we're in my science classroom, only this time my relationship feels like the experiment.

"See?" he asks. "Just then. Where'd you go?" He shrugs.

"I'm here!" I say and shuffle forward so I'm just an arm's length away. "It's only—"

"Only that you're not." His voice isn't unkind, not upset. More confused. "Did I miss a memo? I thought I was supposed to get here, to campus, ASAP so we could . . ." He puts his arms around my waist, the heat from his palms penetrating the fine cotton of my T-shirt. I try not to focus on his usage of ASAP as one word rather than an abbreviation. In my journal—and to Chris—I've spewed my grievances about people who pronounce it "a-sap." Here, in the murky swamp light with Charlie, I annoy even myself with my ramblings, so I try to explain.

"I want to be here." I bite my upper lip. "I do. All week I've been waiting for you, you know, counting down the hours. . . ." He smiles at me. "See? Now I feel stupid. It sounds silly. Oh, here I am in English class counting the minutes . . ."

"I never made fun of you." Charlie's confusion spreads across his face. "Where's this coming from?"

I sigh and back up, then look around us at the multiple sinks, the eyewash centers, the lab counters and solid floor. Outside, the chapel bells ring, informing all of us who haven't been signed out for the night that there's less than two hours until curfew. I've been using up my minutes overthinking everything rather than throwing myself into the night with Charlie. "Okay, I know I've been kind of out of it. It's not intentional. Not that this makes it any better. But I've been writing so much, and trying so hard . . ." I look at my shoes. "And I felt like I was trying to hide my high school status from you—"

"Um, Love?" Charlie licks his lower lip, eyeing me adorably before going on. "You realize it's impossible for you to hide that, right? I mean, it's not like we met off campus and I don't know the real you. I came here." He points to the floor. "Here. To high school. And not just any one, but the one where my famous brother is hailed as one of the best people to grace these halls." He sticks his neck out, pigeonlike, for emphasis. "I think you can safely say I'm okay with our age difference. And with the fact that to see you, I'll have to retrace the Parker-trodden path." He sighs. "Which, as we know, isn't top on my list."

Something occurs to me as he says this. "Then why Harvard?" I scratch my neck. "If you don't want to repeat Parker or follow in his footsteps, why not enroll someplace else? Carve your mark at Princeton, or Brown, or Stanford?"

"First of all, we're not talking about me right now— we're focusing on you. Second of all, good point." Charlie hoists himself up on one of the soapstone tables, his left hand resting on the swan's-neck faucet. "The tricky part about sibling rivalry is wanting to be free of Parker, like I was in high school. He was here; I was at Exeter. But it didn't stop the inevitable comparisons—by my parents, by mutual friends—like those guys on the Vineyard, Henry Randall and his pack."

I haven't heard that name in a while, and it dawns on me that even though my world should get bigger with college approaching, the prep school world makes it smaller, all those names and faces reappearing when you least expect it, all the *do you know*s to come over the years. Charlie turns the faucet on and for a second I wonder if he'll wash his hands, but he just fiddles with the hot and cold, then stops. "The only reason I went to Harvard was because it won me over. Not because Parker was already there, but because on my tour, it felt right."

My mouth forms a very small *O*, and I nod, imagining what it will feel like to tour campuses in a few weekends, the questions I need to think about before my interviews. "I keep hearing about that—the feeling that something just fits . . . but I just don't know if I'm that kind of person."

"Are you talking colleges or something else?" Charlie pats the table next to him. I go and sit near him, with the sink between us. It's small, and not particularly deep, but it might as well be a moat for all the touching it allows.

"Everyone says you 'just know' when you've found the right place. But what if I'm just such a thinky person, such a list maker of this versus that, pros, cons, middles, that I can't do that?"

"Can't what?"

"Can't relax and just give in to the feeling." As I say this, I suddenly know I'm talking about more than just colleges.

What if I can't do that with relationships, too? Didn't I stop all of them in the past? Fine, so Robinson Hall cheated on me and turned out to be a sophomore mistake. But then with Jacob I could have pursued it, but I chose an internship instead. Next up was Asher Piece, whom I left in London and who then dropped me. So maybe that would have kept going if I'd stayed. But maybe not. And now Charlie. As though he can read this doubt in me, Charlie hops down, his shoes scuffing the poured concrete floor, and inserts himself between my knees.

He puts his palms on the back of my neck, his hands leafing about in my hair, his fingers sending ripples of pleasure from my scalp to my legs as he plays with my hair, then kisses me. "Can you relax in this?"

I lean in so my face is on his shirt, wanting to take in that mixture that makes him smell like him. Sometimes, when I'd finish work at the café and crawl up to bed by myself this summer, I'd sleep with something of his—a sweatshirt, a T-shirt—just so I could breathe him in. My list of what he smells like: cornflowers (not in a perfumy way, but those flowers are clustered near his beach cabin), Nevr-Dull (brass polish he uses on the boat), lemon Joy (he washed his hair with it on boating overnights), chocolate, cinnamon, and the salty ocean. I press my nose into the yellow broadcloth of his shirt, sniffing. My heart and my nose come up empty, though, when I get the whiff of only Tide. And not the ocean kind.

"Look, it's bound to feel weird while we get used to this back-and-forth thing," Charlie says. "I'm in ... My world's kind of different—classes, my housing situation, no rules . . ."

"I'm sorry," I say, and then shake my head into his chest. "I keep wanting to apologize. For all that—the picking me up at my dorm, that I can't just decide to go to the Square and hang out with you." I pause. "That I can't sleep over . . ." I'm speaking into his chest, muffling the words, especially the last few, just in case calling the bedding situation (or lack thereof) to light only makes things worse.

Charlie arches back so he can see my face. "Did you just make reference to the lack of physical proximity?" I nod. He raises his eyebrows and frowns. "Well, then, I guess it's over. If we can't sleep together tonight—in fact, right here and now—I guess we're done."

"Okay." I laugh. "I get it."

"It just is what it is, Love. How great would it be if we could just be summer bound forever? You a coffee wench and me a poor but honest fisherman." He touches my hair.

"It sounds like the start of a fable." I smirk and pull him back, my legs wrapped around his waist. Like this, I can believe we are a couple, no matter the distance, the age inequalities, our past relationship mistakes, our "old friends" Jacob and Miranda.

"Yeah?" Charlie looks at me, but with that guy expression of half being aware of the words coming out of his mouth, the other half being sucked into *the look*. That prephysical trance. "So what's our moral?"

I tap my forehead. "In film world, this means I'm thinking."

"Just like Lucy Honeychurch in that movie we were supposedly watching?"

"You knew her name?" I thought he'd never seen that movie.

Charlie nods. "I took a film course called Agrarian Visions. I used *A Room with a View* in my thesis." I blush. Every time I think I'm informing Charlie of something new, or expressing myself for the first time with him, it's like he's heard it before. Now I feel redundant even with my slim knowledge of movies. "Not that I didn't thoroughly enjoy your espousal of the film's subtext. A."

"A?"

"My grade. For you."

"What do I have to do for extra credit?" I joke. He puts his fingers on my lips and I'm torn between wanting to nibble on them and the subtext of our own story. Is he the teacher to my student? Then, before I can let my inner critic come on full force, he leans me onto the soapstone so I feel the stone's coolness at the same time he's on top of me. There's something amazing about kissing while lying down, such a connectedness. All prior worries and feelings of being somehow less than present disappear. He's all mouth and hands, whispering words to me that give me chills as strong as the physical moves do.

I kiss him back, not minding the hard surface I'm on, almost unaware of our surroundings save for the quiet drip of water into the sink. I guess Charlie didn't tighten the tap.

"Can I?" Charlie whispers while in the process of taking off my shirt. I nod, feeling Charlie's hands on the back clasp of my bra (a position, it should be noted, that takes no small amount of abdominal musculature on both our parts, what with my having to arch my back, and him being on me but not so on me that I can't breathe).

"Charlie . . ." I give in to the moment, to the feeling of being wrapped up in him, so wrapped up that I pepper the physicality with a question he can't answer. "Am I going to lose my virginity to you?" The sentence makes its way from my brain, where I thought it was tucked away to consider at other times (lying in bed at night, bored in class), to the air between us. Why does that question come to me for consideration when I'm *not* with him? Maybe spitting it out now is my way of espousing the need to connect it—that string of words—to the actual person and act. So now I've asked it, and the words hang there, suspended as if in a cartoon bubble, while we continue to kiss. Charlie props himself up on his forearms, looking down at me.

"Did you just ask me what I thought you asked me?"

"Yep." I look at him. "I did, in fact, say that out loud."

My shirt is off my body but around my neck, bra undone, my heart racing for a ton of reasons, Charlie's pressed against me, and to make a point he asks in a very clear voice, "You're asking *me* if I'm the one—*the* one—you'll have sex with for the first time?"

This time, the words more than hang in the air: They echo, overly loud, with his enunciation. Right after Charlie's posed the question back to me, an unpleasant surprise: A small cough tells me we're not alone. And while I'm in full view on top of the lab table, I can't see the door in its entirety.

"Oh, shit, sorry," says a voice.

I hear this from the doorway without knowing who said it. From where I'm lying (half naked, of course), I can just see the floor and two pairs of shoes near the door. Charlie bolts upright, jumping cleverly behind the counter so only his upper body is viewable, and I grab my T-shirt and roll it down as the intruders walk into the room. My bra dangles like a useless limb from one side of my shirt.

"Oh, hey, Love, sorry to bust in on you."

I stick my arms into their proper position in my shirt just as Chloe Swain presents herself in front of me.

"Hey." I smooth my hair behind my ear. I say *hey* like we've brushed by each other in the hallway. Not like she's just seen me kind of naked, in a very compromising position. Not like she just heard Charlie ask me about losing my virginity, and not like Jacob's right next to her.

"Hey." He says *hey* like it's been years since we last tuned in on each other's lives. Maybe that's what it feels like—when you go back to school after summer break and you see that person out of context, that it's been eons. I flash back to seeing him make out with Chloe at the fair on Martha's Vineyard, all those reflections of them in the hall of mirrors, slamming me.

"We were just . . ." Chloe giggles and slinks her arm around Jacob's jean-clad waist. She shrugs so we all know we're in this together, this unintentional double date, all of us sneaking illegally for a campus hook up before the dorms beckon.

"It's fine." My blood races around my body as I adjust my foot into the flip-flop that had flopped off and wave my hands. "We were almost done." Cue regret of word choice. Done with what, exactly? "We're heading out anyway."

For the few minutes of overlap we've had with Jacob, Charlie's been quiet. He emerges from behind the soapstone slab with his hands in his pockets, in a nearly identical stance to Jacob. Charlie is a vision of crumpled academia, and Jacob, earthy in a grey T-shirt so thin I can see his tanned stomach underneath, looks incomplete without his guitar. Oh my God—I have my own Cecil and George! Just like in the movie downstairs. Only, Cecil is so prim he's ridiculous on film and George is like a puppy he's so enthusiastic. But still.

"We'll let you go, then," Jacob says, and just like that I'm reminded that I don't have him and Charlie. Unlike Lucy Honeychurch and her conflicted suitors, I have just the one—and he's tugging at me.

"Okay, well." I suck in air so hard everyone hears. Then I counteract his use of the pronoun we with my own. "We'll see you back at the dorms, then."

"So, you never did tell me the name," Charlie says.

Our hands are clasped, swinging just slightly, as he walks me back to Fruckner. I couldn't get a ride with him without signing out officially and I couldn't find Mrs. Ray, so we hoofed it up and back. It's not bad, really, to end the evening strolling with your boyfriend, even if the air is sticky and the heat oppressive.

"The name of what?" Now that we're out of the science building, away from Friday Night Flicks and hookup surprises, the night feels bigger, better.

Charlie stops. He touches my face. "This whole time, the whole distraction thing?" He kicks his feet against the sandy grit on the pavement. "All I wanted to know was the title—of your story." He smiles at me. "For Chaucer."

I stretch my arms up into the sky, wishing it were cooler, wishing we were back on the beach, or that it was summer, or that I knew—just somehow could find out—what would happen with us. "You're so nice to ask, Charlie. Really." I stand on my tiptoes and kiss him.

"So?"

"'What You Might Know,'" I say, and nibble a bit of skin on my top lip. "I keep changing it slightly." The temperature hasn't dropped, and I'm hot. The kind of hot that invades you whether you're fully clothed or, say, seminaked on a science lab table. But I digress. "It's not set in stone. . . ." In bed or walking to campus I've played with the title, debating the merits of the words.

"It's a good title." He doesn't say more, which I take as a sign of respect.

The noise of our shoes on the pavement sounds louder than it should, making me feel a certain emptiness. All that looking forward to seeing Charlie all week only to have it go by so quickly. We walk past the cemetery, where giggles and a few decidedly undead noises filter into the night air. By the time we reach the circular driveway for Deals, Bishop, and Fruckner, I'm bursting with the warmth, and back to wishing we were at Charlie's cabin, where the sea air comes at a fast clip, instantly making you long for an oversized sweater.

"So you're not going to tell me what it's about?" Charlie puts his thumb on my chin, right near my lower lip.

I look down. Okay, so maybe I took the respect too soon. It's not that I don't want to share the story with him, but that I don't want to share it with anyone. The doubt I have about my writing is too raw. Those words on the page are too new. Even if I just sketch the plot for him, I'll feel like I've let something go. And I can't do that yet. It's almost like if I do, I won't get into Chaucer's class. A silly mind game, admittedly, but I need all the help I can get. "I was just thinking how much I wish we were in the driveway near your cabin." I kiss his thumb and he retreats it.

"She said, cleverly deflecting his attempts at finding out about her secretive writing." He wipes his forehead with the sleeve of his shirt, making me wonder why he doesn't shed the Oxford and just wear the white T-shirt. "Could it be hotter?"

"I'm not being secretive." I brush my bare neck, glad now for not having extra weight on it, but still missing that summer part of me. "I'm just not ready to delve into it, okay? And no, it couldn't be hotter, because if it were I'd actually dissolve. My dad's been fielding calls all day from irate parents."

Charlie uses his chin to point to the dorms. "Still no

AC? I remember Parker once tried to convince his dorm to sleep on the roof. Smart."

"Probably not a solution." I shake my head. "Obviously the buildings at main campus do. And the newer dorms up there do, but not our sweet historic houses here." I pat my thigh as I speak, as though comforting the out-of-date dorms. "And all I was really trying to say is—with the heat, and seeing you . . ." My voice trails off.

Charlie holds my shoulder and locks his eyes to mine. "I know. It's like we should be back there, on the Vineyard, but . . ."

We're not. We both know this, so we don't say it, as though uttering those two words (well, one word and one contraction—does that count as one or two?) will only prove what we feel.

"Looks like the masses are returning." Charlie looks over at Bishop, the middle house, where guys are filtering back from campus. Near Deals, a couple of day-student cars are parked with their headlights on, their doors open. Everywhere, people are complaining about the overwhelming heat.

"Ah, curfew," I say. I check my watch. "Lucky me! Back to the dorms."

"See?" Charlie shrugs. "Now if I say, oh, you'll have fun, I sound totally condescending. But if I agree with you about how lame dorm life is, I sound like a dick. Or worse, I'll give you a complex and you'll think that I think it's lame that you live here and—"

"This is way too complicated a scenario for my brain

to process with these temps," I say and point to the oversized thermometer that's rooted in the ground near the flagpole. Rumors abound about this flagpole, about how it's a legendary meeting point for postcurfew activities and graveyard excursions. But you never know with prep school lore, what's real and what's the product of many a night spent fantasizing about life beyond the dorm walls. "Suffice it to say I will miss you. And thanks for coming."

"I know you're working the rest of this weekend, but what about the next couple?"

I scratch my head, feeling sweat on my scalp. I want to shower before bed, even though it won't have a lasting effect. "Yeah, sometime soon, right? I have my first—" I stop myself from telling him that I will be visiting his esteemed place of learning, that Harvard is first up in the interview process.

"Your first what?"

With both hands, I secure the longer pieces of hair at the front behind my ears. "It's nothing—it's just, like, the first few weekends here are so busy and I should—"

"Right. No problem." Charlie scratches his stomach, lifting his shirt just enough so I can see his tan line and the soft, lighter skin that hides underneath his shorts. Will we? Will he be that one?

"Well, if you decide to change your mind . . . and get out of here for the day, you could meet me in the Square two weeks from tomorrow." He holds his palms up like he's expecting payment, so I slap him ten.

It's not that I'm embarrassed about still being ensconced

in the college process, but more a fear that if I involve
Charlie in it too much, I won't be able to keep my vision
straight. That is, I'll like Harvard too much because Harvard equals Charlie. Or, if we're fighting, I won't give it a
fair shot.

"I wish I could." I touch my stomach, feeling the slick
of my shirt on it where my sweat acts like glue. "But with
papers and those pesky things known as college applications . . . Sorry to even bore you with all that. Can we just
play it by ear?" What I don't add is my hope: that I get
accepted into Chaucer's class and have another writing assignment, more than one. That if I get accepted I'll write
something I can use for the Beverly William Award. Even
though Chaucer's class would ultimately add to the bog-
gage of work, I'd welcome it. If I get in, it will mean I
am one of those six people who trek to Chaucer's place,
who even though they seem to have little else in common,
always note one another's presence in the dining hall or
assemblies. A sort of elite writer's group. "I don't mean to
plague you with my senior suckage."

"You're not." Charlie squeezes my hand, his palms still
the slightest bit rough from the earlier part of summer
when he still fished and sailed. Soon he'll have those hands
of winter, pale and soft from only working at a desk. He
kicks at the ground. "But what you're confirming is that
you'll be absent from the first annual read-a-thon."

"Two weeks from tomorrow, right?" I give him a par-
tial smile but don't tell him I'll be on his campus, nervous
as anything in my interview clothing. Let's just hope the

heat's broken by then. "Sadly, I will have to miss that scin-
tillating event. I do so hope you make lots of money for
the charity, though."

"Just picture me—sitting in the yard in the heat along
with the squirrels and anyone else who signed up for it."
The read-a-thon is an admirable, if slightly passive, event
Charlie got involved with to raise money for inner-city
schools that need books. Like the cancer walk I did, he's
gotten donations, and for every page he reads aloud (to
squirrels, presumably) he raises funds.

"It's kind of a funny image—you, with some leather-
bound tome in your lap, fending off the heat wave . . ." I
fight laughter.

"Hey—it's not that pathetic. First of all, I'll be reading
Lady Chatterley's Lover . . ."

"Ohh, steamy!" I say, half in mock shock.

"Yeah, I had to pick something with sex in the title to
inspire people to come." He grins. "Um, word choice?"

"Nice." I put my hand on his chest to feel the thump
of his heart and the heat rising from his skin. My sweet,
community-minded Harvard boyfriend and his innuendos.
His commitment to reading and to me. Sigh.

"And at least I won't be alone, mumbling to myself." He
coughs and wipes the sweat away again. "I mean, at least I'll
have Miranda for company."

I take my hand back from his chest upon hearing her
name. Right then, my staid vision of my boyfriend doing
boring reading for a good cause, looking perspiration damp
and slightly kooky reading aloud in the yard while students

tour the campus, gets washed away. In its place—a lurid, steamy, sweat-hazy reading in which the characters leap from the page and inspire Charlie and Miranda to do some, um, pruning and weeding of their own.

"Miranda's doing it?" I ask and wish for the backspace button on *doing it*.

"It was her idea." Charlie takes his keys out of his pocket, signaling it's time to go. "She's so charitable. I admire that about her."

Do you admire her honking breasts? I want to ask, even though I have no idea what the woman's chest looks like, nor should I care. But I do. Just like I wish it were still summer, I wish I'd never heard about Charlie's old friend, never let his past interrupt our present.

"Well, good luck with it." I manage to keep calm while sweat drips in thin rivulets down my spine.

"Thanks." He kisses my forehead, no doubt tasting the salt, and remaining oblivious to my paranoia. "If you feel like dropping by, do. Otherwise . . ."

I nod. "Soon?" Charlie nods. Then I remember something. "Hey, just out of curiosity . . . did you have dinner with the chancellor the other night?"

"The dean. Sure, yeah." He sounds nonchalant, his lips pulled into a straight line. "Why?"

I cross my arms over my chest and lower my voice. "Was there someone there . . . Do you know Lindsay Parrish?" Just saying her name to him makes me queasy.

"Chapel Parrish's little sister?" Charlie's hair is damp, darker at the edges from sweat. I fight the images of him sweating further with Miranda, or worse, checking out Lindsay in her dressed-to-thrill ensemble from this week. "Vaguely."

"Oh." It's the best I can do without sounding catty. "She's in my dorm."

Charlie sighs and pulls at his collar like he's got a tie on, perhaps remembering all the times recently that he has. "From what I can tell, she seems gracious."

Is she a house? A still image from one of those architectural mags that describe entryways as "gracious." "So you spoke with her, then?" I think back to Lindsay's sneer after she paraded by my room with Chili.

"I hardly noticed her, to tell you the truth. But then— your friend—Chili?—she was there, and that sort of got us to talking."

Now I get it. Clever Lindsay with her gracious manner brought Chili along not only to steal her away from me but to get a better intro to Charlie, since she knew Chili'd met him on the Vineyard. "Chili's great!" I say, just to sound enthusiastic and avoid clawing at Lindsay. If I'm going to be jealous of Miranda, and allow myself that indulgence, I can't overdo it with Lindsay, or to Charlie—and even to myself—I'll be way too possessive.

"Chili's a nice girl. And Lindsay—well, she spoke very highly of you." Charlie's teeth are bright in the darkness. "And I couldn't agree more."

I smile back, but inside, I feel a certain clenching, knowing Lindsay is up to something, further ingratiating herself into my life when she knows she's not wanted. Could she just be looking at the Ivies and making small talk with him? Yep. But is it more likely that she's elbowing her way past me and setting me up to fall? I have to think it's a strong yes. I loop my arms around him and turn my face up so he'll kiss me. "So, when is our next . . ."

"Meeting? Face-to-face? Get-together?" Charlie snorts. "Aren't you the one who said play it by ear? Imagine if we had real travel involved. A guy in my house is seeing this woman who lives in Tokyo. Now, that's long-distance."

"I know. I know we're only a few miles apart." But I like knowing. Having that date fixed in my mind gives shape to the next weeks. A bright side after slogging through so much work.

"What about a week from Wednesday?"

I make a face. "Am I supposed to know about that date without consulting my book?" I grin but then pout. "I'm only slightly joking. There's so much to do—"

"You're the one pressing for a time and place."

I poke him in the stomach and he instinctually bends at the waist. "I only said when. Not where."

"Well, I'll tell you both." He puts both hands on my shoulders, pressing down on them as though he's trying to plant me into the ground. "Relationships work on realities, not theories, right? So how about the reality that you meet me the Wednesday after the read-a-thon in the Square and I give you a little tour."

I wriggle free from his grip. "Off campus?" I bite my lip, thinking that now I'm entering the lying zone, whereas before I was only not telling him about my upcoming Harvard visit and interview.

"That"—Charlie grins—"and more."

More. Oh. My tongue traces the outline of my mouth. "It's a date. I get out at one thirty on Wednesdays, so I'll just . . . sign out and . . ."

A kiss ends our night, and Charlie walks to his car, leaving me with a host of thoughts running sprints in my head.

In the grassy oval, clumps of boarders head toward Deals, Bishop, and my own little abode, Fruckner. You can tell from the swaying of bodies who's been drinking, minitoothpastes in their pockets to hide the smell; who's been studying, the weight of their bags hunching them over; and who's been hooking up, their bodies cozy together. In the halo of light by the flagpole I see my roommate, Mary, with Carlton Ackers, a few other campus couples, and then, far back in the haze of bugs and heat, Jacob's easy stride next to Chloe Swain.

The heat of shame and embarrassment doesn't really hit me until Charlie's car is out of the driveway. While he's there, on the grassy oval, kissing me good-bye and promising to call/write/think of me (the long-distance triad), I'm fine. Protected by some relationship bubble. But as soon as he leaves, beeping once, in the latest eco-car (having eschewed the gas-guzzling red pickup for something city and enviro friendly), I'm a mess.

The intense humidity creeps onto my skin, mixing

with bubbles of fear. Jacob knows I'm a virgin. Or could. And does it matter? Did he really hear? I imagine him and Chloe conferencing about my lack of sexual experience and then decide I'm giving myself way too much credit—like I'm what they're going to talk about while on a hookup mission to the science building? So I have the virgin eavesdropping thing bothering me, and also the reality of it—Charlie and I never completed that conversation. So now, kicking through the dewy grass oval on my way to Fruckner, I'm left to wonder by myself until—

"Hey, Bukowski!"

I turn around, sure that my shame is visible from the outside. "Oh, hi, Mary." She's in a sporty tank top and mesh shorts that only accentuate her height. Standing there together, she and Carlton seem fit for some teen athlete magazine, all sweaty and smiling, chastely holding hands with a basketball caught between them. "Hello, Carlton."

He's not someone I've ever really spoken to, but now that I'm rooming with Mary, we're suddenly buddies. Dorm life is like that, I guess: Instant overlaps lead to hallway communications that never would have occurred, broadening or shrinking your social life all of a sudden. Carlton gives me a jocular wave, squeezes Mary's hand, and then says, "Sweet potato."

"Corn on the cob," I say, just because it seems equally irrelevant.

Mary chuckles and Carlton gives a knowing grin and walks off toward Bishop. "Oh, those Bishop boys," she says in a voice-over advertising way.

"They're something else all right!" I add, finishing the fake promo.

She casts a final look over her shoulder and elbows me toward Fruckner. "So, you ready to go home?"

Home. Four letters. A mile away. Literally. "I am. But not to there." I point to our darkened window. I picture my room at home, and this time I don't miss the physical comforts—my own bed and knowing I can eat and sleep when I please. This time, I'm sure it's the comfort of knowing my dad is nearby that I long for. Not being with him necessarily. Just having him downstairs or on the porch.

And he's still nearby, only it doesn't feel that way. He's made it clear by sticking me in the dorms that there's a division now, one that started when Aunt Mable got sick, and kept going while I was in London, and then grew. I know this happens when you get older, but I can't help but feel like my dad's insisting on it for other reasons. That he harbors a desperate need for me to be able to cope on my own like he had to after my mom left. Now that she—and Sadie—are back in the picture, I wonder if he'll change his mind. "I could really use a night's sleep in my own bed."

Mary twists her mouth, fighting a big grin. "I hear you. I could also use a giant fan or a block of ice." She stops, listens for noises, checks over her shoulder, and then bends down so she's closer to my height. "We have to lie low, okay? Tonight you'll tell me about the sordid adventures of College Boy and Writer Girl. . . ."

I laugh. "Okay, but only if you'll indulge me with the

epic poem known as the four-year relationship you have
with Mr. Sweet Potato . . ."

Mary puts her finger to her lips, shushing me. "This
weekend, as I said, we chill. Like before a big game—rest
our muscles, so to speak. Then soon, after a couple weeks'
worth of hard work . . ." She tucks her chin to her chest
and eyes me furtively. "Then, next Saturday, you'll come to
understand the full meaning of Sweet Potato."

Chapter Eleven

♡

By Sunday, chapel dinner looms not only because it signals the end of the weekend, but because my story is officially due to be placed in Mr. Chaucer's hands. The heat hasn't broken, and all of us—the boarders from the west side of campus—make the haul up to main campus, soggy in our formal gear. The guys have their required blazers draped over an arm or held by a finger over their shoulders, the arms of their shirts rolled up. Like most of the girls, I'm in a sundress just so I can keep cool. I borrowed the dress from Harriet Walters down the hall after she came and asked for "that flowery shirt you wore that time" and I actually knew what she meant. Before the walk up here, Fruckner was ablaze with more heat from hair dryers, girls running around half dressed in search of a suitably alluring outfit, and lots of clothes swapping.

"It felt like—I don't know—some scene from a boarding school movie," I say while Mary swats at a bug and Chili fans herself with an actual paper fan.

"How do you think movie people come up with ideas?" Harriet asks. "From life. Art, life, the clichéd conundrum. Damn, it's hot."

The steady stream of Fruckner, Bishop, and Deals people moves slowly past the graveyard, past the main buildings, and finally down the hill toward the big dining room for our family-style dinners.

"Maybe it'll be something good." Mary sniffs the air once and holds the door open for us.

I look at her with my eyebrows raised. "Maybe it'll be roasted *sweet potatoes*." I keep hoping she'll clue me in to what the words mean—the untold code of starch.

She shoots me a look and then glosses over it. "I prefer *homefries*."

"Me, too," Carlton says, clearly getting her hidden meaning. He swats Mary's butt as he walks by. Following closely with him are guys I saw on the Vineyard—Nick Samuels, Jon Rutter, and then Jacob and Dalton.

My blush mixes with the heat of outside as I wait my turn to go in. Jacob. My virginity. Chris appears next to me. I've told him everything from my weekend, so he knows just what to say.

"Look, either he knows or he doesn't. He heard or he didn't. And does it really change things? No." Chris looks at me, his face pleasantly flushed, as if the stifling temperatures haven't fazed him. The reality is, I know he and Haverford Pomroy did their own version of Friday Night Flicks but at an actual movie theater, unbeknownst to Haverford's boyfriend, Ben, who was studying all night.

My best friend's a cheater, the other man. But at least he seems happy.

"You have the crush high written all over your face," I say and touch his cheek.

"Does it show?" Chris backs into the doorway, and I follow him, past Mary and her assigned table, where there are no clues as to what Sweet Potato might mean, and past Harriet Walters and Chili, who are sharing Chili's fan.

"I'm at table sixteen," I say and scan the room for it. On each of the long polished tables are metal placecard holders, each one sprouting a number. Every week the tables are shuffled so that—in theory—all the students get to know one another, mixing with other class years and new faculty members.

"I'm at nineteen. Prime real estate." He smirks, also looking for his table. Thoughtfully, the powers that be don't put the tables in order, so there's always a group of people standing where we are, at the edges of the room, furrowing their brows, their gazes wandering to table after table until they find their rightful place.

"You did not just make a math joke," I say and shake my head. With one hand I keep a firm grip on my story. New title: "What We Don't Know." I look for my table and for Mr. Chaucer, figuring I'll dash over to him, hand him my story as he ordered, and sneak in a few sentences of how hard I worked and what it's about.

"I did. I guess spending extra time in the science lab is paying off," Chris says, giving a verbal nod to his advanced physics section—another overlap with Haverford. "Oops, sorry to bring up that place."

I roll my eyes, thinking back to the cool soapstone slab, the way it felt on my bare skin. The sound of Jacob's *hey* when he saw me there.

"Oh," Chris says. "You're over there—by the big window. And Chaucer's over there. . . ." Chris flicks the pages of my story and I flinch like he's touched a sprained wrist. "Jeez, nerves much? It'll be okay. Just give it to him." Then he goes back to looking for his seat. "And I'm—oh, poor me. I'm at the no-reservation table." He points to the worst seating, the table closest to the kitchen, forever getting the churning heat from the ovens, the shouts of the disgruntled workers, and bumps from the students on serving duty. Freshmen—the class IVs—all have to carry the water trays, the food, the plates, out to each table, where the faculty member plates the food. "At least I'm not serving. Save me a seat in chapel?"

I nod as Chris heads for his crappy table and I walk slowly to mine. The tables by the windows are illuminated by the early evening sun that still lingers in the sky. I focus on the small round placard that has *16* printed on it, trying to get past the fact that Mr. Chaucer is the faculty "anchor" at my table, and among my tablemates are Jacob and Dalton. Of course. I sigh, knowing Chili will quiz me endlessly about what Dalton wore and what he said and if her name ever came up. She watched him at the batting cage behind the gym on Saturday, pretending to study while checking out his swing—among other things—and her crush is stronger than ever.

"Happy to have you at sixteen," Mr. Chaucer says and gestures for me to sit down at the far end of the table.

I move to try and sit closer to him so I can explain my story and the work that went into the writing. "Hi, Mr. Chaucer. I have the—"

Mr. Chaucer welcomes two other people and promptly points for them to sit in the chairs next to him, cutting me off. I wonder if it's intentional but try not to take it as an affront.

"Good weekend?" Chaucer asks the table. It's standard fare for prechapel dinners. I used to come to this meal with my dad; the only difference now is that I don't get to keep within me the surety that, after the mediocre food and service, I get to leave. Part of this new experience for me is a night like tonight, where I'm not equal but separate; I'm just in it like everyone else.

Only, I have the crushing need for Mr. Chaucer to take my story and read it right then and there, and listen to my side comments. I lean forward, trying to get his attention. "Mr. Chaucer, I have the—"

"So, who saw *Room with a View*?" Chaucer asks, accepting the water tray from a freshman and then sending her back to fetch the food.

"Aren't you missing an article there?" Dalton helps himself to water, then reaches across to my glass and fills it. He's in good spirits, not grumbling about the weather like everyone else.

"Aren't you the gentleman?" Jacob considers Dalton's move while Dalton waits for Mr. Chaucer's response.

"Ah, yes, I dropped an *a* back there. Sorry." Mr. Chaucer goes so far as to lean down and mime picking something up from the floor, when sunlight spills over the oriental rugs and hardwood floors. "Did anyone see *A Room with a View*?"

"Nope." Dalton drains his glass of water and refills it right away.

Jacob looks at me, head-on, for the first time since I was semishirtless, my virginity echoing all around. "I wasn't at Flicks."

Maybe Jacob was there but doesn't want to admit it. Maybe he's protecting me from the embarrassment of that night by pretending he wasn't there. That he didn't see the movie or me. Or maybe he just doesn't care. I hold my story under the table, hoping it isn't getting wrinkled, and take a sip from the water Dalton poured for me. He's hard to figure out, that one. I'm not sure if he's well-mannered and that's why he poured the H_2O or if every act of his is a subtle form of sarcasm. Jacob's stare persists. The freshman appears with a tray of food.

"I saw the movie," I say to Mr. Chaucer, and then glance back at Jacob, who flicks his eyebrows up. "Some of it. I saw some of it."

Chaucer begins dishing out manicotti and steamed broccoli. When he's filled a plate he hands it to the person next to him, and she passes it, and so on down the line until the plate's circled almost all the way around and we each have a hot meal. "Some? Didn't it hold your attention?"

"It wasn't that," I say, faltering. "I'd seen it before. I love that movie, actually."

Dalton smirks, sliding a bite of pasta into his mouth. Mr. Chaucer checks that we're all served, takes some for himself, and looks at Dalton. "Mr. Himmelman, do I detect an all-too-knowing sigh?"

Dalton looks up from his plate. Jacob's eating, despite the fact that the last thing any of us feels like is tucking into a steaming dinner when it's almost one hundred degrees outside. At least the dining hall is air-conditioned. Chapel isn't, and Chris and I will need to find a spot at the back to avoid breathing in the pungent odors. My appetite is usually strong, but today I haven't felt much like eating. Either I miss Charlie, or I feel worried about work, or else the heat's just put me off food for now.

"It's just . . ." Dalton wipes his mouth with the cloth napkins used on Sundays. "It kind of figures that you'd like it, that's all." He gives a small smile, then shrugs.

Jacob looks at me. I wish I knew what he heard, if he heard. What he thought about finding me in that room with Charlie. The irony that he was heading in there with Chloe to do basically the same thing.

"What does that mean?" I point to Dalton with my fork for a second, then think it's rude, and put it back on my plate. In my journal from when I was in London, I have a list that includes bad table manners (I was going through a very faux-upper-class Brit invasion) and I can picture my handwriting: *Do not use utensils for gesturing.* All of those lists and journal entries and lyrics and beginnings of writing are stacked in my bedroom at home, squirreled away out of sight. And now I have a real story, one with a middle and an end, ready for reading. With my fork back on my plate, I look at Mr. Chaucer and try again with my story. "Mr. Chaucer—I have the—I wrote my—"

"No, really, Dalton, I'm curious—what does all this mean? Are there types of people who flock to Flicks? Or is it that you think Love, in particular, likes that movie?"

Again my efforts to hand off my writing have gone interrupted, which is annoying. But I, too, admit to wondering what Dalton means.

"Yeah, Dalton, is she—what—an E. M. Forster groupie?" Jacob laughs.

"It's like this." Dalton pushes his plate away, drinks more water, refills, and then starts. "Some people like stories—books, plays, movies—about ideas, and other people like them about reality. They want to see themselves portrayed or else they want to live out a fantasy that takes them away from their lives."

"But *A Room with a View* is both." I glug my water, then wipe my mouth. "There are ideas, like thinking versus feeling, religion versus nature, and so on, but—"

"But the whole movie's a statement." Dalton leans his upper body in over the table, making it seem like he's really invested in the conversation. "Sure, it's nice to look at, and the accents are swell, but it's no *Simple Men* or *House of Games*."

Jacob intervenes. "I don't think you can compare E. M. Forster with Hal Hartley or Mamet."

I can totally see why he and Dalton are friends—Jacob's got music as his territory, Dalton's got books and writing, and they meet in the middle over film. In an instant I can see adding myself to their friendship, being the girl who refreshes their banter, changes their straight line to a triangle. Then I mentally bonk myself for having such thoughts—not that they're impure (well, maybe just the tiniest bit; I mean, they're both incredible looking in very different ways)—but because they're a closed society. Dalton and Jacob have roomed together since freshman year, and though they're widely liked and accepted into various social circles, they kind of have their own language. Probably like me and Chris.

"You have it all figured out, don't you, Dalton?" I say it matter-of-factly, my fork in proper usage as I attempt to pick up a piece of manicotti. The floppy pasta won't stay speared, though, and falls back into a mound of tomato sauce, sending a spray of small red dots onto my borrowed dress. Can you say *dry-cleaning costs*? Dalton doesn't respond to my comment but looks at me long enough that I know he's heard it.

"First of all," Mr. Chaucer says, swallowing a spear of broccoli, "you can compare anything. You, Jacob, I seem to recall, wrote an essay contrasting the works of Shakespeare, Bob Dylan, and LL Cool J."

" 'Maternal Figures and Images of Courtly Love by Three Cool Dudes'—God, I was such a sophomore loser." Jacob laughs. Dalton joins in, raking his hands through his hair and causing more than one girl at a nearby table to gawk. More evidence of their cool society that I'm not a part of. The kind of guys who can refer to themselves as losers because they're not. I start to laugh anyway, but then I think about Jacob in our class III year. If he was such a loser then, in his opinion, doesn't that make what we had then—first a friendship, then more—loserly, too?

"So how, exactly, does this relate to Love?" Mr. Chaucer watches our faces.

Jacob's gaze returns to me, and I feel that same burning—does he know? Does he care? And then something new. Why do I care so much? It's so easy for me to write off my fumblings usually, and I'm not someone who minds minor public humiliation. Then I realize, this isn't that—it's private. The most private. I look at him and dare to raise one eyebrow. *Do you know?* I ask with my eyes. Does it matter—to me, to you, to anyone?

"It is my contention," Dalton says, beginning to stack his plate and the plates near him even though it's not his job, "that Love is the kind of person who gets fixated on an idea and then has trouble letting go."

"Don't we all do that?" Chaucer asks.

"Sure. But . . ." Dalton looks at me while he scrapes manicotti remains, tidying up the table while the grateful freshman waits so she can clear. "But Love likes the conflict. That tugging you get inside over which way to turn." He looks at me and I'm completely sucked in to what he's saying. "Lucy Honeychurch's struggle between two guys can be reduced to a cliché—the thinking guy and the passionate one. But Love, and people like her, live not for the

decision over whom to choose, but for the struggle itself."
He takes a breath and helps the freshman with the bowl of
fruit salad she's brought for dessert.

My appetite is instantly gone, my stomach twisting. My
story is probably wrinkled from being sat on (I figured
this was better than the alternative—being on the table
and getting splashed with tomato sauce), and I'm deeply
puzzled. "What makes you think you even know me?" My
jaw is set forward in disbelief. Not that what Dalton said is
bad, necessarily, but that it's true.

"It's just a hunch," he says and scoops strawberries, blue-
berries, and chunks of cantaloupe into small white bowls,
usurping Mr. Chaucer's job.

The rest of the meal continues with talk of classes and
the heat. "I can't take it much longer," Mr. Chaucer says.
"I'm from Canada—we don't get this kind of humidity."

I half listen, feeling the pages of my story underneath,
the pangs of knowing that Dalton was at least partly correct.
I do like that struggle—those *what-ifs*. They make me feel
human and alive. The fruit in front of me is of no interest;
in fact, my stomach feels seriously crampy suddenly—not
in a menstrual way, probably just nerves. My hands are
clammy. My head aches. Then again, I've had too much
crammed into my brain space for my own well-being.

Mr. Chaucer leans down the table toward me and asks,
"So, you've got something for me?"

"Yeah," I say, sighing. "I wanted to tell you before, but I
kept getting—"

"It was intentional." Chaucer sticks out a hand and I

place my pages in his grasp. There's a moment where he has yet to cinch his fist around the story, when I could still yank it away and have all that anxiety around it disappear. Tear it up and go back to senior fall without the tempting writing class. But I don't. I let him take it, fold it, and tuck it into his brown leather briefcase.

"Intentional?" I ask, still feeling slightly sick. Inside, there's not just cramping but actual pain. I press my hands into my abdomen under the table, hoping this will help.

Other tables begin to empty, students standing, stretching, dreading going back out into the heat and up to chapel, where it'll only be worse.

"You wanted to sit here"—Chaucer points to the chair currently occupied by someone else—"but I knew if you did—"

"She'd just end up explaining the story, right?" Dalton stands up.

I look at him. "How do you know?"

"Because we all did that." He brushes his hands through his hair. The closest color is the brown of a Chesapeake Bay retriever, like the one who lives in Whitcomb House. In the dining hall sunlight, the brown of Dalton's hair is flecked with reddish hues and his eyes are the palest of blue. Unusual.

"Dalton's correct, Love." Mr. Chaucer stands up and most of our table does, too. "It's not that I don't want to hear about your story. Actually, that's exactly what I don't want. I only want to read it. If you have to tell me about it to prove it's good, then it might not be. Or if you have to explain what happens verbally, then you need to go back to the narrative and see what isn't translating. A lot of the time when writers are getting started . . ." He looks at me and tilts his head, going for peacekeeping. "I know you're not totally new to writing, but still—oftentimes writers feel the need to explain their work, when the best explanation should come from the writing itself. Does that make sense?"

I nod, knowing they're probably right, only wishing I had one more chance to reread my story. I think about how it ends, the last two lines:

Out past the mooring lines, Amelia could see the dipping and rising of the waves. And farther, something darker than the water itself, lurking underneath.

I can't explain what I want there to be lurking underneath, or that Nick Cooper (the fictional one, not the real one I know from London—and from whom I expect a letter any day) may or may not have loved her, and that she may or may not be harboring some secret. All I can do is say, "Well, I hope you like it." Then, with a sigh, I add, "God, that sounds dumb."

"It's never dumb to hope that people like your work," Dalton says. He has his hands on the back of the chair he sat in, waiting for Jacob to eat the last of his fruit. "Dude, you spearing them individually or what?"

Jacob glances up at Dalton. "I like to take my time with food—what can I say?"

"Unlike with other things . . ." Dalton and Jacob share a guy moment, but I take it in. Then Jacob sees me watching and flicks something at Dalton under the table—which I know only because Dalton flinches.

"I'll get to this tonight, Love." Mr. Chaucer motions to my story, which is now housed in his bag. "I promise. And I know it wasn't an easy task—coming up with a whole story that quickly." He looks at me with a certain degree of pity, which I take to mean I have no shot in hell of getting in.

"It would mean a lot," I say. "Not that you want me to explain—again—why I need to be in that class. But it's just—"

Mr. Chaucer whips the story pages from his bag and waves them. "This has to do the talking for you. Okay?"

I watch him leave, see other faces I know marching toward the heat, and then have a view of my father, in his blazer despite the temps, holding the door open with his long arm. I decide what I want most is to see him, maybe even deal with multiple body odors in chapel and sit with Dad up front. So I wipe my mouth a final time on my napkin and decide to make a move toward Dad, which is when two things happen at once.

One: As I go to stand up, pushing my chair out from the table with the back of my thighs, Jacob picks the exact same moment to stand up. Across the table, his green eyes shift from his now-empty bowl to my face, and suddenly it's perfectly clear: He heard. He nods to give me confirmation of what I suspect, then lets his gaze rest on me a few seconds longer than it should, which is when—

Two: I fall over.

Not in the tripped and fell way, but in the *holy shit, now I'm on the floor* way, and I don't know why.

"I'll walk her up to the Health Center," Jacob's saying to Mr. Chaucer when I rejoin the world.

"Yes, that sounds good. You can just—" Mr. Chaucer is interrupted by the sudden appearance of my father.

"Daddy!" I say and don't care how I sound. He comes over and relieves Jacob from his next-to-me position.

"I take it from your pallor that you didn't just trip and fall." Dad crouches down next to the chair someone— Jacob?—placed me in.

"My stomach feels terrible," I say. My hands are clammy, and I'm sweating even though I feel cold.

"Maybe she has food poisoning," someone offers from the side.

"Why don't we let the kind people at the Health Center figure that out," Dad says.

Then I get it. He hasn't hugged me. Hasn't swooped me up and said, *I'll take her home.* He hasn't acted parental; he's acted like a concerned administrator. And because of this, and the stress of the story, and that Jacob heard, and that Charlie had dinner with Lindsay even though it meant nothing, and because I'm boarding, and because I have to apply to colleges and Mrs. Dandy-Patinko said my map sucks, and because I still don't know what Sweet Potato means, I start to cry.

Chapter Twelve

♡

My father stands, looming large above me, his hands braced at his sides.

"No."

It's not the answer I want to hear. "But, Dad, I'm . . ." I flop back onto the pillow and give a moan worthy of at least an Oscar nod, if not an actual award. I'm not usually over-dramatic, but in this case I feel I have to be. Being stuck in the infirmary—aka the Health Center—is bad enough. But being exiled from there when there's no room at the inn is unbearable. "Dad, please!" I sit up and look around at the bodies splayed out everywhere. The heat has taken its toll with exhaustion (like mine) and true heat stroke (worse).

"All the beds are filled, the floor space is, too, and I just don't see that keeping you here is an option." Dad's tone is administrative, the same one he's been using to field phone calls from parents demanding air-conditioning for their kids. You'd think with an endowment like Hadley has, the dorms would have been upgraded years ago, but they weren't. It remains one of Hadley's quaint charms. While other prep schools are building out and up and re-sembling cookie-cutter high-end chain hotels, Hadley is still the vision of New England it once was. But the sleep-ing conditions bite.

"But you're saying I can't go home. So what can I do?" I put my hands on my forehead, feeling dizzy and wishing he'd just let me rest in my own bed. I'd recoup, read, lounge in my boxers and ratty T-shirt, watch some reruns, and have Chris bring me homework and gossip. It sounds like a spa in comparison to right now.

Dad reaches for my hand and helps me up from my temporary cot, which is immediately claimed by another near-fainting person. "Look"—his voice is hushed, his tone now conspiratorial—"I have a crisis situation here. The board of trustees is about to mutiny, the parent league is in an uproar, and I have to get things under control."

"And where does your sick daughter fit into this?" I rest my hand on his arm for balance but wish I didn't have to. "It seems so simple—why not just shove me back at home and deal with the rest of the stuff you have to do."

"Love, you've read the handbook, haven't you? Just be-cause your parents—or, parent—" He stops, singularizing himself so as not to bring my mother, Gala, into the pic-ture. "Just because I live on campus doesn't mean you can just flee home whenever you feel like it."

"I hardly think that this—"

"Right now, sure, there's a viable excuse. But what about the next time, when it's not sickness but . . ."

I sigh and let go of his arm, steadying myself on the cool white wall. Through the doorway I can see a nurse checking someone's blood pressure and a line of students waiting to be seen by the on-call physician. It is packed. "You don't want me confusing issues, is what you're saying."

Dad nods. "Exactly."

"So, then, what?"

He pulls me to the front door, giving a nod to the nurse, and then we're back outside on the Health Center porch. At one point, this was the headmaster's house, a cottage with a hearth and teacups. Now it's got none of those charms save for the porch, which calls to mind rocking chairs and homemade lemonade.

"Uhhh," I say, feeling nauseated in the heat all over again.

The chapel bell rings. "Here's what we do." Dad smacks one of his hands into the other like he's planning a military mission. "I go to chapel as planned. You will not stay here, and you can't go home, but I will give written permission for you to remain in the dorms tonight during chapel and then during the day tomorrow."

"So you're saying it's better for me to be unattended at Fruckner than to be home in my own bed?"

"You won't be unattended," Dad says. He waves his arm, signaling across the street. "You'll have Mrs. Ray there to check up on you. Heat exhaustion doesn't last long. You'll feel better in a day or so." He brushes his hands. That takes care of that, I guess. He clears his throat the way he does when there's more he hasn't said.

"What, Dad?" The heat prickles my skin, sending tingling waves down my arms.

Dad furrows his brow. "I wanted to let you know that in a couple of weeks . . ."

"Yeah?" I wait for him to say something—like he's going to ask his girlfriend, Louisa, to marry him, or that he feels the need to accompany me to Harvard, that he's going to check on me at the dorms and let me come home.

"I'm going to look at colleges," he says.

Even in the heat and feeling sick I have to speak up. "Oh, you know, I really think I want to—"

"Not with you." Dad holds on to the porch railing and tilts his head up, keeping a steady watch on the last students and faculty heading into the arched chapel doorway. "With Sadie." He looks for my reaction. "All summer you came to terms with Gala, and I'm sure you'll continue to explore that relationship . . . but I had news, too."

"I know," I say, sure of how new and confusing it must be for him to suddenly be parent to more than one child. More than just me. "It's a good thing. You're right to do it."

"Phew." Dad swipes his hand across his brow. "Not that this is optimal timing for telling you, but I just thought you might wonder where I was, and— Well, anyway, I'm going to meet her in Michigan. Try to get to know her a bit."

"With the college tour as a pleasant backdrop just in case the conversation stalls?" I give him a weary look, and then sigh. I wish I could just go home. "So, when is this again?"

"A couple weekends from now."

From across the street, away from the masses already huddled into chapel, I see whom my dad waved to.

"Hey!" Jacob comes bounding across the road and up the five steps to the shady porch. Sweat drips from his forehead. His *hey* brings me right back to Friday night and how surprised he seemed then.

Dad gives me a perfunctory hug and hands Jacob a set of keys connected to a Hadley Hall chain. "Mr. Coleman . . ." Dad doesn't say anything else, but Jacob nods. Clearly they've made prior arrangements.

I lean on the porch railing as my father makes his way over toward chapel. He's clearly dealing with major stress about the weather—one of the only things on campus he can't control—and with other, more internal issues that I'm not a part of. I don't need to be, but it's bizarre nonetheless. We're usually so in tune.

"So." Jacob gestures with the keys. "Wait here."

He leaves me in the heat of the evening, wondering if he'll come back, and disappears in the direction of back campus, where the utility buildings are.

When he returns, it's not on foot but in one of Hadley's golf carts. White, and with the Hadley crest on the side, the small thing hums while Jacob leaves it running and helps me into the shaded passenger seat. The carts aren't for golfing, but for helping elderly alums during reunion weekends, or a student who breaks a leg during ski practice. But right now, it's my convalescing vehicle, and it's perfect.

"Thanks." I keep it short while Jacob steers us along the side of the road, the haze of fading sunlight and a puff of heat remaining between us.

"No problem. I mean, I couldn't exactly leave you there, fainting in the dining hall."

I put my feet up on the plastic dashboard. My borrowed sundress trails down onto the golf cart's floor. "I think fainting might be too strong a word."

"Too dramatic?" he asks. The motor's whir sounds like music in the background, and I can see Jacob's chest rise and fall with each breath. I look away, over my right shoulder, to avoid watching. "So . . ."

I shake my head and keep looking right as we near the graveyard. "Just don't, okay?"

"I was only going to say—"

I grip the metal handrail and bring my knees up to my chest, barely able to stay in the seat. "Please just don't say anything."

Jacob stops the golf cart. We sit there, across from the graveyard, both trapped in our own minds. "I won't." He looks at his lap. "Not about *that*."

Any lingering doubts I had about just when exactly he came into the science lab on Friday night are gone. "Now you have to say something. About something else. Anything else." I put my face in my hands. "And then take me back to Fruckner. I feel like crap."

"Okay . . . how about—remember the Vineyard? And sitting on your roof, with you singing? And being at the fair, before it started—in the bumper cars?"

"Of course I remember," I snap. "It wasn't like it was years ago. It was months. Weeks."

Jacob's dark curls move even though the air is still. He turns so we're facing each other, the keys jingling in the ignition. I'm sure this isn't what my father pictured when he asked Jacob to make sure I got back to the dorms safely. "Well, you don't act like it. I mean, you act like nothing happened."

My hands fall to my lap and I look him in the eyes. "Nothing did happen, Jacob. That's what I remember. We had a lovely time—"

"Lovely? What kind of word is that? Who are you, Lucy Honeychurch?"

I picture it, that scene in the movie when passionate George finally grabs her in the field of blooming flowers, the air thick with lust and haze, his act of ardency met with surprise. But Jacob doesn't do that. He doesn't reach for my clammy hand or try to kiss me. He just waits for my answer. "Didn't we decide to be friends?"

"That's what I mean, Love. You haven't been exactly cordial of late."

I lick my lips. "It's been awkward, that's why. You've got Chloe now and it doesn't seem like—"

"There's room for you." He says it in the affirmative. "There is. On Friday when I—"

"I thought you said you wouldn't bring that up." I turn away again, focusing on the graveyard, wishing I had my aunt Mable to call up after this. That she could comfort me. Then a thought clicks. I could call my mother. I could call Gala.

"I won't." Jacob starts the cart up again, keeping quiet enough that I know there's tons he's not saying. He turns the small wheel and pulls into the driveway, the tires crunching on the gritty road.

"If I were feeling better I'd take the wheel," I say. I want to show him we can be friends, that I want to. Only, there is that other side to us, that deeper part, and I can't extricate it completely.

"Maybe when you're better," he suggests. He cuts the engine when he's right in front of the Fruckner door. Then he looks up at the illicit porch off my room. "That's your room, right?"

"Mine and Mary's, yeah."

"Cool." He puts his lips together, hiding his teeth and God knows what else. Then he moves his hand and I'm sure, positive, that he'll put it on mine. But he just drapes his arm over the back of the seat. "I want to be friends, okay?"

Feeling shaky from the sickness and from the conversation, from handing my story in, from wondering what the answer is to the question Jacob overheard, I prepare to leave the cart. My dress feels like a sham, and so do I. I want to be that person who borrows dresses and runs through the halls and flings off worries and can be friends with the boy she liked so, so much. But I'm not sure I can be. "Okay," I tell him. From my face I hope he gets what I'm feeling, but you never know what people are going to infer, or what they're going to overhear, and if it matters in the long run.

Chapter Thirteen

The next day goes by faster than I expect. In the morning there's the initial rush of girls showering, eating breakfast, and making too much noise for me to sleep off my heat-induced nausea, and then afterward, a calm. The quiet coats the house, and I fall asleep until late morning, only getting up for water and to call Gala collect. She accepts, and I tell her about almost everything, much to my surprise. She's more than sympathetic, and even though she doesn't know the key players as well as Mable might have, she offers this:

"You know, it's been my experience—and I can't speak for you—that I can't hide my thoughts. So if, say, I were in your shoes but suspected I had certain feelings for Jacob lurking beneath the surface, I wouldn't be able to be his friend, either."

"But I don't. Have those feelings, I mean." I hold the pay phone to my ear, wishing we were allowed to have cell phones so I could talk from bed. The house is so still, I keep expecting a horror movie soundtrack to cue up.

"Right," Gala says. "I know. I'm just saying—and this will sound very loaded from someone in my position"—read: someone who dropped out of my life and my dad's—"but be true to yourself. You're the one who's stuck in your life, who benefits from things and suffers if you rely on someone else's vision for how things should be. Respect those feelings that lurk beneath."

Those words. That's how I ended the short story. That there might be something lurking beneath the ocean waters for Amelia and Nick Cooper. And what am I really hiding from myself? "Thanks," I say. "It's so quiet here it's ghostly."

"You should probably get to bed," she says. "Listen to me, sounding like your mother." Cue massively awkward pause. "I am, I know . . ."

I'm out of it enough not to overreact. I mean, the woman is my mother, and one of the things I learned from Aunt Mable's treasure-map journey this past summer is that you can't alter the past. You can wrestle with it, duke it out, but you can't change it. "It's okay. . . ." I breathe deeply, feeling my fatigue as I speak. "Thanks for listening."

"And I'll see you at Thanksgiving, okay?"

This is news to me. "Really?"

She takes a breath and I hear the sound of pages moving in the background. I don't know if it's sheet music that she's working on or a calendar or the newspaper. All I know is she's on one coast and I'm on the other and my father and sister will soon meet in the middle. "Didn't your father mention anything?"

"Not about that, no." I feel weak all over again and decide I'll grab some crackers from the pantry and sip more water and go to bed. If I can't be in the Health Center and I'm not allowed home, I may as well take advantage of my empty room. "But you're coming here?"

"Yes. I have my ticket."

"Good." It's another of life's curveballs that I have her, on the phone, where this time last year I didn't even know where she lived. "But, Gala?"

"I know," she says.

"What do you think I'm going to say?"

"Keep the postcards coming."

"Yeah, that."

We end the call and I wonder about everything she said. Not the Thanksgiving part—that feels good. She'll be here, and maybe Sadie, too, and Dad and I will have to put the fun back in *dysfunctional* and cook a turkey. Suddenly that doesn't seem so overwhelming. Because I know how I feel about it. What does feel huge, though, is that scene I wrote about for Mr. Chaucer. Those characters, on the beach, with lots of unknowns out in the water.

In my room I have the windows open, but there's no breeze to speak of. Outside is a vision of the heat wave— the once-green lawn is edged with brown. The plants have wilted, and even in the shade the campus dogs are panting and miserable. I look at my watch. Noon. If I were at school I'd be eating lunch, navigating the dining hall and trying to prove to Jacob I can be his friend. Or prove to myself. Chris and Chili and Mary and Harriet Walters and Dalton—they're all up there, proceeding with their days while I stay here, stagnant. And I have no e-mail access so I don't know if Chaucer's read my story.

Gala's words stoke something in me, causing my mind to whir and my pulse to pick up its tempo. When I revisit lying there with Charlie, asking him that question, I realize the person I was really querying was myself. And, even in my sickly fog, I know that the answer can't possibly be in the affirmative. How could I sleep with him if I have any doubts whatsoever about feelings lurking beneath my own emotional surface? I stretch my legs out on my white duvet, heat coating all of me, and play mind Ping-Pong with scenarios. I like Charlie. A lot. Don't I? In the small frames of it, I do. Like when I saw him at the ferry last spring or being with him all through the warmth of the summer months. Even seeing him on Friday night. If I think about our relationship in segments, I come up with a positive feeling. We like each other, it could be serious, and blah blah blah into the future. But when I back up and think of my whole life as one big moment stretched like a canvas, big as the white-hot sky outside right now, everything changes. Seeing high school, summers included, as one long segment, I see how much a part of it Jacob is. Or has been. And how, no matter what, I always seem to come back to him. Or our unfinished business.

It's so confusing. All this thinking, and for what? Just to plague myself with doubts and indecisions? I reach for a piece of paper on my desk and jot down a line:

One of Amelia's biggest problems was her inaction.

When Poppy Massa-Tonclair taught me in London, she had me read piles of books about writing. At the time, I wondered why? Why not just write actual fiction or poetry? But having written the story for Chaucer, I can see why. And having written that line for another Amelia story, I can begin to understand that everything I'll write, even stuff that's set in Mongolia a hundred years ago (which, um, I know nothing about so I certainly wouldn't pen that instantly), will still be filtered through me. Am I Amelia? No. But do I think writing a story about a person who may or may not do things, may or may not feel things, means something? I do. That much I know.

I lean back on my pillow and start to fall asleep. In that nap haze, I'm woken by voices outside. By the flagpole, in the sun, I squint to see them: Chloe and Jacob. Meeting by the flagpole like in Hadley lore. Except it's daylight and they're loud. Probably they love each other already and are yelling it for the world. Chloe yells something and I can see Jacob reach for her. I put my hand over my eyes as a visor and lean into the window for a better view. She pushes him away and then they hug. I'm still half asleep, but even then, if I'm really very honest with myself, it stings. Just seeing her touch him. Like she did in the science center, casually, her arm at his waist. Even though it was years ago, I still can recall the way it felt to have Jacob's hands tangled in my hair as we stood, kissing for the first time, outside of Slave to the Grind, Aunt Mable's coffee shop. Has too much changed? Not even enough? I wonder. Then I fall asleep.

★   ★   ★

When I wake up, I feel much, much better, healthy even, but confused as hell. It's dark out, and so hot I think I have blankets on me but I don't.

"Finally!" Mary says from her side of the room.

"Why is it so quiet? What's going on?" I sit up and feel my heart pounding hard, like I've overslept and missed a class.

"Don't panic—you just slept away part of your life. No biggie." Mary cracks a smile. "Go shower, grab your sleeping bag, and come with me."

"Huh?" I check my watch. Past dinner, past a lot of things. "I'm hungry."

"They'll have food there," she explains and, before I can ask, shoves shampoo and conditioner my way. "Your dad did it."

"What?" I try to shake off the sleep and confusion. I grab clean clothing and my hairbrush and realize the rest of the dorm is empty when I get into the hallway. "What's my dad doing?"

"He's making Hadley history," Mary explains as I grab my towel. "It's the first ever sleep-in. The trustees finally pressured him, I guess, and the HVAC guys are already almost done with Deals."

"HVAC?"

"Heating, ventilating, air-conditioning. My cousin's a contractor. Anyway, they're doing all-night AC installation, and as a result, the unlucky—or lucky, depending on your point of view—are out of Deals, Bishop, and Fruckner tonight."

"And just where are they putting us for this sleep-in?"

"The board wouldn't spring for hotels. Pity. I guess some people signed out to day-student houses, but most of us are at main campus." She pats her sleeping bag and takes mine for me. "In the science center."

Dorm parents and the resident faculty members have done their best to keep us segregated by dorms and gender, but it's to no avail once the lights are out. As soon as the chapel bell rings ten times, the scurrying starts. Like mice—big mice—we all adjust to suit our needs. Mary disappears to wherever Carlton is. Groups of girls cluster near one of Mrs. Ray's unbirthday cakes, laughing and then being shushed by another group of girls. The shushing only makes a group of guys from Bishop laugh harder.

My sleeping bag is unfurled right near the scene of Friday night's crime (breaking and, um, lack of entering?), and I've slept so much during the day that I cannot sleep now. I wish the whole school were here; that way Chris and I could whisper and he could catch me up on anything I might have missed today. You miss one day of school and it's like the social order has changed—or at least, that's how it feels. Plus, he might know about Chaucer. But probably not.

"Are you sleeping?" Chili asks, plopping herself down next to me. "I'm over there." She points in the half dark to one of the physics rooms. "Sophomore territory."

"You can stay here; you don't have to be quarantined."

Chili shrugs. "It's okay. So, you feeling better?"

"I am." They've cranked the AC up so high that I'm actually chilled, and I stick my legs into the sleeping bag. "Anything new to report?"

"Nothing major. Just the usual breakups—" Chili bites her lip.

"What—spill it," I command.

"It's over. Ben and my brother."

"Seriously?" I think back to Chris's grin at Sunday dinner, how happy he was. "And Chris?"

"Haverford—to my surprise—was totally honest with Ben. Told him everything—about hooking up with Chris over the summer—and insert breakup speech here: it's done. And our boy Chris has himself a Pomroy."

My pulse speeds up for him. "Bet he wishes he lived in the old dorms; then he'd be here." I look around at the disarray of sleeping bags, the makeshift beds people have thrown together from sheets and pillows, some towels.

"But he's not," Chili says. Then she bends down, eyeing something or someone. "But you know who is."

I don't have to look to know whom she means. "Chilton Pomroy, I am a taken woman." It occurs to me that Charlie has no idea I'm about to spend the night here, and that I haven't seen his place of residence, either, that long distance kind of means not knowing everything all the time. That I could have called him during my sick stay but called Gala instead.

She stands up. "I know. I'm just saying. Gotta go—lest I defect to seniorland."

My sleeping bag rustles on the concrete floor. Lying

here, with the foreign sounds of other people breathing around me, I feel like I'm at a Hadley party, like Crescent Beach. With my eyes closed now, I can imagine it: the start of this past summer when I woke up there, in this same sleeping bag, next to Jacob. How I thought we'd re-found something there. I open my eyes and turn on my side, listening to quiet chatter, and then I think I hear, softly, strumming.

The way cartoon characters follow the scent of food cooking, all noses forward, a cloud of smell pulling them, I sit up and let my ears lead the way. Around the side of the lab, past the physics rooms, past the door to the photo labs where I first got lost as a freshman. All the way, I keep listening. The open ceilings and echo-prone rooms make it possible to find the sounds.

Sure enough, up in the solar balcony that overlooks where I was lying, I find them.

"If it isn't the superheroes themselves," I say to Jacob, the one strumming, and Dalton, who types furiously on a laptop. I'm not sure why I used the word *superheroes*, but that's what they are, a dynamic duo, able to scale enormous heights or sing or make snarky comments.

Without looking, Dalton asks, "Which heroes would we be, exactly? And don't for a second call me Robin."

"He has sidekick issues," Jacob explains. Then he points to his chest and mouths, "Batman."

"You could be Strummer Boy," Dalton offers from his workstation. I stare at the lighted screen, wondering what he's writing. He has the luxury of knowing he's already in the Advanced Creative Writing class. It dawns on me how polite it is of him not to have brought that up. He hasn't rubbed my nose in his literary talents but hasn't shirked all mentions of it either, which is pretty cool.

Then I think since Dalton's in Mr. Chaucer's Comparative Lit section, he could, in theory, know if my story's been seen. "Dalton?" I ask.

"I have no idea if Chaucer's read it." Dalton keeps typing.

"How about you, Strummer Boy?" I ask. "You didn't happen to bump into Mr. Chaucer—"

"And just happen to ask about your story?" Jacob picks single strings on his guitar. I'm thankful I don't know the song he's playing, if it even is a song. "No. Doubtful that Chaucer'd even tell us, anyway."

"I think Little Strummer Boy suits you." Dalton sees me looking at his screen and shuts the laptop more than halfway. He looks at me. "You're either in or not—not much else you can do now except wait."

Wait. Great, more inaction. I feel my feet on the solid floor and wonder if they could take root. I am a potted plant, I think, for all the fervor with which I embrace life.

"How about Super Typing Kid flies out of here." Jacob keeps playing while he says this, the usual banter between them strong and fluid enough that without questioning it, Dalton packs up and leaves, giving us both a nod on the way out.

After Dalton's gone, his footsteps echoing as he descends

the open staircase, I realize I have no plan. "I have no plan," I say aloud, hoping this will crystallize one.

Jacob stops playing. The guitar rests in his lap and he drapes his arm over it, lovingly, familiar with every string, each fret, the hairline fracture in the thin wood of its body. "And you need one?" He looks at me.

He looks at me the same way he did outside Mable's coffee shop two-plus years ago. The same way he did at Crescent Beach three months ago. The same way he did as we sat, grounded, in unmoving bumper cars on the Vineyard only one month ago. At least I think it's the same way. One thing's clear to me, however: I want it to be the same way. And maybe that's the key to writing and to love and even to having sex for the first time—you have to know yourself.

"Maybe I don't need a plan," I say. Then I think but don't add, *Maybe I already have one.*

People talk about just knowing and they talk about gut feelings, and right here, even though I questioned my ability, I unroot my legs and feet from the concrete and sprint—metaphorically speaking, of course. In reality, I did move—but just over to the balcony.

"Well, I know a good plan store if you need one," he says and goes back to the guitar.

"I still have feelings for you." The words leak out one by one. All those months, years even, of thinking this, of writing it in the privacy of my journal, of perhaps fiction-alizing it in my story, and here it is—the truth is coming out of me at the first-ever Hadley sleep-in. That's what's lurking underneath.

I lean on the concrete balcony. It's thick and cold and affords a view of sleeping students. While I'm in the slow-motion moments that follow my six-word declaration, I notice something. Straight across from me, at ceiling level, are shiny orbs, all of the planets in order, each one strung from an invisible point.

"Planets," I say softly, pointing to them. It seems big to me, somehow, meaningful, that I never noticed them before. That I was lying there on the soapstone table with Charlie and never once saw the blue-green of Earth, the murky marble of Neptune, the brightness of the sun.

Jacob starts to play, then sings. *"Satellites gone up to the skies / thing like that drive me out of my mind."*

" 'Satellite of Love,' " I say. "Lou Reed."

"Yep. The single from his 1972 album *Transformer*." Jacob brackets his fingers to form chords, mumbling further lyrics.

"Bowie produced that album, you know." My hands are clasped together, pretty-please style, but the rest of me feels very calm.

"I still have feelings for you, too, Love. But I think you know that."

Jacob keeps playing, his voice soft with the lyrics, and I don't join in. I stay where I am. When the song ends, Jacob does that thing where he slams his hand over the strings to silence them suddenly, then gently puts the instrument down and comes over to me. He faces forward, looking out at the swinging planets, and I face in, toward the quiet guitar, thinking about all the music that's passed between us. About what happens next.

"I'm waiting for a lot of things," I start.

Jacob leans on his forearms, not touching me, his face and eyes away like it'll be easier to speak this way. "I heard everything."

"I know." I take a breath. "It's embarrassing, okay? That's why, in the golf cart, I couldn't—"

"Love, I get it. Doesn't take a genius to know that the sex thing's kind of a touchy subject." He pauses while I laugh a little. "I know, bad word choice."

"I don't care that I haven't had sex, you know? That's not it. It's like, I didn't want—I don't want you to . . ." I turn around so we're both at least facing the same way, with a view of Saturn and its rings and tiny Pluto. "So, what'd you think, when you heard it?"

Jacob swallows and rests his chin in one of his hands. "I thought—oh, shit."

"Hmm, eloquent."

"Well, that was the first thing—you know, I didn't want to walk in on you, but Chloe—"

"Right, Chloe." I picture them hugging at the flagpole today.

Jacob stands up straight, stretching his arms like he has any hope of touching those planets, and then starts to reach for my face. His hands are nearly there, almost on my cheeks, and he pulls them back. My stomach lurches, thinking about him touching me, and I bite my lip. "Big night." He takes a step back.

"Yeah."

"We should probably reconvene at a later date?"

All we exchange is a look—a look that tells me he won't make a move and neither will I until I speak to Charlie. Until, until, until. So much for action. "Is it possible to like two people at the same time?" I ask.

"Completely possible. Likely, even. For a little while, I guess." He shoves his hands in his pockets. "But if we do this . . . if we become a *we*—for real this time? It can't be right now. Not like this."

In my mind, as we part, I can hear the songs he played. He goes down the stairs first, leaving me to think about what comes next. All those galaxies we've yet to explore.

Chapter Fourteen

♡

There is no reason in the world not to like Chloe Swain. She's categorically fun, pretty in a nonthreatening way, able to catch a ball and paint a landscape in a way that suggests if not true talent then an acceptable mediocrity, and she's the kind of person who laughs easily—which means the times she's been present and I've made a joke or comment, she's rewarded me publicly with a true guffaw. The only possible thing I could list in my journal about her is that she is a constant fiddler. Not in the bluegrass-slap-your-knee kind of way, but in the tiny-movements-all-the-time kind of way—tapping her pen on the tables, drumming her fingers, twirling her hair, flicking the corner of the notebook, opening and closing her lip-gloss tube. These are not egregious actions on her part, and yet, in the middle of learning about peace treaties, her minuscule fiddlings are enough to make me wage an invisible war.

"I can't sit next to her anymore," I tell Chris when the bell rings and we're being herded down the corridor to yet another fun-filled class that will result in too much homework.

"Jealousy sucks, huh?" Chris slings his backpack over one shoulder.

"Thanks, Mr. Sensitive." My mouth tucks into a pout and I stop for a drink of water. Chris stands by, watching me sip. "What?"

"Nothing." His voice goes up a register, which I know is his *I'm hiding something* tone.

"Spit it out." I wipe my mouth on my hand and check my watch. "I have precisely two minutes before I have to bow at the altar that is creative writing."

"Today's the big day—that's right." Chris tries to deflect my curiosity onto the well-worn subject of my prolonged courtship with the ACW class.

"More than a week I've had to wait." I shake my head. "So unfair. Here I am dealing with colleges and the upcoming campus interview crazies and I still don't know about my future."

"None of us knows about our future." Chris looks at me like I'm nuts.

"No—not like that. But, in August, when I decided to try and get into his class—I made up my mind. Writing. That's what I want to do. So when you find out what you want to do, you—or at least I—want to get started right away. Like you and a certain someone . . ." I smile as Chris smiles about his new boy.

"ASAP?" Chris asks, saying the letters as a word, which he knows will annoy me.

"Charlie does that—for real." Pointing out such a little flaw now seems silly, especially given the fact that I've spoken to him only once since my intergalactic adventure with Jacob, and I'm no closer to clarity about what to do. "I have to tell him, right? Just call him and say that I like him . . . of course I do . . . but that I—" The bell rings. "What the hell am I thinking?" I grab Chris by the shoulders. "Help me. I mean, I like two guys—one's supposedly my boyfriend, and the other one's taken anyway. So maybe I shouldn't say anything, just go about my—"

"He's not taken." Chris says it fast. "You're not supposed to know, but now you do."

My mouth drops open as students shuttle by me to class, jostling me this way, then that. "Jacob and Chloe?"

"They broke up when you were sick," Chris explains, his hand over his shoulder like it happened long ago instead of just a week. "And I would've said—especially given the circumstances with you and J—but Chloe swore me to secrecy."

"I'm your best friend."

Chris sighs. "We're going to be late. The truth is, I didn't think you could deal with one more issue. I was going to dish it out right after your meeting with Chaucer."

My meeting. Right. "I have to go!" Then I suddenly smile. "He broke up with her?"

"By the flagpole. Total Hadley cliché." Chris turns me in the direction of Chaucer's room. "Maybe now you don't care so much if she flicks her pen cap and twirls her hair?"

Up in the hall, Chris sees Haverford. They're pretty

mellow in terms of announcing their relationship to the Hadley public, but Haverford's grin speaks loudly. "I have to go, too."

"Did I tell you I'm glad things worked out for you two?"

Chris nods. "Not in so many words, but yeah." He walks a few paces down the hall toward Haverford, who's already decked out in his Hadley soccer gear, his cleats clicking on the linoleum. "And, Love? It will for you, okay?"

I speed away, down the steps, out the side door, and over to the faculty room where I'm supposed to meet Mr. Chaucer. In less than five minutes I'll know my writing fate. I could have my Wednesday and Sunday nights suddenly taken up with secret society meetings, feeling a part of the smallest group of the best writers on campus, the ones who go on to publish books and edit anthologies. Or I could be negged with the simplest shake of the head. I imagine Mr. Chaucer's slow back-and-forth *no*, the gesture he rarely uses in class except when he thinks we're getting way off track. He doesn't shake his head; he sort of tilts and shakes, like he's trying to lessen the negativity.

Which is just what Mr. Chaucer does when he sees me. He walks out of the faculty room eating a slice of banana bread so pungent I feel like I've eaten some, too. I take a deep breath like I'm about to swim into oncoming waves. Then he shake-tilts his head again, and no matter how I try to buoy myself, my confidence flags. I've already been discarded without so much as a *thanks for trying*. All of this makes me fairly certain I am ill prepared for all those college rejection letters, the ones that start with *While we appreciate your efforts. . . .* Note to self: Must apply to actual schools prior to getting barred from going.

"I could try—" I start and then reel the words back, remembering he doesn't care for explanations.

"Here." Mr. Chaucer pulls my story from his brown briefcase. "Walk with me to Maus Hall. I have to hand in some recommendation letters."

One of them could be mine. He's one of the teachers I asked to write on my behalf, and I still need to get two peer recommendations. It drives me up the wall that I'll never know what was said by either camp.

I take the story and hold it out, flipping through it to see if he made any comments. "You didn't mark it."

"I didn't."

Probably not marking it shows just how much he disliked it. I go a little ways in front of him and then stop, so he stops, too. On the quad, fall is finally kicking into gear. Long pants, tanks tops gone, the air sliced with cool, the sunlight dappled and lower in the sky. Now that the dorms are finally all air-conditioned, the weather is temperate. Wish it were that way for my emotions.

"What could I do to make this better?"

Mr. Chaucer looks uneven as he holds the weight of his bag over one shoulder and tilts his head, frowning. "What makes you think you need to?"

"Well, I'm not in the class, right? And I've got enough humility to know that I could try again. So, can I?"

He shakes his head again, sorry. "No."

My heart is in my feet, all hopes of writing dashed. Probably I should tell Poppy Massa-Tonclair not to bother writing my recommendations, not to nominate me for the Beverly William Award. It's futile. "Well, thanks, anyway." I wonder where I can go on campus to curl up, fist-tight, and be upset.

"Love?" He looks amused, and also baffled. A smile forms on his lips. "You know I'm letting you into ACW, right?" He waits for me to confirm.

"But you—"

"Didn't get a chance to tell you before your pessimism took over?"

I give a half laugh, the slow rise of happiness and excitement building in my belly as I wait for the reality to hit. "Okay. True. But you shook your head."

He keeps walking and we wait for a car to pass before crossing the street that separates upper and lower campus. "I only shook my head because this—your story—it wasn't what I expected. It's wrong of me, I know, to have pre-formed visions of what students will bring to the table, and if anything, this proves to me I have to let those go."

"I'm in?" I try not to squeal like a little girl getting cotton candy, but since I love cotton candy and I'm accepted into ACW, I can't help it.

"You are. Number six." Mr. Chaucer holds up fingers to correlate with my entry into the class. "You know it means extra work, and deadlines, and lots and lots of revisions?"

I nod. Then I wonder what he thought he'd get from me. "Did you think I'd write a story set in high school?"

I trot next to him, not quite puppylike but close enough. "I work on the lit mag, remember?" The campus literary magazine, *Fusions*, considers all the submissions anonymously so no one gets preferential treatment. The main problem isn't always the quality of the writing but that the stories never leave campus. Girl likes guy or the other way around or friendships get strained, but it's always loosely veiled visions of Hadley Hall.

"This is my stop," Chaucer says when we're on the stone steps in front of Maus Hall. "EEK!" He thumbs to the building. "You'll need to report to the class this Sunday, then again on Wednesday." He pauses. "You can ask Dalton Himmelman if you have any questions."

"Dalton?" I wrinkle my nose. I knew he was in the class, but I didn't know he was the go-to guy. But I'm in. All that work, all that worrying—a huge relief washes over me.

"Yes. And just so you know, he read your story." Chaucer doesn't apologize for this, as if handing off my private work was no biggie. Then he sees my dismay about this. "We all read everything in the group. So get used to it. You won't be able to hide under that anonymous cloak."

I mime throwing off a heavy cape, which I know I'll have to actually do when it comes time to meet. "Did he like it, too?" I ask and wish I weren't so interested in getting praise. But there you go; I am. And for some reason, from him especially.

Mr. Chaucer lets his bag drop from his shoulder and starts up the stairs. "He did." He walks up to the double wooden doors and reaches for the brass handle. "Only . . .

he didn't think there was as much lurking underneath as the writing suggested."

"What?" I need further info on this.

"With those characters—Amelia and . . ."

"And Nick Cooper," I fill in. I can't wait to tell my dad about the class. And Gala. And Chris. And Jacob. And Chili. The world, basically. It's only after I go through the names that I realize I haven't even thought of telling Charlie. And he was so good about asking after my writing. Note to self: Deal with dwindling long-distance romance or perish.

"I liked them together. That ambiguous last scene with them on the beach? How we know that underneath it all, Amelia really loves the guy." Mr. Chaucer opens the door and I can hear college chatter from inside.

"And Dalton?"

"He wasn't convinced."

Chapter Fifteen

Settling into a routine just happens. You think you won't, that the newness of each season or year will stick with you, but everything fades out—and faster than you think. There's the blur of classes, assignments, hasty lunches, furtive glances across the quad/room/field with Jacob. Some phone tag with Charlie, me taking longer to return his calls because of our lame phone system but mainly because I can feel things crumbling. There's an old stone wall behind the Lowenthal Outdoor Gymnasium (aka the LOG), and when I'm treadmilling or crunching, I stare out at it, amazed it hasn't toppled yet. Apparently it's been in semidisrepair for years. Some things are like that, I guess, collapsing over time—and maybe that's what I'm letting happen to my relationship with Charlie. Talking to him feels distant. The time I met him in the Square for a milkshake was brief and terse—not platonic, but not connected, either.

"I never thought I'd tell you this much," I say to Mary

on the way down to dinner. Fruckner House has its own industrial kitchen, and along with unbirthdays, one of the house traditions is eating sit-down meals thrice weekly.

Mary and I arrive in the dining room in time to sing "Happy Unbirthday" to Becca Feldman, who shakes her booty like she's at a club rather than a same-old, same-old dinner. Mary leans down, whispering, "Well, I'm glad to know you—and spill my guts, too. You don't think it'll happen, that roommate thing. But it does—I mean, we're cooped up nearly twenty-four seven, so what else are we going to do except bond, right?"

"Bond or perish," I say with a mental nod to Lindsay Parrish. If she and I had ended up rooming together, no doubt my emotional well-being would have been thoroughly disrupted. She's joined the staff of *Fusions*, the literary magazine, and I'm fairly certain she has little or no interest in the written word. Chris thinks I'm being paranoid, but my instincts tell me that LP is set to invade every area of my life—right down to my extracurriculars. Good thing she can't get into ACW. A slight panic grips me. She couldn't, right?

"Have some food, Love." Mary gestures at me with a forkful of mashed potato.

"Sign me up." I reach for my own plate o' starch.

The unbirthday proceeds, with the cake set aside for after the meal. With each forkful of mashed potatoes, I feel the minutes draining away, pulling me closer to getting out the door and over to my ACW class. More than once Lindsay has tried to stop me by threatening dorm meetings (she decides when these blessed events occur) and upset me by

announcing loudly that she has "co–head monitor issues
to discuss with her co–head monitor." I'm definitely not
being paranoid. The girl's a raging nightmare.

Most of the time at dorm dinners, Mrs. Ray heads the
table, presiding over all of us, while Mary makes me laugh
and Lindsay makes it clear she'd love to stick her fork in my
eye rather than into her few paltry lettuce leaves. Tonight
is no exception.

"Just in case anyone's searching for me after dinner"—
Lindsay chews her lettuce and swallows—"I'll be having
parietals in Jacob Coleman's room." Mrs. Ray opens her
mouth to remind us—yet again—of the parietal rules,
but Lindsay keeps going. "We just have so many issues to
discuss." She gives me the pleasure of looking at my face
and motioning to my chin with her manicured talons. (Of
course, they're not long talons because long nails scream
mall and Lindsay is far too pedigreed for that; hers are of
the carefully sculpted oval variety glossed in barely there
pink.) I swipe at it with my napkin and of course have potato sludge on it. But I don't let anything show.

"Gee," Mary says to Lindsay, "I hope you can get all
those issues sorted out, what with all the freshmen needing
your help here tonight."

Mrs. Ray takes a sudden interest. "What's this?"

Mary puts on her innocent face—easy for her since
she's so friendly and open. "Oh, I was overhearing the new
freshmen and how they could really use a hand getting
used to writing five-paragraph essays. You know, the Hadley gold standard."

People use that phrase, *Hadley gold standard*, when they're pressing a point. Mrs. Ray bites the line, however, and touches Lindsay's arm. "Lindsay, it would be very courteous of you—as the dorm head—to spend the time with them tonight."

Lindsay's displeasure spreads from her neck tendons to her hands as she mutilates the next piece of lettuce. Perhaps if she ate something, she wouldn't be quite so cranky. "I really must meet with my co–head monitor." Note how she uses the possessive and doesn't mention his name, just in case Mrs. Ray thinks there's any funny business between them. Which there isn't. Right? I carve a pattern in my potatoes as though this will clarify any lingering doubt.

Mrs. Ray taps her knife on her glass. "For those of you needing help in the area of the five-paragraph essay— good news! Lindsay Parrish will be available tonight after dinner until lights out." Mrs. Ray smiles at Lindsay, unaware that she's ruined the girl's night. And made mine just a bit better.

I smirk into my starchy food and nudge Mary under the table as a thank-you.

Lindsay mumbles into her salad, "Gold standard, my ass."

"No," Mary says. "Mine is, actually."

I crack up as I clear my plate and head out the door.

Mr. Chaucer's apartment is in a section of campus everyone refers to as the Stables, even though there are no horses to be found. Used to be, Hadley had a team of workhorses and the wealthiest students kept their own carriages and top-of-the-line stallions and mares. This was hundreds of years ago, though, when getting off campus meant saddling up. Then, in the 1950s, it became chic again for students—girls, especially—to own horses, and they added a few small barns near the paddock. Now the paddock is still ringed by a wooden fence, but it serves as an entryway to faculty housing.

The large barn holds a bunch of faculty apartments, and each of the single stables was converted into a tiny house. Mr. Chaucer lives in one of these. The stable houses form a semicircle, with Chaucer's on the very far left, set back from the grassy paddock, shouldered by the woods.

The moonlight is dim now, the night sounds just starting. Branches crack when I step on them, grass swishes with my steps, and some sort of creature digs in a compost heap. I hold my notebook to my chest, take a breath, and go inside.

Midway through the evening, this is what pops into my mind:

I am guilty of thinking too much. Of planning out how things should be to the point where if conversations or kisses or dates or beach trips go differently than I pictured, I'm not as happy. This is something I've been fixing, slowly. But despite many days and times that I've fallen into that trap, my ACW class is exactly what I pictured—only better.

The living room is small, and somehow, even though we are landlocked, the wide, unstained wooden plank floors, the windows trimmed in cracking blue paint, the sea-chest coffee table and hurricane lamps, all make it look like we're clustered together by the ocean.

"I liked the use of symbolism," Linus says. He sips green tea from a plain white mug and leans over the round oak table.

The six of us—seven if you count Chaucer—are dispersed through the small room. Sara Woods is on an ottoman, her dark hair pulled back as she rereads Priss (short for Priscilla, slightly unfortunate nickname, though if rumors are valid, not applicable) Giggenheim's story. Priss and Oscar Martinez sit in two chairs near the ottoman, while Mr. Chaucer stands and occasionally paces the room. Avenue Townsend (Avi for short, which suits him much more than his rock-star-sounding name, given to him by his rock-star parents), whom I know from the *Fusions* staff, hasn't taken his coat off. He sits chewing on a pencil and worrying the edges of his sleeves. His demeanor is like his writing—intense and dark with moments of funny.

Stacked in neat piles are student papers, books, and, by a giant old dictionary, the applications for the Beverly William Award. I try to ignore them.

"Any more rain in here and it starts to be biblical." Dalton Himmelman reaches for a bite-size brownie at the same time I do and our hands brush for a second. He's on the floor with his back to the wall and I'm not so much next to him as diagonally across from him with the snack tray in the middle. So far, I've been pretty quiet. I'm new and don't want to burst onto the ACW scene too harshly.

I'm more interested in the whole atmosphere—on campus, but feeling off, something intellectual but that has so much emotion involved.

"Biblical? It's not like she's got an ark in here." I nibble the brownie the way I eat all baked goods—edges first, then the softer inside afterward.

"It doesn't have to contain an actual Jesus or six pairs of animals to connote . . ." Dalton ends his sentence by eating. Everyone takes turns baking, and Mr. Chaucer provides the drink.

"Well, I wanted the point of view to be—" Priss starts, but Mr. Chaucer does his combination head shake and tilt and she's instantly quiet. One of the rules that's been explained is that you can't comment on your own story. You write it, hand it in with copies for everyone, and get to listen to every word people have to say. But you can't be your own footnotes. So Priss gives an embarrassed smile and looks down.

"Anyone else?"

Linus proceeds. He's smart, the editor of the serious campus paper, and known for his grades and perfect SATs, if not for his sense of humor. "It needs work." He looks up and addresses us all. "That's my honest opinion. You have to use the principles of effective composition even in a creative context." He goes on to explain why, in very academic terms, until Mr. Chaucer interrupts. He leans on the old dictionary, causing me to eye the applications again. Weird to think that one of them will have so much of me in it. I wonder who else will apply. Probably the entire senior class. Linus gives me a side glance. "You have to be tough in here." I nod.

"Love can handle the constructive criticism," Dalton says. He grins at me. He and I spoke before about how that term, *constructive criticism*, is thrown around the way people say *no offense* and then proceed to offend you. As though under the guise of constructive, people can be honest and say you suck. I grin back.

Mr. Chaucer pats the dictionary as though it's an old friend or a dog. "There's the payoff. The good part, if you will, of this group. And since Love is new to our meeting, I'd like her to see how we end our sessions, just so she's not freaked out at the possibility of having her creative writing hacked to bits when it's her turn." Chaucer refills my cranberry juice spritzer and explains. "Despite the food and drinks, our circle is no picnic. Sometimes, your piece will be ripped apart. And it's not a good feeling."

"Trust me," Sara says, rolling her eyes and gripping her pen tightly. "But it happens to everyone."

Mr. Chaucer goes on. "So at the end, after your poem or story or play has been examined and put to the verbal test, we do the kindest thing."

"Burn it?" I joke. People laugh.

"No. Praise it." Mr. Chaucer sits on the only chair left— neither Dalton nor I wanted to take it—a butterfly chair in the corner. "Priss, I think you have a remarkable talent for pacing. You know just when things need to happen—the right dialogue, the perfect action." He hands his copy of her story back. "Well done."

Linus goes next: "Priss, you have a great way of hooking us in, getting the reader to want to know what happens."

Everyone delivers the praise face on, not shy about it. I notice that the criticisms were said in the third person, but the praise is direct. This strikes me as gentle, too. None of these people—with the exception of Dalton—are people I really have reason to hang out with—except maybe Avi for editorial meetings—or even talk to. But now I'll be one of them; nod to them over casseroles at Sunday dinner, brush past them in the hallway, and wait in line with them for coffee at the student center.

"That's true." Dalton nods, brushing his chocolate hair out of his eyes. "Page turning. It's a quality I need more of in my own writing." He casts a self-deprecating smile toward Priss. "You really have that part down."

"I'm just a really big fan of yours, Priscilla. You know that. And even though I didn't love this story, I still think you're amazing." Sara crosses her arms. The group is small enough that each week is devoted to close reading of just one person's work. By adding me, Chaucer lengthened the process, but no one seems too put off. I just need to brace myself for the all the construction that lies ahead for me and my writing.

Everyone turns to me. I clear my throat and hold back a minibelch from the fizzy cranberry spritzer. "I'm new, obviously, and I'm sure I'll feel kind of timid—"

"You? Timid?" Dalton gives a disbelieving look.

"I'm not sure what exactly I like about this story." I look at Priss, then at Mr. Chaucer. He nudges me ahead with his eyes. "And I know that's not helpful because generalities don't make you better; they just make you question yourself. But . . ." I hand her story back. On her lap, Priss has a pile of copies, all with notes on them, each one marked up for improvements or with suggestions. Already I can't wait to have the same pile back on my lap after I've gotten a chance to submit. All those comments and notes directed at my writing, which up until now has gone largely unread.

"Can you tell us the line you liked best?" Chaucer suggests. "Sometimes if you don't know what to say, showing an example of the writing that worked for you could be the key."

I take my copy of her story back and quickly flip through it, all eyes watching me. But even under pressure in here, it's a good kind. The excitement that runners get before they sprint, or actors do before a play. Buildup, but not negative.

"Here." I point to a section. "On the eighth page, when you say 'mile after mile, the dust kicked up behind the car wheels but the Milagro Café was still in view' . . . It's small, I know, but I like how you're so clear about the picture. Telescoping, almost, on what you want us to find."

Priss smiles. "Thanks. Telescoping. Good word."

We end the session with a discussion of scheduling.

"Dalton, you'll be next week." Mr. Chaucer points to him. I breathe a sigh of relief. Even though I'm excited, I'm not quite ready for it. "Then Love." He checks his teacher planner. "That'll be right before Columbus Day."

This rings a bell in my mind and apparently in Chaucer's, too, because the next thing he does is wordlessly distribute the applications for the Beverly William Award. It lands in my lap, flapping like a bird's wing, and for a second I don't even look at it. I watch the room, taking in how everyone has hold of his or her application, how *constructive* suddenly just got competitive. Only Dalton casually shoves it into his notebook without looking. "Then after Columbus Day we'll get to Sara and so on . . ." Mr. Chaucer opens his front door, letting a gasp of cooler air in. Then, when we're all standing and ready to go, everyone waits before leaving.

"Okay—quotation of the week." Mr. Chaucer recites from memory. "'Reading makes immigrants of us all. It takes us away from home, but, most important, it finds homes for us everywhere. . . .' Hazel Rochman."

Dalton whistles as we leave the paddock area. I think about the quotation, about finding a home and how that's what I hope to do at school, with my writing, even with love. The whistle carries through the air. The extra weight of the BW Award application makes me ever mindful of how much I have invested in applying.

"Is that 'Rain Falls for Wind'?" I'm kind of shocked— not just that Dalton knows the band the Sleepy Jackson, but that he likes the music enough to whistle it.

"*I've been drinking and thinking of you . . . ,*" Dalton sings, remarkably on tune. "What's not to like?"

Our feet rustle through the leaves. The other ACW members head back to main campus while Dalton and I, the only ones from the west dorms, head the other way. "I thought you were . . ." Dalton tucks his notebook securely under his arm, saying nothing about the application he so carelessly shoved inside, and leads me not back the way I came via main campus, but a back way. On the far side of the paddock, he lifts a metal ring off the gate and swings it open. I can almost imagine horses here, riders practicing jumping or whatever they do exactly during lessons.

"You just have me pegged as Sidekick Boy."

I run my tongue along the inside of my teeth, thinking about that comment as Dalton walks into the darkness of the woods. "I know you're not Robin to his Batman. Really." I duck under a branch and keep following him. "And by the way, don't lead me to the swamp and do something you'll regret."

"This isn't a murder mystery," Dalton says. "But that's one of the reasons I like walking this way. You can't really, during the day, because technically we're trespassing on that person's land." He points through the thick pines to a house, all its windows lit up. "But it makes me think about home."

"Why, you live in the woods?" I ask. "How very Robert Frost."

Dalton doesn't give me a quick response. He lazes into growing up on a farm, with his academic parents, with three sisters. "It wasn't idyllic or anything—I mean, it can get boring when you're fourteen. But as a kid, it was awesome." He pulls back a branch so I can walk by. "And I love visiting there. We have wicked sledding contests in winter."

"You, on a sled, shrieking?" It's a funny image, almost too sweet—for someone who always has an edge, always has something extra to add.

"In the interest of full disclosure . . . there might be some mulled wine involved." He laughs.

"So, you like the Sleepy Jackson. . . ." I pause, realizing I'm filling air with chit-chat rather than saying what I want. "In the interest of full disclosure, I have to say that maybe I did peg you as Jacob's whatever. I mean, it's how I know you, right?"

And it's true. Over the years he's always been there, just off to the side when I've gone to talk to Jacob, or on the Vineyard when we hung out. At assemblies or in a class here and there. It comes as a revelation that only recently have I been adding to the once-slim file in my brain marked *Dalton*. "I'm sorry, I think." I stop walking, the wind catching the edge of my scarf, making it dance of its own accord.

Dalton turns, looking taller in the darkness, his eyes still so light blue they appear nearly silver. "Your story—for Chaucer?"

"The one I wrote in two days to get into the class?" I make a mental note that I mentioned the haste with which I wrote it to remind him it might not be my best work.

"It's you and him, right?"

A sound somewhere between guffaw and snort comes out of my mouth. Nice. "*No*. No—it's not. It's fiction. A short story."

"Right, of course. But"—Dalton punctuates his sentence with a click of his tongue—"in every fiction there's a kernel of truth, isn't there?"

From my waist I pull my worn-in Hadley sweatshirt and slide my bare arms into the double-lined cotton. Right then, I know that's how I feel about ACW, that familiar comfort. Of being surrounded by something that could be trite (a high school writing class, a Hadley article of clothing) but turns out to be perfect. "I don't know what I think about that truth-in-fiction stuff. Amelia and Nick Cooper are just figments."

"I think," Dalton says, still not moving, "that that's the problem with them."

"What?"

"They don't jump off the page. You know, come alive and feel so real you could know them or grasp their fingers." He puts his hands together. "And in good fiction— the best fiction—you can. Touch them, I mean."

I rest my chin on my chest—an awkward position but one that affords a certain amount of shyness and warmth. "So you're saying you don't believe in Amelia and Nick." I wonder if underneath those names I really do mean me and Jacob, all that stuff about them kind of being together in the story and kind of not. And if Dalton thinks this, too. If he's trying to tell me something.

"I just don't buy it. The two of them on that beach. All that water underneath the proverbial bridge." He snaps the branch back and it rustles the pine needles.

"So you don't think once people—characters, I mean— have that much history they can surpass it like Amelia wants to?" I picture the character I made up with her hands up, her feet on the sand, waiting for me to tell her if she's real or not, if she and Nick Cooper will really be joined or if she's destined to comb the beach for polished stones and glass by herself.

Less than a mile away from us right now, Jacob is strumming his guitar or doing homework or playing foosball in the Bishop common room, maybe thinking about Chloe Swain or—maybe—me. And farther away, Charlie's off doing whatever it is he does when he's not with me. It used to be fishing or repairing his boat, but now he lives a life at college that feels for some reason even less related to me. So maybe Amelia and Nick are a loose version of me and Charlie, unable to meet fully on that beach, wherever that is.

"What did Mark Twain say?" Dalton thinks. "Not trying to be pretentious or anything, but my dad—he's an English professor."

"And just what did your dad, by way of Mr. Twain, say?"

"The difference between the right word and the nearly right word is the same as that between lightning and the lightning bug." Dalton switches his notebook to the other arm. "You're applying, of course?"

I swallow. "Yeah. You?"

"Yep." He says that the same way Jacob does and I wonder who started it—who brought what to their room freshman year and where the dividing line is between them. "Long shot, though." He waits for me to catch up, then explains. "But I figure—any lesson in writing is a good one."

I take that in. "You never know—you could win it."

"So could you." He whistles again, then stops. "Like Twain said, it's a subtle but huge difference."

This applies to him and Jacob, too, I think. How being with Dalton kind of reminds me of being with Jacob but isn't the same at all. How, like lightning bugs or lightning, it would be a mistake to clump them entirely together. We leave the cluster of trees and wind our way toward the dorms. Rather than passing the graveyard, this way we go past the track, the swamp where the campus dogs like to play, and Dalton talks. "I think you'll like the class. Meetings are one of the best parts of my week."

I don't ask what the other best parts of his week are; I only breathe out relief. "I'm just glad I'm in." Cold air fills my lungs with the seasonal shift. "I just want to be good at it, you know? Be able to write something that blows people away. Or maybe not even that major an impact. Maybe just something people like. Something I like."

Dalton nods. "That is the goal, isn't it?"

"You nervous that you're up at bat next week?"

As we approach the service road that nudges up to a path behind the grassy oval, Dalton stops. First I think it's for dramatic effect, but then I realize he's got something in his shoe. He hands me his thick notebook while he deals with the pebble.

"This looks pretty all-inclusive." I hold his book close to me, feeling that it's sacred somehow, all that writing—those parts of him, of myself—we never share.

He takes it back, slowly, looking at me while reaching for

it. "I've been writing so long, sometimes I forget I haven't put all the stories on paper. Or I wonder what's real in my day-to-day life versus what I've inferred."

I grab his arm, enthused. "I do that, too. I spend so much time trying to give the characters dialogue that makes sense but that means something, too, that I'll be in class or at the gym or something and put way too much meaning on everything."

Dalton imitates us both. "Pass the salt." He furrows his brow. "Now, does she mean pass the salt, or is she making reference to my salty attitude, or that day we spent on the Atlantic?"

"Exactly." I sigh. "It's exhausting, really." I motion with my head to Fruckner. The downstairs lights are off, girls are all in their rooms—their stomachs filled with unbirth-day cake—and I will soon be in mine, belly smiling from the brownies, and mind lit with potential ideas. "I'll make sure to keep your day life . . ." I pause and shuffle my feet. "I mean, what I know of your day-to-day life—out of your stories. I won't read into them too much." I say this, won-dering if he'll do the same for me. Or if he already did.

"Good deal." He starts to walk toward Bishop, and then stops. "You think you'll continue with Amelia and Nick or try a different story?"

I shrug. "Don't know. Is it better to go back and revise or leave it and move on?"

"Depends . . ."

I picture Amelia on the beach waiting but also know there are other ideas, places, I want to write about, descriptions and tensions I've yet to explore. "What about you? What will I have the pleasure of reading next week—an old story of yours or something new?"

Dalton's yards away now. The grass seems blue in the moonlight, the flagpole bright. "Maybe a combination."

"A drunken sledding story?" I suggest, giving him a grin based on my great night, that good fit when your life feels tucked into place.

"You never know." He stands there, near Bishop's front steps, waiting for me to move the last few paces toward Fruckner. I imagine Dalton going inside, treading the path up to his room, and finding Jacob there—how they each have stories complete with dialogues and characters. Will Dalton tell him about ACW? Or does he keep that close to his chest, poker-faced about his writing the way Jacob is about his music? Briefly, I wonder if I'll play into their conversation tonight. Or maybe guys don't talk like that, spilling secrets while the moonlight seeps through the sides of the shades. I open my mouth to say good night, to thank him for the walk back, but by the time I do, he's just gone in, leaving the door partway open behind him.

Chapter Sixteen

"This is the last fall Field Day!" I say while Chili sprints the length of the football field. Days have washed by, bringing homework and time spent hanging out in the dorm. Now, though, we're all benched, bleachered, and stuck on the grass while we wait for more events and games.

Chris and I are off to the side, sitting on a grassy hill, having already competed in a rousing game of capture the flag. "You say that like it's a bad thing."

"Aren't you the slightest bit sentimental?" I pull my knees up so I can lean into them. "I keep thinking about all the things we won't do again. All those lasts."

"What does that mean?"

"Like ... when it was the last September twentieth, or the last time I'll have those back-to-school jitters." We focus so much on firsts, I sometimes wonder about lasts. Then I think about telling Dalton this on the way to ACW this weekend. He'll know what I mean, in a writerly sense, how first everything—sex, love, spelling bees, driving a car—all those times get top billing. But what about lasts? The last time you felt a certain way or ate licorice or cried until you had nothing left. Or took part in a semifun day, a remnant from when people still hauled tractors across the Hadley fields and had burlap sacks for reasons other than Field Day races.

Chris shoots me a look of disbelief. "You don't think you'll have tons of jitters going to college for the first time? You will."

"But it won't be the same." I sigh, looking out at the field that's scattered with players, the ongoing games and bright red plastic cups filled with water littering the view. "All those days of high school you wake up and you know what to expect—and then, after all these ones we have now, we won't know."

"That's the beauty of college—or of life after Hadley. Not knowing." Chris pulls out stalks of grass and chucks them into the air. "Is this because you're not falling prey to the Hadley sickness?"

I slouch. "Maybe. It's just—everyone seems all set with college. You've got your top two places. You've got your middle ones, and even a few lesser-ranked colleges you'd be okay with. Mary's been scouted by UConn for basketball, so she's all set. They even sent her a sweatshirt." I scan the track and field for other faces, other stories. "Linus—another one of Chaucer's disciples—he's bound for NYU or Columbia, then no doubt to Iowa for fiction. Jon Rutter's got his pick of places; Nick Samuels had been professing his adoration for Princeton since before he even started here." I gesture to Nick. "He's already wearing orange and black socks. . . . I could go on and on." I lie back on the grass, my limbs in the soft green. "I can pick through the entire senior class and it seems like everyone knows what they want and where they need to go. Except for me."

"First of all, you've done your apps. That's just so annoyingly prompt of you I can't stand it. Plus, it only seems like that—that everyone's sorted." Chris touches my knee and I sit up. "But you know, maybe that's your thing. Maybe not knowing is what you need. The rest of us"—he sticks his arms out, pretending to gather up the masses—"we're just lemmings in the college process."

"Maybe," I say. "Maybe I'm just chickening out so I don't have to deal with being disappointed."

Chris furrows his brow. "First of all, it's early yet. You could change your mind after interviewing. You know, get a spark of interest somewhere."

I nod to him, agreeing. "You don't know how much I want that award." My voice is small, soft, like admitting how badly the Beverly William Award pulls at me will only make not getting it worse.

Chris leans forward like he needs me to say it again. "That's huge—you want something." He raises his voice. "Hello, Field Day participants. Love Bukowski wants the writing award." He smiles like a proud parent. "It's just great to hear you actually vocalize a desire."

I swat his megaphone hands away from his mouth and laugh. I do want it, though. I want the recognition, the knowledge that someone thinks my writing is worthy, and, most of all, the freedom that comes with it. The award is for young writers to travel and write, and comes with the assumption you'll have a book by the end of the stipend money. A book sounds incredibly far off. But applying for the award doesn't. In fact, it's soon, and my plan is to ask Mr. Chaucer to recommend me after the next ACW meeting, though I suspect I'm not alone in asking this.

Chris squints at me. "Now, just what other desires are lurking in there?"

I don't answer. How can I muddle through the swill that makes up my emotional baggage? In my pocket is a scrap of paper that I tore out of the phone log. Someone wrote "Love B. got a call from Charlie. No need to call back." First of all, the fact that anyone put my last initial down is funny. Like there are other Loves. And second of all, I've been toiling endlessly with the *no need* part. Is that Charlie saying "just calling to say hi"? Or is everything with him just so banal that if I never called back, he'd be fine with it? Either way, the scrap of paper feels small in my fingers. So does the memory of being with him.

Down the hill, Mary swigs from her sports drink and waves. She has yet to reveal the very covert Sweet Potato meaning, but as I look she gives me a thumbs-up. "Go, team!" she shouts. Then she points to something in front of her. Then I get it—not today. Tomorrow. Sweet Potato. I return the thumbs-up, even though I feel a little asinine not knowing what I'm agreeing to. Mary's over by the rest of the supersporty girls, all legs and ponytails, taking Field Day way too seriously. Really, it's an excuse to have a half day of classes, but they're decked out in head-to-toe Hadley gear, big *H*'s painted on their faces. Maybe it's sweet, too, that school spirit, but I know if I wore the *H* it would just seem like I was trying too hard, or like I had to do it for my dad. Dad's not even here today. He left a message for me in my mailbox, an index card with his flight information and the approximate route he'll drive with Sadie. When I don't think about him, I'm fine. But when I picture our previous squash matches, or sitting by the ocean this summer with our iced coffees, my intestines feel empty. Or maybe intestines are always empty and I mean something else.

"I hope he has fun," I say, not explaining whom I mean to Chris.

He doesn't need my words. "Sadie has every right to have your dad for the weekend. Just like you have every right to have her mom in your life."

"It's not like I mind. . . . I just want it all, you know? The family, the friends—"

"The boyfriend," Chris suggests, spying his own over the field. "Check out Haverford and the potato sack race. Too funny."

I stand up, examining my legs for grass marks, and pulling my long sleeves over my arms. I got hot when we were running, but now I'm cold. "Yes—I want the boyfriend. *The*. Not *a*."

"So you want the King of Hearts, not the prince."

"Something like that." Tomorrow I'll be dressed up— or if not *up*, at least better than I am now—all ready for my Harvard tour and interview. And looming ahead is my turn for constructive criticism and praise at the ACW class. I'm curious to find out what Dalton's writing is really like. I've read two poems and one story of his in the literary magazine, but *Fusions* isn't ACW, and I have a feeling all of us in there will share more than anywhere else. Thinking about Dalton leads me to thoughts of Jacob and how, like Amelia and Nick Cooper, my abandoned characters, I haven't leapt off the page to do anything. What's the lesson learned there?

Chris hands me a red plastic cup and I take a long drink from it. "Did you tell Charlie yet?"

I hand the cup back. "We've talked on the phone—about other things . . . but not that. I keep putting it off. Because I don't know what to tell him."

"How about—you were a summer fling?" Chris holds his hands up. "Oops—sorry, that was harsh."

"He wasn't just that. He isn't. Present tense."

"Well, you better figure out who and what everything is soon. You said it yourself—fall's here; it's partway done already. Your last one at Hadley." Chris overemphasizes so I know he's kidding, but part of it's true. When it's down to the wire, you want to make it as real as possible—with real meaning that counts. "Make this year count!"

"I'll do it tomorrow." I check my watch as though it could suddenly put me a day ahead. "After my interview. I'm there, right? Charlie has his read-a-thon." I say *Charlie* like I'm saying tuna fish or something just as blah.

"Ohh—and you can see the legendary Miranda." Chris stretches, leaning far over to the right before he's called to the track for the relay race. "Ten bucks says she's a hairy troll and you've been paranoid for nothing."

"You always say I'm being paranoid, and nine times out of ten, you're proved wrong." I stick my hand out. "I'd be happy to take your money."

The breakup. I feel decent about my decision. It's time. I've put it off. Not that I'm one hundred percent committed to ending everything with Charlie, not that I relish the thought of hurting him or losing him. Only, I'm very sure I can't be involved with him exclusively and still have feelings for a certain dark-haired guitar player who is currently eyeing me from the track. There are, as I have noted before, many songs about making up your mind over two people, or having lusty thoughts about one while being with another. But none of those is quite what I have.

"Am I ambivalent?" I ask Chris.

"No . . . well, maybe some." He flips my hair so that it's parted on the other side, doesn't like it, and flips it back. "You just have to try out a few relationships and see what sticks."

"So I haven't found my superglue, my peanut butter, my . . . name something else sticky?" I try the same thing with his hair, but he backs up.

"All I can say is that when I'm with Haverford—even when I was with him and not *with* him—I got this overwhelming sensation."

"Eww . . . I might not want to know."

Chris punches my thigh. "Shut up. Not like that."

"Okay, like what?" He gets a look on his face and I have

to retch. "Oh, you are not going to say *a fit*—what are you, Cinderella? Let's drop it, okay?" I laugh, but inside it makes me feel hollow. I thought I had that kind of fit with Charlie, but I don't. And what if thinking I could have it with Jacob is just more unfruitful wishing?

"How is your musical bard, anyway?" Chris tugs me so I'll cast a quick look at Jacob, whose chest is pushed out as he runs through a purple ribbon at the end of a race.

"Pretty quiet." We've been semi-avoiding each other since the sleep-in, primarily, I think, because he's decent and didn't want Chloe to feel worse than she already did, and because I'm still in limbo. "The last time I really hung out with him was the . . . the planet night." I look to the sky like the moon or Mars might appear, but nothing does.

"Hey—speaking of lasts . . ." Chris points to me. "You have to tell me what you want me to plan for your birthday."

I puff out my cheeks and pretend to blow out candles. "Oh, yeah. My last Hadley birthday."

"The big one-eight."

"I can vote!" I say.

"Vote for me," Chris pleads like he's running for student body president. "Or at least tell me what you want so the big day doesn't fall flat."

"Since you're asking . . . just something simple. Like a nice dinner someplace not superfancy. Friends. Not too many."

"I know—you and your lack of wanting full attention. We could pretend it's someone else's birthday. . . ." He smiles.

"I'm not that bad! Plus, you know I'm a sucker for but-tercream frosting. So make or buy a cake." I smile. "And thanks for thinking of it."

"My pleasure."

Over the loudspeaker, outcomes of various events are announced as though anyone really cares, and then up-coming races.

"I'm up." Chris makes a strongman stance, his arms flexed.

"Good luck relaying," I say.

"Good luck relaying yourself. The message, I mean."

I open my mouth to say how punny Chris is, but we're interrupted by a swish of hair and the strong smell of Cha-nel No. 5 perfume, which can mean only one thing.

"Lindsay." Chris fake smiles.

"What message?" Lindsay doesn't miss a beat and with her hands on her hips turns to me. "Anything I should know?"

"Nope." I keep as closed as possible, knowing that if she sees a crack, she swings any door wide open.

"Ready for the Crimson?" she asks. "Isn't tomorrow your big day at Harvard?"

I take a breath as I think of just how big a day it is: the interview, the breaking up, the college tour, the wondering about my future, not to mention finding Jacob after my conversation with Charlie and—presumably—telling him how it went.

"I have an interview, if that's what you mean." I make space between my face and the scent of the Chanel, waving my hand in front of my nose. "It's a fairly common occurrence this time of year."

"Yes," Lindsay says, giving me a full-on look. "Fall's all about interviewing for new positions." She pauses, letting the weirdness of her comment linger. "Good luck with all your endeavors." She sounds like a promotional ad for insurance or something equally banal, but I know she's up to something.

"Don't overinterpret her," Chris warns.

"I'll do my best," I say, imitating Lindsay's tone. "What position could possibly be new for her?" He and I laugh. "Ugh, can you believe Jacob had the poor taste to kiss her?" I try not to freeze in my mind the image of their mouths meeting.

Chris shakes his head. "At least it was just a kiss—and be glad you were abroad when it happened. But yes, poor judgment."

Chris and I part ways and I look across the field to where Jacob and Dalton and the rest of their crew are benched now, talking and laughing. The last Field Day will be over soon. My first college interview will be, too. And maybe other endings. Firsts and lasts, firsts and lasts—those are the words that I hear when I head down for my next event.

Chapter Seventeen

♡

Thoroughly exhausted from just watching Field Day, I tuck myself into a corner booth in the student center to indulge in two of my favorite pastimes: people-watching and writing about it. In order to observe and write down any dialogue (Chaucer's always saying to go out and study how people really speak to write believable stuff), I turn off the iPod. Good-bye to my songs of the moment: The Kinks, "Waterloo Sunset"; Elvis Costello, "Every Day I Write the Book"; and Anne Heaton, "Give in to You" . . . and hello to snippets of dialogue to recycle in my stories for ACW.

"She's not even that nice. . . ."

"But after you try it, don't make it so you can't twist the thing off. . . ."

"Not even. Mrs. Jackson's busting me about turning the paper in late, which—"

I write all of this down in my journal. Not because it's fascinating but because it's not. Sometimes, words and conversations are just regular, and if I'm going to be a decent writer I have to know how to write that way, too.

"... if you say so. Then, fine. But don't waste it with ..."

"Do you think he knows? He might. But maybe not. But maybe."

I look up briefly after this last one. Just as I suspected. Chili Pomroy confiding in another sophomore. I wave. Chili waves back, continuing. I bend down, scribbling so it's not obvious I'm eavesdropping in the name of creative writing. "But if he does know, do you think he cares?" Her conversational partner sighs, both of them dreaming about Dalton Himmelman, oblivious to the fact that they'd have better luck with the sophomore boys currently ogling them from the foosball table.

As I shift in my booth, the most recent Gala postcard slips out from the journal's pages. I reread it, tracing her loopy script with my pointer finger.

Love—

Isn't this picture a hoot? And to think I used to have shoes like these! Be glad you don't have to walk to class in such silly things. Right now, I'm actually barefoot and mailing this from Mexico (brief sojourn to nudge a reclusive artist to record a new song). Hope it gets to you soon!

X, G.

The picture in question is hilarious—a black-and-white snapshot of a woman whose feet are clad in wedge

shoes tall enough to be stepstools, a beret tilting precari-
ously to one side, and a crocheted sweater vest that demands a headline such as FASHION CRISIS. Except that when
this picture was taken, she was probably the height of cool.
I smile, knowing that Gala thought I'd find it amusing and
that she's right. The smile lasts until I hear more dialogue
worth writing down.

"It's like she doesn't even know how dumb she is."

"She can't possibly think anyone—let alone the one she
wants—is ever going to care."

I write that last one down word for word, chewing on
my pen cap until I hear—

"And gross. Is she in third grade? Who chews on pens
anymore?"

Chews on pens. Ahem. That's me. I look up. Chris was
wrong. My paranoia about Lindsay Parrish is well-founded.
She stands there, brows arched, arms crossed, smug.

"Can I help you?" I ask, trying fiercely to avoid blush-
ing. I actually wrote down insults being said about myself!
Note to self: Cross off realistic-sounding dialogue from to-
do list.

"I seriously doubt it." Her gaze rests on my journal pages
until I quickly cover them, slamming the book shut with a
loud slap. "I was thinking I could help you, actually."

I swallow, a sudden burst of saliva heavy in my mouth.
Breathe. Breathe. Why does she inspire such a race of an-
noyance and worry in me? "And just how, pray tell, would
you be able to do that?" And when did I start using words
like *pray tell*?

Lindsay inserts herself into my booth, causing not one but a few surprised expressions from several onlookers. We are not the usual buddies in a booth. "Well, you know you've got this quandary," she starts.

The interview? I'm not sure where she's going with this so I lean back, trying for my best couldn't-care-less pose. "How so?" I put my book into my bag, gearing up to go lest she think I'm game for hanging out with her here.

"For starters, you've got your interview tomorrow."

Bingo. "Yes. All set, thanks so much for your great advice, Linds."

She looks at me as though I'm four years old. It works and I feel dumb. Then annoyed at myself. "Not Harvard. That you can mess up on your own." She leans forward, her hair falling on the table but narrowly missing the glob of ketchup leftover from someone's curly fries. Mine would have gone in. "I'm talking of more romantic pursuits."

Romance. What does she know of my romantic life? Nothing. Except she clearly wants to know Charlie or make me think she does. We lock eyes. Suddenly it occurs to me that she's gazed at someone like I have. Surely she must have felt real emotion at some point? I feel my chest get heavy, a little sad, wondering if she's ever been in love or anything close. "I'd like to keep my romantic life out of this." I make a sweeping gesture between her body and mine. I stand up. "Gotta go."

"Love, wait." Lindsay's voice is stern but not mean.

I wait. For a moment she appears soft, kind even, her head tilted. "What?"

"Did you ever really, really just . . ." Her voice is so normal I feel bizarre. Is this what it would be like if she weren't evil?

"Did I what?" I return the favor with a normal voice but don't allow myself to race ahead to where we're friends and have regular conversations and go to dinner in Boston, or flit off to NYC to her palace house for a weekend. No, I try and stay here. To the one minute she's being nice.

"You always seem to have it together, you know?" She smiles. Normal. Not with fangs.

Oh my God. This is so Disney I can't take it. Except it's so much better than mean. "Really? I always think that you—"

"I'm totally kidding, you fool." Lindsay looks at me as though she's stubbing me out with her heel. Which she kind of is. "In no way, shape, or form are you 'together.'" She does air quotes for that last word.

And right as I'm about to respond and give her a list of all the ways I am so together, she goes on. "And just so you know, don't waste your time with—"

"Charlie's not interested," I spit out. I want to dangle his old T-shirt in front of her, to show her how much he's mine, and then I remember I don't want him to be.

"I'm not talking about Charles Addison," she says. She stands up, too, so we're level—or would be if I were taller.

"Oh, yeah?"

"I'm talking about Jacob. Jacob Coleman." With that, she gives her regular smile, and I feel the bite.

"What about Jacob?" My bag slides off my shoulder and I heft it back up, balancing on the table with my hands.

Lindsay shrugs as if this is a casual name. "You know when you were off in London?"

"Yes, I do. It was a whole semester, after all. Not one I'm likely to forget." I glare at her to imply just how tremendous my time abroad was, and beat her to the punch. "And I know about you and Jacob."

"Really." Lindsay says it as a whole sentence.

The image of her mouth on Jacob's pops up again and I try to smush it away. "So what?"

"Nothing," Lindsay says, eyeing the booth. She takes a step and then adds, over her shoulder, "I just thought you'd care that we slept together." She watches my face for a reaction. Somehow, I manage to keep it together for three whole seconds before my heart starts bouncing and jolting. "Especially, you know, since you guys wrote about your virginity—and how precious it is." Now it's Lindsay's turn to wait.

I compose sentences in my head. Real ones. Ones that sound like real dialogue from real people. Real people who are shocked and not entirely believing. "You're lying."

"That mail table in your house—wasn't very protected. Shame no one ever gave you and your dad a proper mailbox."

"You took my mail?" I think back. "That's illegal." Then it hits me.

"You were leaving for London—"

"You took it?" As I was getting on a plane to London, Jacob said he'd mailed me something important. A letter. One I know now I never got. "You're faking it."

Lindsay's face says otherwise. "Sadly for you, I'm not. Ask him. Ask the man himself."

"Show it to me. Produce the letter." I want to think she's making it up. That she's only ever kissed him. That all these months I've consoled myself with thinking they didn't really hook up, they didn't really have anything, she doesn't really get to me. But maybe they did, and she does. "Why? Why would you sleep with him?"

"The word *revenge* ring a bell?"

My mind sorts through files of why and what for, and then registers. "Because of Robinson Hall?" Lindsay's face changes the minute she hears his name. "God, Lindsay, that was so long ago, and it meant nothing."

"Sure." Lindsay's body looks stiff and angry, her hands clenched. But before she can be at all vulnerable, she cocks her jaw. "And that's how I feel about Jacob."

"But I never even slept with Robinson," I say, defending myself.

Lindsay clears her throat on her way out. "More's the pity. At least Jacob and I had fun. Ask him."

I don't want to ask Jacob. I can't. "Show me the letter."

"Maybe one day," she teases.

Her footsteps scrape the floor as she exits, leaving me with surprise, a bit of horror, some lingering doubt, and a hand smack-dab in a blob of ketchup.

Chapter Eighteen

♡

Saturday begins early, with the usual rounds of getting showered, dressed, and ready for whatever the next hours hold, with the added bonus of anxiety thrown in. I walk to the T, take it all the way into Harvard Square, and crunch through the leaves toward Byerly Hall, where the campus tour starts. On my desk I found a note from Mary that read, *Good luck today—and smile—we've got tonight!* It's nice to have a roommate for this reason—the notes, the well wishes, the shrugging off of yesterday's Lindsay run-in. I've liked being with Mary. And tonight, I can only assume it's time for Sweet Potato.

The black metal gates frame the entryway into Harvard Yard. In my boots, black pants, and bright but not-too-bright sweater (I read that you should wear something colorful so that you make a mark on your interviewer, but not too bright lest you create a visual disturbance), I take a minute to inhale and exhale before going inside. Around me, undergrads clomp through the fall air on their way to study or shop or have coffee. How can life continue on when I'm facing such huge possibilities like where to plant myself for the next four years? Times like this, I hear Aunt Mable's voice: *Because it can. Because you just keep going.* Which I do. But—

How can everyone look so relaxed when I've bundled up so many nerves that it's all I can do to walk? In each face I see, I check for Charlie, even though I know he's already hunkered down in the yard somewhere, reading for charity and no doubt fending off the miraculous Miranda. Curiosity gets the better of me and I take a quick peek through the gate to see if he happens to be right there, but he's not.

"Ms. Walters," I say when Harriet's next to me.

"Just keep moving. Pause too long and you'll lose the nerve to go in." She was on the T with me, but we didn't technically come together. Checking her out now, I see she's cast off her hippy-gauzy skirts and Indian-print tops for the day and looks like she did last year, all poised and together.

"Did you leave the peaceful sixties back at Hadley?" I ask, giving her the sign with my fingers as she tugs me through the gate. "You look nice."

"Thanks. I figured that my temporary foray into stonerwear might not be an accurate representation of the woman I am." She slides some Chap Stick on and offers me some, which I accept.

"And just who is that?"

"Good Lord, who knows." She checks her hair for signs of any strays. "Who can say who they will be?"

"Then why the bravado?" I sidestep a pile of dog poop,

glad that for once I haven't fallen or spilled or stepped in something foul before my interview. The leaves overhead make the yard idyllic, a vision of fall the way it is on film or in the catalogs. "Man, no wonder they have you tour now—it's beautiful." Even though I've been here many times before, it feels different right now. Not like I'm trespassing. But that it could be my school, my yard, my rightful place. Or not.

Harriet turns on her heel and puts her hands on her hips. "You'll need some sort of bravado to get through the interviews. I did all mine—this is my last." She gives me the once-over to see if anything needs fixing before we meet up with the rest of the tour. Apparently, I meet with her approval. "I'm applying here early decision. At least, that's my plan. What's yours?"

My plan. My map, chart, sketch, strategy. "Tour, interview, breakup?"

Harriet nods like it's official. "Good order. No breakups prior to interview—don't want to expose yourself before being quizzed."

I nod but don't tell her how I'm feeling, how that inner conflict sucks and breaking up stings, even if you're the one doing it. I picture Charlie at Hadley and feel semisick but picture him in the summer and feel sad, like ending things means losing everything we had. Which I guess it does. I check the time. "We should go. I don't want to be late. Early decision—that's so . . . binding. . . ." I can't imagine doing that, committing right away to a single place. But then again, maybe I haven't found the right place.

"Yeah . . ." Her shoes click on the stone ground. "But you never know. I could see something on the tour that would completely make me change my mind."

Here is what all campus tours boil down to: architecture ("The library was built in 1708 by a mercantile sailor"), a few random facts about students tailored to the specific place ("We're a pretty studious/fun/athletically inclined/ enviro/international bunch!"), and one message ("You want to go here"). All of it's only mildly useful because what you need to know you pick up between the facts, underneath the strong sell from the tour guides. After the required information session, during which Harriet Walters takes notes and I listen for signs that this is the school that would be right for me, the tour starts.

"This is . . ."

Insert name of building and its function.

"We always have . . ."

Insert name of specific tradition—snow sculpture contests, science experiments, the largest outdoor omelet competition.

Not that I'm not enjoying myself. Without a doubt the school is gorgeous, famous, historic, and very difficult to get into. With every fact and story that comes from the tour guide's mouth, the interview gets closer and closer. What if this is my first choice and I can't get in? What if I clam up and can't explain where I see myself in five years or whom I admire most or which historical figure influences me in my day-to-day life? And what if I can't even concentrate because I know that afterward I need to find Charlie and tell him?

Harriet whispers to me as the tour guide explains the residential houses. "Love, you look way too nervous. It's not good for your complexion."

I pinch my cheeks—Aunt Mable's old trick for looking less pale on a moment's notice. I wonder if she learned that from my mother in college and what I might learn when I'm there. Or if. "But I am too nervous."

"Then bag the tour and collect yourself. Seriously." She raises her eyebrows and removes her wireframe glasses so I know she means it. "You know your way around here. Go get a coffee—or no, no caffeine. Just go do yoga or something and meet us at the end."

As the herd of touring enthusiasts moves on to the next place of interest, I hang back, then slink away, hoping no one notices. Instantly, a bit of the pressure eases up and I walk a few yards without feeling weighted by stress. Past Widener, past benches filled with students, I head for the gates on the other side of the yard which I know will lead me to Bartley's Burgers, site of many days and nights in my life. Harriet's got a good head on her shoulders, and gives good advice. The tour won't shed much new light, but walking around does. I could be here. This could be it, right? I indulge a momentary fantasy in which the interviewer loves me so much that he or she announces I'm already accepted. My spirits soar, then I think about how even if I do that, I still have to find Charlie and deal with that, not to mention the fact that just because someone says you're accepted into something doesn't mean it's the right place for you.

Rather than use the minutes I have left before the interview to further fantasize at Bartley's, I veer left instead, and find myself in a side yard that's dotted with large sculptures and further decorated with Shetland wool sweaters and jeans, all worn by current students who hold textbooks and soak up the warmth of the morning sun. A feeling of peace starts to fill me. If I could bottle it up, keep it for the interview, I'd be fine. Only, just when I start to do that, I see that one of the dots on the grass way over in the corner is familiar. Feeling like a bad spy, I go closer, ducking behind the ancient elms for coverage.

Charlie and his read-a-thon in full action—close enough that I can hear the words. Close enough that I can see the other readers and the listeners, as well as the sign behind them that announces the event. I check my watch. Is ten minutes too little time to break up with someone? I feel like a bitch but know that in this case, now that I've seen him, Harriet can't be right. I have to do this now if I'm going to make it through the interview without bursting.

I walk over, knowing I look interview ready and hoping that after all's said and done, Charlie doesn't think I dressed up for dumping him. What constitutes the correct clothing for dumpage? I broke up with Robinson Hall in something stained. Ugh. Thinking of him leads me back to Lindsay and Jacob. It can't be true. Is it? I pick lint from my pants. When Asher ended it I wore a new pink T-shirt

I've never worn since. Will these black pants go the way of the castoffs?

Oh, dumping him—he looks so sweet on the ground, the book in his lap where my head has rested so many times, his hands on the pages. What if those feelings I had for Jacob were just passing?

I look to the blue sky and know it's not true. Those feelings haven't passed for more than two years. But Lindsay and him? No. Maybe. I suck in the cold air. I have to do this. I stand a little ways off, behind the group, with a view of their backs, all anonymous sweaters and shirts. And I'm about to make my presence known, by waving or saying hello, but I don't want to interrupt.

I scan the people next to him to see if Miranda is there, if she's touching him, if that hunch I had about her was correct, and they are more than just old friends. Then I get proof: from the front row of listeners, a mop of perfectly tousled hair and a scarf whose print announces its brand name. The woman and her hair lean forward, too close to Charlie for my own comfort even though we're about to break up. I mean, he doesn't know that and yet there's a female so close she may as well be on his lap. Which, until said breakup occurs, is my place. I step forward. Miranda. I shake my head. Note to self: Never buy the old-friend excuse.

Then I feel a tap on my shoulder. I spin around thinking it'll be Harriet or an irate tour guide, but it's not.

"Love?" A woman with a big smile and a pixie haircut extends her hand to me.

My face says *Do I know you?* but I reach my hand out
anyway, wondering if maybe Harvard plants random inter-
viewers on campus to trick you. "Hello . . ."

The woman laughs. "Oh, sorry. I know you—or feel
like I do—but you don't . . ." She makes a name-tag shape
on her chest. "I'm Miranda." She looks at me with something that registers as pity, her eyes full of knowledge. But
of what? We shake hands and a chill runs through me, my
gut pulling me back to where Charlie is seated. If she's
Miranda, then . . .

I get a better look now at Charlie. The read-a-thon
banner undulates with the wind, and as piles of leaves swirl,
the hair, the scarf, the girl in the lap—she turns to face the
crowd, sitting as close as she can to Charlie, and after taking the book from him so she can read, slips her legs over
his. First she leans on him, then into his chest. He holds
the book for her and they sit linked like one person. One
intimate person.

Miranda looks at me, whispering so as not to disturb.
"You know her, right?"

I nod, and gulp for air. "Yeah. Lindsay. Lindsay Parrish."

Three hours later and I'm finding solace in a frappé and
burger at Bartley's, my ACW journal in front of me, only
slightly smeared with ketchup. Harriet's been across from
me, working in silence for a while. She's attuned enough
to know I'm in no mood for chit-chat. I don't even like
that word.

"Another hour and we'll go?"

I nod. Another hour will give me enough time to obliterate Harvard from my list, finish some math homework, and finally end the story I'm working on. In it, a farmer in the 1930s deals with a flood and has to save all the animals he can. I know it runs the risk of Dalton calling it biblical, and Chaucer hating it, and Linus Delacorte being critical because he hates all stories with animals, but I have to know I can finish it. The ending has been tricky because I don't know if any of the animals survived and what it means if they do or don't. I want to have created a character—the farmer—who, as Dalton phrased it, jumps off the page. And I think I have. But I can't figure out that damn last line.

The barn's small gate held behind it a cluster of chickens. Soon the water would reach them, and the Holsteins, too.

Am I really writing about cows? I ask myself while tapping my pen on the page. Is that the lesson I'm learning? Part of me feels badly about leaving Amelia and Nick Cooper on that beach with everything still unsettled.

"Still going for early decision?" I ask her. My pen is poised to write, if only that last line would come. I bite my lip, flinching when I bite too hard, and wishing I didn't feel quite so betrayed on a day when I was supposed to be the breaker-upper. So Lindsay's more than just "gracious" to Charlie. Or that's the way it looks.

"Definitely." She looks happy, settled. "What about you? Did you see anything on the tour to make you go one way or the other?"

"You could say that." I sip my frothy drink. The

interview went fine, but I had that out-of-body experience of watching myself interview. A disconnect that
maybe didn't show—I held up my end of the questioning
and gave respectable answers, but something was lacking. I
guess that's how you know it's not your top choice. I want
to feel knocked over by a place, totally sure.

I wave a now-floppy French fry around and flick back
to the image of LP and Charlie. With certainty I can say
this: It's not that Lindsay is all over him. It's not that he
never told me about her coming to the read-a-thon that
gets me. It's not even that now, instead of having a college I
love and a guy I'm broken up with, I have only the image
of my nemesis and my summer love together. It's that yet
again my actions have been foiled. Each time I think I've
made a decision—like with Jacob and the planets, or even
choosing a college—one gets made for me.

Chapter Nineteen

Back in my room, Mary's at her desk with her history book open.

"I'm doing a report on the suffragettes," she says before I've even dropped my bag.

For the first time this whole fall, when I walk inside, drop my bag, and shed my shoes, I realize I'm actually happy to be here. Away from the Square, away from Lindsay and college interviews and unpleasant sights. No pangs of elsewhere, safe in my hideout.

"Go, female power!" I say and raise a fist. Then I flop onto my bed.

Mary stops writing and pivots in her chair so she's facing me. "Did you get the 'Hadley Hall is known as a feeder school for Harvard—how do you stand out amongst your classmates?' question?"

I nod. I've been so distracted by the sights I've seen that some of the interview details have slid by. "That one and many more. It went okay, though. All things considered."

I dish it all out to her, the nervousness, the tour, meeting Miranda and seeing LP and Charlie, rehashing Lindsay's virginity claim on Jacob from yesterday.

"So all along it wasn't Miranda you had to worry about." Mary talks like she's an inspector on a crime show.

I neaten up my desk, enjoying the feeling of knowing my homework is almost done and the next ACW class is tomorrow. If only I could get the last line of the story. At least Dalton's up this week. I still have a week to make my story worthy of inspection. Math—check. History—check. I've even studied those lame Hadley facts in case I have a test in my campus history class. But still no last line. Maybe I can't finish it because I haven't taken care of my interpersonal situation.

"I'm going to call Charlie and get this over and done with," I announce. "It's the only way."

"Right on, Sister Suffragette." Mary taps her text with her pencil. "And then . . ." She gives me a wicked smile and cackles.

"What?" I grab my bag of coins for the pay phone. How do you start a breakup? Oh, yeah. *We have to talk.* Or, *I've been doing some thinking.* Or, *Lindsay Parrish is a mean, haggy whore.*

"Tonight's the night." She puts her finger over her lips.

"Really?" I raise my eyebrows. "You mean there's a light at the end of this stressful day?"

"There is a light. And its name is Sweet Potato."

Having taken the stairs two at a time, I arrive in the phone room but find it's in use. The foreign students hog the line all day during the weekends, taking advantage of the rates and the time zones. I make it clear I'm waiting and then sit on the porch with my bag of change. If my dad were here, I'd suggest we go apple picking or hiking. It's that kind of afternoon. But he's off with Sadie. Thinking of them together makes me smile—a quiet kind of hope for a family that's different but complete somehow.

I stare out the window while I wait for the phone. Over in the green oval, the white flagpole stands straight into the blue sky. When I saw Chloe and Jacob hugging there, they were breaking up. This makes my heart lift a little, until a nearly duplicate vision appears before me.

Chloe and Jacob, oblivious of who's watching, hug in the fall afternoon as they share an apple. Talk about biblical. Dalton would have a field day with that one. I study their actions—Jacob's got his hands in his pockets, but she's draped on him. It could mean nothing. They broke up. They're just doing that postbreakup friendly thing until enough time passes and they can ignore each other without appearing callous. Except it's kind of close for people who aren't dating and who aren't predating (e.g., flirting and frolicking). My insides churn.

From behind me, the door opens with a squeak. Dalton sidles up next to me, having emerged from inside my dorm. "I was just dropping by to say hello," he says. "Check on your story. See if Amelia and Nick Cooper reached a resolution. But you aren't in your room."

"The rumors are true," I tell him and stand up, trying my best to ignore the PDA on the oval. "I escaped. You are observant." I slide my feet on the rough stone steps. "I sort of dropped Amelia and Nick. Moved on." I think about my cows and chickens in that flood and suddenly the story seems ridiculous.

"Really?" Dalton looks dismayed. "You're just going to leave them there, without any SPF?"

I smile. "Amelia tans without burning. She's got fictional skin."

Dalton clicks his tongue and grins from the side of his mouth, an action that makes my heart race. Jacob does that. Did he do it with Lindsay? Did she notice? Does it matter? "That—right there. That expression . . ." Dalton touches his face to see what I mean. "Your, ah, roommate does that." We both sneak a glance at the oval, where Jacob and Chloe are staring at the sky together. I've never really brought up Jacob before, but I feel comfortable with Dalton now.

"Oh, the sideways grin? That?" Dalton does a double take at my face, checking for hidden meaning.

"Yeah." I stumble over my words. "Jac—he always—it's just something I've noticed. Sort of a trademark grin . . ." I exhale loudly. "It's funny how roommates take on each other's traits. Mary lines her shoes up now, just because I always do that. And I've found myself doing a nod I never did before, which I think I stole from her." I demonstrate the nod now.

"Well, just so we're clear, it's my grin."

"Huh?" I look at him and think back, flashcard fast, on all the times Jacob did that side grin that my heart melted, that my insides went loose. How I looked for Charlie to have that grin but he never did, as though he'd misplaced the action. Turns out, it wasn't his or Jacob's to lose.

Dalton pulls his wallet from his back pocket. From inside the worn brown leather he slides a small black-and-white photograph of four kids in a row, each one leaning back on the next in the snow, a long wooden sled underneath them.

"Sledding race?" I ask, my finger resting on the edge of the picture.

Dalton nods. "Me and my sisters." He peers closely, showing me. "Check out the expression."

I point to the toddler version of Dalton, who looks remarkably similar, same melted dark chocolate brown hair, same pale eyes. Exact same sideways grin. "Okay, so you're the original grinner." I hand the photo back, thinking about how it acts as his proof. What do I have that proves who I am, that proves the lessons I've learned? There's no way I can use my flooding farmland story. It's not real. It's not me. "Maybe I will go back to Amelia and Nick. . . ." I shrug. "Anyway, I thought you were the one whose story will be in the spotlight this week."

"Yep—that's me. A walk-on part in the high school show."

"What does that mean?"

He cracks up. "I have no idea. But suffice it to say my story is done."

I snap my fingers. "Just like that? You just went back after last week and wrote it?" He makes it sound so easy, as though no effort is required and the words will just adhere to a premade idea.

He sits down on the stone steps, his legs out so that his shoes are near mine. We're comfortable together after the ACW classes and our walks. I think I've also been speaking with him so much because I can't really talk to Jacob, who upon last check, showed no sign of coming over to me and Dalton, preferring instead to chill further on the grassy oval.

Dalton gives me a grimace. "So, you're in tonight, right?"

I stare blankly, for real, until I clue in that he's referring to Mary's mission. Then I play up the vacant stare. "I have no idea what you mean."

"Good. Then we're all set, Sweet Potato."

"Oh, so I have a pet name now?" I raise my eyebrows. He called me Bukowski that first day of classes and I knew it was because he and Jacob must have called me by my full name way back in sophomore year. People do that sometimes, not wanting to use my first name because of its emotional component. "Fine. You can call me Sweet Potato." Dalton and I waver in the fun space between comfortable and flirty—intimate with our conversations but decidedly not with our bodies. He's not one of those guys that's continually touching and gesturing while talking—either absentmindedly or on purpose.

"Look, if you need to be one of those girls who has a weird-ass pet name in order to feel cool and accepted, so be it. Sweet Potato it is."

"Funny," I say and stick out my tongue. "I think I'll pass."

"Too late," Dalton shakes his head. "You're stuck with it." He cups his hands into a foghorn. "Everyone, this girl is from now on known as Sweet Potato."

I blush at the spectacle and because it makes Jacob look over at us for more than a normal amount of time. Does he think Dalton's watching over me? Does he imagine we talk solely of him, of the years' worth of angst and crush? Or does he not even care?

I bow my head. "Fine. Call me whatever you want and I will respond. I'm a retriever like that. . . ." I hold my hands down like paws and pant. "Speaking of which . . . we're getting a dog. Tomorrow. To train." I explain further. "It's Fruckner's community service project for the fall. That plus a fund-raiser later on."

"So you're going to do what, exactly, with this dog?" Dalton looks amused, his lips curling up while his eyes stay half lidded.

"We have to follow the rules that Guiding Eyes for the Blind sends us . . . but it's kind of cool." My voice rises with the description and I realize I'm actually excited about having a puppy. "I volunteered to be the main caretaker. But, it's kind of like writing—I mean, you're supposed to make sure that the puppy experiences all this stuff: walking on a variety of surfaces like rugs and wood and gravel. And that it plays in different spaces, and gets to know a certain amount of new people."

"Socialization and more."

"Right."

Dalton bites his lower lip and looks at the grassy oval. I fight the urge to look there and focus on him instead. Chili will want a report anyway, on what he wore and so on, still caught up in her Dalton crush along with half the school. "You should bring the puppy to ACW." He pauses. "That is, if you survive tonight, Sweet."

I fake grimace at the nickname. "Yeah, right . . ."

"No, seriously. We could walk it up and back—that's a bunch of surfaces right there. The gravel by the service entrance, the paved road, the wooded area, the stony paddock."

I nod and take it in. All along I've been gathering the details from the walks, and it's nice to know that Dalton has, too. That they're a part of his ACW experience. "Sure. When we get her—or him—that'd be good."

I jingle my bag of coins and take one last look at Chloe and Jacob, who are now playing catch with the core of the apple they shared. For people who aren't together, they are so chummy I want to barf. The daunting task of breaking up with Charlie stands boulderlike in my path to a good time tonight—whatever it is we're doing.

"Anyway—puppies, writing, snacks. What else in life could one possibly need?" Dalton asks.

I study the slant of his broad shoulders, the curve of his neck. Tans are fading now and I can see the skin Dalton will have in the winter, the color of whole milk, a perpetual flush near his jaw. "What else?" I smile. "Oh, yeah . . ." I'm about to say he forgot love, but it sounds loaded, like we talked about. And just in case he's analyzing the dialogue for deeper meanings, I leave it out even though I know I want it. "The Beverly William Award? Just a suggestion."

"Right—one for you and one for me." He deals out invisible cards that are supposed to signify the stipend.

"Why, thanks. I'll put it on my mantel next to my Pulitzer."

"So." He puts on an indecipherable accent. "Sveet Potato. Ve vill meet later."

"Yah." I nod to him, wishing the breakup were done, that I knew what to do with Amelia and Nick, that Jacob would stop touching Chloe and that Lindsay Parrish would vanish in a cloud of Chanel. Dalton has one foot on the upper step, the other on the lower one as I head inside. We pass by each other as usual, with no touching, no good-bye, just a look. Past him, I can see the edges of the grassy oval and I know the biblical images of Jacob and Chloe are still there. I wonder if Lindsay really did steal his last letter to me. If she hadn't and I'd read it, would everything be different? Dalton coughs, bringing me back to him.

"And Love?" He looks out at the oval and back to me. "They're back together. Just so you know."

He doesn't say this with vengeance or snidely or with any of the sarcasm-laced lines he's so famous for. It's just a fact. Pure and simple. Presumably the reason for his drop-by visit. Chloe and Jacob were broken up, and now they're back together, glued like a plate split down the middle. I nod at him, conveying my gratitude just with my eyes. At least he had the courtesy to tell me. Not that Jacob and I had a deal, but that's what I took our conversation in the balcony to mean. Turns out, I was wrong.

I don't react to the news, at least, not verbally. But the bag of coins suddenly feels anvil heavy. I take it into the phone room with me, aware that I'm about to commit a relationship sin by breaking up on the phone. Asher did that to me and I hated it, but what else can I do? Seeing Charlie in person would only be worse. Even if Jacob's with Chloe, it doesn't change my indecisive interior. So I drop in the money, warned by the operator that this buys me two minutes, and wait for him to pick up.

"Charlie?" I press my lips onto the black receiver, my hands shaking.

"Love! How'd it go? Are you in love with the campus or what?"

In love. Hardly. "Well, I wouldn't say that—"

"Oh, you have to give it a chance." I hear him open a window. "God, it's amazing out today, isn't it? Did you ever have one of those days when you just can't stop smiling?"

His tone is so up I feel even worse about what I'm about to do. Then I think of Lindsay's cashmere on his chest, and ripples of anger roll through me. "Charlie—I have to tell you—" Images of being with him on the Vineyard come flooding back, but I push them away, leaving them to sink like the farm animals in my story.

"The read-a-thon was a big success. I just got back, actually. And I know we'd talked about getting together tonight. . . ."

We had? I search back over our conversations and come up blank. "I don't think we did—"

"But I can't. Turns out, I have tons of work. And I'm kind of hosting, too."

Hosting? Is that what you call it these days? My mouth is dry. My legs feel weak. Then I do it quickly—like ripping a Band-Aid off. Which is maybe what Charlie has been. "We shouldn't be together."

Silence. It feels long. The ticking away of seconds. Every other sound except for Charlie's voice resonating—birds outside, nearby chatter, then the operator asking for more money. The coins drop in with a gentle clinking, and finally Charlie speaks. "Just like that? No fading out, nothing?"

"You don't sound surprised." My chest feels heavy, and time feels long. The time since summer, since his visit, since it felt really right.

"I figured we'd end things at the Silver and White," he says. "If we're being honest." He takes a breath. "Then, when I saw you—you just weren't—"

"I wasn't what?"

His sigh is heavy and long. "We want different things."

"So now we're moving on to clichés?" I feel sadness and frustration rising in me. Can't he at least be clever in the breakup? Witty? Make me feel both reassured we're doing the right thing and amused at the same time? I know I'm being unreasonable.

"Aren't all breakups clichéd?"

I pick at a piece of flaking plaster on the wall, digging

my thumbnail in and picking off tiny pieces. "What about Lindsay Parrish? As long as, you know, we're being so honest." I clip my words, waiting for his response. People always want a good ending, one that's clean and leaves them friends, but the reality is if things were so great, you'd be together.

Charlie takes so long to respond, I have to put in two more quarters. Now I'll need to get more change before doing laundry. If only I could go home, do a couple of loads while watching TV . . . but I'm not allowed. Then a thought occurs to me: My dad's away and I have a key. Chloe and Jacob are together, the breakup sucks, and all I want to do is curl up while my clothes get clean. This is senior year. So much for Sweet Potato—I don't know if I'll be up for any covert missions after this. And after seeing Jacob and his newly reunited touchy-feely girl.

"As I said before, Lindsay Parrish is merely an acquaintance. One who supported me by showing up to the read-a-thon today. She's just a friend of the family and I'm being gracious." There's that word again. Definition: genial, affable. Why, then, does it translate to me as a noun: being of or pertaining to sex regarding family friend Lame Piranha?

"So now you're angry that I didn't? I had my interview, for God's sake." Now I'm pissed off. We break up and he gets to have a romp with Lindsay, not hurting over me, while I have laundry fantasies. What's my problem?

"I understand why you couldn't come—I just wish you'd had the guts to break it off in person."

I can hear him licking his lips and it dawns on me that

I'll never touch them again, never even get close probably. I might not even ever see him again. Even though he's eighteen miles away we would have no reason to over-lap anymore. "I'm sorry. Charlie, you know my feelings for you . . ." I pause. What do I say?

"Were in the past. Or weren't steady. Anyone could see that. Even Parker warned me this summer." The thought of his brother knowing my feelings before me is unset-tling. "Clichéd as it is, I think you're right. We had a good summer."

A wave of sadness descends on me. The heat is gone from the air, and those months with him are, too. We aren't angry; we're just over. "We did, right?"

"Yeah."

That's how we leave it, sitting in silence until the opera-tor demands more, always more, and I hang up.

Chapter Twenty

Very few actions make your pulse bypass the speed limit like breaking rules in such a big way that you could get expelled. Then again, you only get to be a senior once. At least, that's the reasoning Mary's using to lure me out the window, down to the balcony, and out to the flagpole.

"I thought the flagpole thing was a Hadley myth," I say, my voice in a hiss-whisper.

"In all good myths there's a truth, right?" She holds her arms up to me as I shimmy down the side of the balcony. She's comfortable enough with the procedure that I know it's not her first time.

"That's what Dalton said." I follow her, creeping with my shoes off so they don't scuff on the pavement. We are as quiet as spilled water, lurking in the shadows.

"What did I say?" Dalton whispers, making us jump.

"Nothing," I fidget, my heart pounding from nerves. "Just that whole truth-in-fiction thing."

Dalton gives the grin I know now is his and then looks away. "Looks like we've got company."

The headlights from a campus security van swing into the driveway and the three of us crouch down behind a boulder, trying to curl up out of sight. I will get expelled, my father will kill me, I will have no chance in hell of either getting into college or even applying for the Beverly William Award. "I'll never get that stipend now!" I whisper to Dalton.

"Hey—at least this way you'll have something to write about!"

"Shut up, both of you!" Mary says as the van stops. The guard comes out, checking around the grassy oval for anything suspicious while we sweat it out in the shadow. I know Mary must be panicked because if Carlton or anyone else involved in tonight's postcurfew mission comes out now, they are screwed. Then, just as quickly as the van came in, it leaves.

"Who the fuck miscalculated that?" Haverford Pomroy's voice breaks the night quiet.

"My bad," Chris owns up. "Thought I double-checked the drive-by schedule. Must've read the weekday schedule rather than the weekend." Then he turns to me. "Hello, Sweet Potato."

I smirk at him, feeling decidedly excited in the deliciously illicit air. "So Dalton told you my new name?"

Chris looks confused, then looks at Dalton, who shrugs. "No. You are, in fact, Sweet Potato."

"What?" I'm totally baffled.

"Ready?" Chris asks everyone.

"Ready." Harriet Walters appears from behind Bishop House with Jacob and Carlton, Mary's boyfriend.

"All set." Jacob and Dalton give each other the guy acknowledgment of sticking their chins out, and Jacob holds up a set of keys on a Hadley key chain. To me he asks, "Recognize these?"

I furrow my brow, then shake my head. Then, quickly, the group moves as one organism, and we're on the service road behind the dorms. Jacob dangles the key from his fingers, the same fingers that have plucked out so many songs on his guitar for me, the same fingers that have most recently combed through Chloe's hair and not mine.

"Will someone tell me what's going on?" I ask, my voice sounding louder than I intended.

"Shh." Dalton leans forward.

In the darkness behind the tool shed I see a campus golf cart and it sets my mind in motion. "So—you took the keys?" I ask Jacob.

"Borrowed."

"I copied them in the Square today," Harriet says.

"I've had them since that day," Jacob says, thumbing behind him like the day he took me home from the Health Center is right next to us. "Figured they'd come in handy."

Chris and Haverford climb on the back of the cart, while Harriet follows Mary to the second row of seats. "Here," Dalton offers, pointing me into the same seat I sat in when Jacob drove me that day. Back before I'd admitted feelings for him, before Charlie and I had broken up, when

I still didn't know if I'd get into Chaucer's class, or how it would be one of the highlights of my week.

"Again, can someone explain?" I fold my knees up so there's room on the other side of me for Dalton.

He climbs in, jostling me a little. "Sorry." He puts his arm around the back of the seat—in effect around me—as Jacob drives.

Once the cart is a little ways away from the dorms, Chris makes an announcement. "Thank you all for coming on this mission. . . ."

I turn so I can see him. "You did this?" I look at Mary. "I thought you were the one planning this. . . . What is this exactly?" I look at the road as we approach the back side of main campus, the dorm lights off, the chapel's distant flickering bulb that stays on all day and all night. "For the last time, could someone explain where we're going?"

Jacob speaks up, leaning forward over the wheel so he can look for a second at Dalton. "What did Yogi Berra say?"

Dalton shifts his weight. Excitement buzzes through all of us, the whole heavy golf cart full of Hadley students. "When you come to a fork in the road, take it."

"This," Jacob says to me as we chug along, "is the fork, and we are—as they say—taking it."

Surprise is a vast understatement to what I feel when Jacob turns the golf cart into my driveway. My house. My real home, not the dorms, is in front of me—its yellow exterior still yellow even in the moonlight. The sky is one of those autumnal ones, clear and high, the stars as bright as holiday lights in the open air.

"Sweet Potato," Chris says, poking me as he jumps out of the still-moving golf cart, "welcome home."

Inside my house, the plan is clear. Balloons, cake, and presents all await me.

"Happy birthday!" Chris says.

"But it's not for another ten days!" My smile is wide as I take it all in: the group of friends who risked everything for me, the gifts, the feeling of being in my house. "So . . . just to backtrack?"

"We knew your dad was away. . . ." Dalton starts.

"I knew your schedule," Mary adds, "and that you'd have your house keys."

"And we took care of the golf cart," Jacob says. "We figured it's faster with less chance of being caught than hoofing it."

"And to cut to the chase, you're worth it." Harriet crosses her arms over her chest. Who'd have thought that a girl with all As who's doing early decision at Harvard would help in a high school heist?

"Well, thanks—all of you." I look at each one of my friends and then go to hug them as Chris and Haverford set up the food and beverages in my very own kitchen.

"Keep the lights off," Chris reminds us. "Key lights only." From his jacket pocket he pulls a bunch of key chains, each with a button you can press to illuminate the darkness. I hug him, then hug Haverford, then move on to Mary and Harriet, who giggle uncharacteristically.

"I've snuck out before," Mary says. "But never to have cake. It's perfect." She gestures to the room.

"Hey," I ask, noticing a flaw in their descriptions of who did what. "How'd you guys get in here, anyway? I have the key." I display it.

"I stopped by your room," Dalton says. In the inky dark he's taller than normal, his voice articulate and soft. "Remember?"

"So you invaded my privacy. . . ." I joke while finishing my hug with Harriet.

"For a good reason," he says, his light eyes even lighter as he smiles.

"Cake's almost ready." Chris sets out plates for all of us. The only people I haven't hugged are Jacob and Dalton.

"Hey," Jacob steps forward, his canvas jacket still zipped halfway. I wonder if Chloe's worn it. "Happy birthday."

I put my arms around him and expect to melt as we hug, to feel that familiar twisting in my gut. I could lean in, whisper about him and Lindsay, if it's true. If they. When they. Why they. But I don't. She either has the letter or she doesn't. They either did or they didn't. Either way, I feel something different. When he hugs me back, the particles in the air have changed. I have changed. I picture Amelia on the beach with Nick Cooper, waiting for him to explain what's really out there, lurking in the water.

A dark fin rises from the water.

"Look," Amelia says, standing suddenly so she can point it out to him.

"Where?" Nick follows her point but can't make out the fin amidst the waves.

I stand there, hugging Jacob but writing in my mind. I know then that I have the rest of Amelia's story but that I'll forget it if I don't write it down.

"Guys?" I say to everyone while Haverford hands out candy bags. I take mine and smile. Chris knows me well enough to plan not just a cake but bags with licorice and Swedish fish, and spearmint drops that only old ladies are supposed to like. All my favorites. "I'm so thankful—and psyched to be here. . . ." My heart pounds, still with the thrill of possibly getting caught, but also because writing inspiration has struck. "But you've got to excuse me for one second. If I don't write this down, I'll—" I cut myself off and dash out of the room, taking the spiral staircase I used to take every day up to my bedroom.

There, right in the familiar setting, I grab an old journal from the stack by my bed and fling it open. I write the lines that I thought of while hugging Jacob and push off the weirdness of not feeling what I thought I would when we did. I'm not aware of how much time has passed until I notice I've filled two pages with tiny scrawl.

A knock on the door breaks my creative trance. "Don't mean to mess up your inspiration," Chris says, "but you've got a party to get to."

"Right." I close the book, confident I can get back to the beach and mend Nick and Amelia once and for all after I've had some cake. "I just got carried away."

Chris smiles. "I like when that happens to you—it's rare, you know?"

I stand up, taking my journal with me. It's the one from

sophomore year, a plain composition book with a few pages I'll have to copy at the back. "Do you think I'm too reserved?"

"I wouldn't say that." Chris starts down the stairs. "But it wouldn't kill you to burst out a bit."

This reminds me of writing, of the characters jumping off the page, like Dalton said. Tomorrow, I'll hear his story, and next week, I'll hand mine in. Both of those pieces will probably be competing for the same award, one that would change both of our lives forever.

"Fine," I say. "Then I'll burst."

I take the stairs fast and enjoy every bite of cake, each chewy strand of red licorice, while the whole group of us talk and laugh, the hours racing by.

Later, I'm back in the kitchen, gathering all the trash in a black bag we will later deposit in the Dumpster behind the gym. Laughter erupts from the other room and I feel myself being watched.

"How's it going?" Jacob watches me collect paper plates.

"Good," I say and mean it. "What about with you?"

He nods and looks at the counter where my journal sits next to my bag of candy. "What's in that thing, anyway?" He touches it and I flinch. "I can remember sitting in your room before summer started, staring at the pile of journals you had. I always wanted to know what you put in there." He looks at me.

I burst out of my skin, jump off the page. "Read it, then, if you're so curious."

Jacob looks like I punched him. "What?"

I shrug. "It was a long time ago, sophomore year, wasn't it?" I picture sitting in Mr. Chaucer's English class with him back then; then I picture singing with him on the roof of my apartment this summer. This time, in the memory, I realize something: Next to him in Chaucer's class was Dalton. And waiting for him in the car down on the street while we sang was Dalton. And today, while Jacob flirted around with Chloe on the oval, was Dalton.

"Yeah," I say and hold the book out for him almost as a dare. "Read it. I'll be back in a minute."

I walk through the living room to find Dalton, but he's not there. "Check your dad's study," Chris suggests. "He's probably stealing books."

They go back to playing some drinking game that involves speaking backward and I look for Dalton. When I find him he's not in the study but on the porch.

"What's this, lonely guy in the moonlight?"

Dalton turns to me, his hands in his pockets, and grins. "Something like that."

"You ready for tomorrow?" I mime writing so he'll know I mean for ACW.

He nods. Then he shakes his head. "I was. I am—no, I was. I think I have to go back and revise one more time."

"So your characters jump off the page?" I ask. "So you can make sure to win that award?"

He sits on the steps, his back to me. "What about Amelia and Nick?"

I sit next to him, the ever-present space between us

still there. Always, there's at least a few inches. I note that I never even hugged him to say thanks for the party. "I just was writing about them. I think she sees a shark, on the beach?"

"And?"

I lick my lips, feeling the cool air on them. "And . . . oh, I don't know. I just hope I can do something with them before Columbus Day." The deadline for applications hangs over me, and I know that right after Columbus Day I'll be thinking about Thanksgiving and my mother and sister's visit, about our odd Thanksgiving, about the award notifications, which happen after the first of the year.

"Can I ask you something?" Dalton leans back with his palms on the deck.

Inside, Jacob could be reading my journal. Or not. Maybe he won't. Or maybe he will, the pull of nosiness too great to overcome. "Sure."

"Two things. The first is . . . what are you doing for Columbus Day?"

"Nothing. God, that sounds lame. I motion to rework that sentence."

Dalton pushes his hand through his hair. He never seems nervous or out of place or uptight. Steady but not boring. Sarcastic but not mean. "Maybe nothing is really something."

"What's that supposed to mean?"

"Nothing. Something. I don't know." Dalton stands up and moves so he's on the paved driveway, the golf cart parked behind him. "So—if you're up for it—a group of people are coming to my house for that weekend. My parents'll sign you out."

"Drunken sledding?" I ask. All of the rest of senior year seems stretched out before me, down a hill that I'm just now seeing.

"Snow in October?" He looks doubtful.

"Anything's possible." I stand near him, looking at my house from a slight distance, and feeling it. I thought coming home would be this great, comfy embrace, but it feels now like I'm visiting—trespassing, even—and that it's time to go. "Sounds fun . . . a weekend in the Berkshires."

"It'll be a full house—you, me, the good folks inside . . ." He points to the house. "Plus Chloe and maybe one or two others."

I picture random couplings, doors opening and shutting, me walking in on Chloe and Jacob. I flash for a second to Linsday Parrish and suddenly I remember something Charlie said during our breakup call. He's hosting. Hosting potential students? He could be hosting Lindsay—she is signed out of the dorms tonight. What if Lindsay and Charlie were more than gracious? What if she beds down with Jacob *and* Charlie? What if Jacob reads my journal? What if Amelia never confronts Nick Cooper head-on? "Has all the makings of a French farce," I say, striving for literary humor. *Amelia finds Nick in the orchard, the trees bare of fruit.* How did an orchard get to the beach? I mentally pinch myself. "But count me in."

"Did you just disappear to writing land in your head?"

I nod. "I can't shake the sensation that I'm missing

something—in the story. That's why I threw the shark in."

Dalton takes his hands from his pockets, the slanting light from the porch and the moon on his hair, and takes a step toward me. "You know you skipped over me, right?"

I pull my head back, pigeon style, surprised. "When?" Then I know. "Oh, right, with the hug."

"Yeah." He stands closer to me than before, his tall frame half a foot away. "Why do you think that is, exactly?"

I look up at him, then turn my head to the side, biting my lip. Stirring way down inside me I feel something—a crumbling of sorts, and a tumbling sweep of lust or crush or something more or in between—something that leaps from the page. Sparks. Electricity. That's what the air is between us. "What, that we don't . . ."

"That for all of our intense conversations, I don't think you've so much as poked me in the arm."

"Oh, like you've been all over me?" I take a step back and raise my eyebrows. "You're the least touchy-feely person I've ever met."

Dalton moves back so he can lean on the front of the golf cart. "Not really."

"Oh, just with me then? Do I disgust you?" I make a joke of it.

Dalton taps the golf cart's nose with his palms. "So, my story—just so you're aware—takes place in high school."

"He said, switching the subject . . ." I pull my arms around my waist, my jacket forgotten inside. "Isn't that the kiss of death?"

Dalton shrugs. "It's the truth, though."

"What's it called?" From inside, I hear a tapping and look back at the house. Jacob's face appears at the window. If I look closely I can see he's holding up my journal and pointing to it, but I don't know what he's saying.

"Sweet Potato." Dalton removes himself from the golf cart. Like lots of things he says, I can't tell if he's being serious or not. "It's about tonight."

Looking at him, I decide for action instead of motion— not the easy way out where I think, think, think, and leave my characters on the beach, but where I do something. "I'll hug you now, if that's okay."

I take a step forward. Dalton stands in front of me, his hands at his sides, and it occurs to me I don't know if he'll be a good hugger, one of those people who pats or rubs your back, or if he'll do the A-frame, where only your shoulders touch. I open myself up and wrap my arms around his back. The hug slides seamlessly from a thank-you hug to a full embrace, bringing me closer to him like good writing pulls you somewhere, my heart and chest pressed into his, while his hands, ones I've never felt before, grip my shoulders. We stay there like that, with his hands now in my hair, my arms wrapped around him like I'm afraid he'll move or slip away. "So what happens, at the end?" I ask, turning my face up to him.

His pale eyes write sentences I will never have to write down to remember, and all of it—the applications, the stories, the lingering questions about Jacob and Chloe and Lindsay and Charlie, my family, the whole rest of senior year—is bottled up into this moment. I keep my face tilted up to him, hoping he'll finally punctuate the instant with a kiss.

All along I wanted my writing to stand on its own—to not involve high school or my life, to just be. I thought Amelia and Nick Cooper were just random characters. Then, maybe I thought they were symbols, amalgams of me and Charlie, or maybe Jacob and Charlie mushed together leading me—and Amelia—nowhere. Maybe that's the biggest lesson of all, about writing and about love, knowing where your motivation comes from, why you act the way you do. What makes up that part of you that no one else ever touches.

"It's you," I say to Dalton. "You're Nick Cooper."

Dalton keeps a grip on me but darts his eyes away. "When I read the story—I asked Chaucer if I could—it wasn't that the characters weren't believable."

"But you said—"

"I know what I said, but it's just that I wanted them to act differently. Only, it's not my story, is it?"

Amelia could see the fin out in the water. Unsure whether it was a dolphin or a shark, she pointed to it so Nick could see. He stood up but didn't bother looking out to the water at what could be lurking underneath.

"It kind of is now." Then I do more—more than just tilt my face up to him. I touch his cheek with my hand, feeling each contour of his face, the slight stubble on his jaw, the easy sweep of his neck and the soft cotton of his shirt.

"Then, try this. Nick Cooper didn't bother with what

was lurking underneath. He could see—and so could Amelia—everything very clearly."

The last moments of my illicit birthday tick on, and the rest of the year tugs us forward, with Jacob pounding the window inside, my empty dorm bed waiting for my return, applications and choices ahead. Above us, the sky appears rippled like seawater, and here, on this planet Earth, Dalton leans down and puts his mouth onto mine. We kiss once and then kiss more, all at once kicking the past to the side and unfurling the future.

During the kiss, and even afterwards, when we're standing in my driveway holding hands in the autumn air, I suddenly get it.

"What're you thinking?" Dalton pushes the tips of his fingers into mine.

"About the Beverly William Award." I nearly whisper this.

Dalton's arm finds its way around my waist. "Really? Not just how much you've wanted to kiss me for so long?"

I feel my mouth wrinkle into a half smile, and I look at his pale eyes. "That, too. But it just . . ."

"I know—you can't control when plot takes over and life sends you inspiration," he says.

"Is that what you are?" I ask, but as I say it, I understand that it's true. Somehow he is the past and present all mushed together. "Everything just feels so crisp, you know? Like I'm suddenly ready for . . . anything." I don't blush or stammer; I just stand there with this new-old boy who gets me, and I breathe in the night air.

"So." Dalton looks over to the house. The window opens, and I can hear Jacob's guitar. He stums chords that in another season might be diluted by breeze of spring birds but right now just float out to where we are.

I have to acknowledge the music. "Elvis Costello." I listen to the words and then sing. *"Almost blue, there's a girl here and she's almost you."*

Dalton nods. "Yeah—he wrote that song for Chet Baker." Dalton clears his throat. "He will get over this, you know."

"Jacob?" I ask but don't need a reply. I nod. "I wasn't really sure there was much to get over." But maybe that's impossible. Maybe your past is always rushing up to you, and your job is to swat at it or ignore it or put it in its place so you can greet whatever's on deck. (Oh, Dad would be proud of my baseball analogy!)

Dalton raises his eyebrows. "I hope I never have to."

Our sides meet. I press myself into him, feeling my face on his sweater. "Never have to what?"

Dalton turns so we're facing each other, and puts his hands firmly on my shoulders as though giving me a pep talk. "You. Love. I hope I never have to get over you." He grins. "Get it?"

"I do. Yeah." I stand on my tiptoes to kiss him, and lose myself in the moment. Then my mind wanders. "You know, if we ended up together—like, long-term—tonight would be our last first kiss."

Dalton breathes in through his nose and licks his lips, humor and his usual bittersweet air playing a duet in his eyes. "The last first kiss?" I nod. "I'm so using that as the title of my Beverly William Award story."

I punch his shoulder. "Thief."

"Good writers steal, bad writers borrow." He grins. "Chaucer told me that."

I shrug my shoulders, all fake disinterest and ingénue pouting. "Doesn't matter anyway."

"Why's that?" He laces his fingers with mine, and I am all at once seeing the moment as a close-up and from a long distance.

"Because." My hair falls from behind my ears, and I tuck it back. What will be happening when my hair is back to shoulder length? Where will things stand with Dalton? What stories will I have written? "Because I already know how my Beverly Williams story starts. That's what I realized when you kissed me."

"You kissed me, too."

"Fine. When *we* kissed." I slide my shoes on the pavement, and the scratchy sound echoes, mixing with the music from inside. We will go back in and have candy and more cake and celebrate my eighteenth year. I tug on his hand, and he tugs me back into the immediate. The right-now. This minute.

"So aren't you gonna tell me? This infamous start to what is surely going to secure you the prize—jointly with my entry, of course, so we can travel the world together and write about our adventures?"

A huge smile overtakes my face at the thought of this coming true. "Okay. So I don't have a title yet, but—you know how you're supposed to write what you know but write it with some perspective? Some distance? That's what I do all the time in my head—why I always say things like 'in the movie version of this.' It's just another way of backing up or focusing in."

"Exactly." Dalton takes this moment not to kiss me—though he looks as though he'd like to—but to straighten my jacket collar. Such a sweet and unassuming gesture. "Let's hear it."

I look at the campus, at my house that isn't mine anymore, hear the noises from inside, and feel myself firmly on this earth, in this place. "Okay. Here goes. This is how it begins. *Just to get this out of the way: Yes, it's my real name. And no, I wasn't born on a commune. In the movie version of my life, there'd be some great story to go with how I got my name—a rockstar absentee father who named me in his hit song, or a promise my real father made to his grandmother in the old country, at least a weepy love story of two people so happy about their daughter they had to give her my name. But there's not—there's just me.*"

Dalton nods, listening intently. "That's it?" He plants a kiss on my mouth and then looks at my eyes, questioning.

"Yes." I nod. "That's how it starts."

About the Author

Emily Franklin is the author of the critically acclaimed seven-book fiction series for teens, *The Principles of Love*; a novel, *The Other Half of Me*; and another series, *Chalet Girls*. She also writes novels for adults, including *The Girls' Almanac* and *Liner Notes*. She edited the anthologies *It's a Wonderful Lie: 26 Truths about Life in Your Twenties* and *How to Spell Chanukah: 18 Writers on 8 Nights of Lights*. She is coeditor of *Before: Short Stories about Pregnancy from Our Top Writers*. She is currently working on a memoir, *Too Many Cooks: A Mother's Memoir of Tasting, Testing, and Discovery in the Kitchen*. She lives outside of Boston with her family.

Visit her or drop her a line at www.emilyfranklin.com.